Discovering Wounded Justice:
CRUEL MENACE

BELINDA D'ALESSANDRO

DISCOVERING WOUNDED JUSTICE:
CRUEL MENACE

BDA BOOKS PTY LTD
A.C.N. 128 320 481; A.B.N. 33 128 320 481

BDA BOOKS PTY LTD

A.C.N. 128 320 481; A.B.N. 33 128 320 481

First published in Australia in 2009 by BDA Books Pty Ltd

This is a work of fiction. The events described here are imaginary; the settings are fictitious and are not intended to represent specific places or living persons. All the characters in this book are fictitious and any resemblance to actual persons, living or dead, is purely coincidental.

BDA Books Pty Ltd
P.O. Box 988
GLEBE, NSW 2037
AUSTRALIA

www.bdabooks.com.au

Hardcover (Trade Cloth) ISBN 978–0–9804548–0–2
Paperback (Trade Paper) ISBN 978–0–9804548–1–9

A Cataloguing–in–Publication entry record for this book
is available from the National Library of Australia

Violence, even in the most favorable case, when it is not used simply for some personal aims of those in power, always punishes under the one inelastic formula of the law what has long before been condemned by public opinion. But there is this difference, that while public opinion censures and condemns all the acts opposed to the moral law, including the most varied cases in its reprobation, the law that rests on violence only condemns and punishes a certain very limited range of acts, and by so doing seems to justify all other acts of the same kind that do not come under its scope.

The Kingdom of God is within you
Leo Nikolayevich Tolstoy, 1894

(From the English translation
by Constance Garnett, 1894)

Discovering Wounded Justice:
CRUEL MENACE

Belinda D'Alessandro

QUIRK OF FATE

The woman refused to take no for an answer.

Not another one! his mind raged.

With mounting irritation, she reiterated her request to the implacable aide. But it was Erik Johannsen's job to filter out the time wasters. And the dangerous.

Not that he saw anything dangerous in the beauty who stood before him. Tall and willowy, with a thick curtain of dark, rippling hair, the woman was clearly English and mature past her years, and her exotic features – the slightly elongated, incandescent dark eyes and striking cheekbones, the small straight nose and translucent complexion – were stunning.

"It's impossible, I tell you," the aide repeated calmly. "Ms. Giordano never sees people out of the blue." Then he added soothingly, "Why don't you tell me what it's about and perhaps I can make an appointment for you – though I must warn you it won't be soon."

The woman looked down at the middle–aged man at the desk and felt a sudden scorching surge of rage and resentment. Did this crazy man really think she was going to walk away now? After all this time?

She moved closer to the desk. "I said I wanted to see Alyssa Giordano – and I want to see her *now.*"

Johannsen wasn't easily intimidated. But as those fierce, gleaming eyes met his own an instinctive shudder ran down his spine. Suddenly, distrusting his earlier judgment, he wondered if he should use the security button placed unobtrusively at the base of his desk. A necessary precaution when one worked for a woman as controversial as Alyssa Madison Giordano.

"Look, as I've tried to tell you, it's not possible—"

The woman cut him short, her voice barely under control. "Then do this for me. Give this to your boss." She took a long, sealed envelope from the cheap raffia bag slung over her shoulder. "Then if she says she doesn't want to see me I'll go."

Johannsen tightened his lips in frustration as the woman dropped the envelope on the desk in front of him. What the hell... demanding overbearing vixen... still, it might be the only way to get rid of her short of calling security. With a curt nod, he rose from his desk and, aware of the woman's silent scrutiny, crossed the room and tapped at the door to the inner office.

Alyssa Giordano was on the telephone, chatting in her familiar quick fire fashion, as he entered the office. He saw her glance up with a probing frown as he passed the envelope across the cluttered desk and signaled towards the reception area. He watched her thick brown hair fall before her green eyes as she cradled the receiver between her shoulder and ear; she continued speaking while he watched she carefully tear open the envelope. A split second later, he saw her eyes grow wide in astonishment as she stopped mid-sentence. The blood appeared to freeze in her veins as she looked at the hand–written pages. *It was impossible... totally impossible...* her face proclaimed.

CHAPTER 1

MENACE GROWING

The luminescent headlights of the imported Daimler cut through the darkness.

He rarely allowed himself the pleasure of taking the wheel but tonight, as he left New York and its worries behind, his thoughts were far from the delights of driving the superbly tuned machine. A pulse drummed agonizingly in his left temple, and his palms were damp around the leather–bound steering wheel.

The traffic on the turnpike was light at that time on a Sunday night, and in less than an hour he had arrived at the turnoff to Millbrook.

As he took the Daimler easily around the curves of the narrow country lanes, he recalled the many weekends he'd spent at Millbrook House in the last eight years. The American Colonial house set in five hundred rolling acres was where he had so often entertained the elite and powerful, cementing the connections which had allowed his empire to expand and prosper.

As Duncan Kennedy turned off the lane and brought the car to a halt in front of a pair of magnificent scrolled gates, he knew that after what had happened in the past week nothing would ever be the same again.

He pushed the electric eye on the dashboard and the gates swung slowly open. He hadn't informed the staff of his arrival, but the red glow of the sensor would alert them. Normally he was a creature of routine and habit, and they would, no doubt, be surprised by this late and unexpected arrival.

Duncan Kennedy's lips twisted in a bitter parody of a smile. Well, there were a few more surprises to come. As he alighted from the car on the curved pebble driveway, he saw the glow of lights from the staff quarters at the rear. Despite the copious staff, no one would disturb him, he was sure of that.

In the cavernous hallway he snapped on one of the two magnificent chandeliers, and then hesitated at the entrance to the sitting room.

Why not? he thought. His courage needed no bolstering – he had made up his mind – yet he saw no reason to deny himself the pleasure of a fine glass of whiskey. His footsteps made no sound on the thick Axminster. Just as his thick hand firmly seized the Waterford decanter, he was disturbed by the ringing of the telephone.

Damn. His face darkened. Not now. Not this evening.

But it was only the internal line. He heard the soft Scottish burr of Robertson on the other end.

"Wasn't expecting you, sir. Just wondered if you required me." The respectful, soothing tones of the perfect servant. A man who knew his job was easier than most and was determined to do nothing to lose it.

"No, Robertson. Thank you. Don't disturb yourself."

Duncan was surprised at the steadiness in his voice. And as he replaced the receiver he thought obliquely how faultless Janet had always been in her choice of domestic staff. *You concentrate on the business, darling,* she would say, *leave the rest to me.*

And as he filled his glass, bitterness again twisted his lips. In the end, it seemed, his wife had proved better at her job than he at his.

He drank the whiskey in one long swallow and, as he placed the empty tumbler back on the silver tray, he took a moment to dwell on the beauty of the room – on the elegant mix of antique and contemporary furnishings, on the superb marble fireplace that had cost him a small fortune to restore, on the Degas that was now worth almost twenty times what he had paid for it.

Material possessions, Duncan Kennedy thought. *Was that the measure of success, realized ambition? What was it all for?* Yet nothing of his material possessions, he knew now, compared to a man's reputation.

His expression hardened as he turned and hurried from the sitting room, the urgency once more within him. In the wood–paneled gun room, where telephone lines were secured and cameras absent, he dialed to disturb another man with the ringing of the telephone. After replacing the receiver, he turned back towards the entrance of the space.

His fingers trembled only slightly as he unlocked the walnut cabinet and lifted the ivory–handled pistol from its padded bed.

*****

He prowled, he planned, and he did everything under the sun to ensure there were no survivors.

Holding the gun in one hand and dragging Duncan Kennedy behind him with the other, as he stalked through buildings around the three–and–a–half–million dollar property, meant that he had to keep his guitar case slung over his back. As the horrifying events began in the late hours of the evening, the slayer forced Kennedy into the barn. He fired the gun to silence the squealing horses as he splashed gas through the central internal passageway of the barn.

He ignited the match and threw it behind him into the barn as he coerced Kennedy into the horse float, to drive it to the mansion's gates before shooting the tires, blocking the entrance to emergency vehicles, ensuring that they would have problems entering the property. It took an hour for the mad man to kill Kennedy's wife and fifteen–year–old daughter, taking his time and taking his pleasure, before laying more fuel and setting fire to the mansion. Then, in front of the security cameras, as the executioner exited dragging millionaire businessman Duncan Kennedy along with him, he gesticulated in defiance and disappeared off–camera, to kill Kennedy outside, then escape.

It was exactly five minutes after midnight when the last shot broke the chilly silence of the night.

*****

The call came through the emergency operator at precisely eleven minutes past midnight.

Sergeant Tim Olsen was the duty sergeant at the station that early morning. He was twenty–three years old and to him the details meant nothing. As far as the former New Yorker was concerned, it was just another burglary turned homicide.

"So that's 506 Sharon Turnpike, right? Is a bus on the way?" He paused a moment for the answer. "Okay, we'll get a car there right away."

Only after he passed on the information did the young sergeant discover that this was no ordinary 10–53.

Oh, God... I have to interrupt the Chief's poker game...

*****

The interruption could not have come at a worse time.

For more than three hours, Hugo Martinez had been dealt lousy hand after lousy hand. Finally, he was poised to end his losing streak. As befitted a man who had plotted his way through the bureaucratic jungle to become the first Hispanic chief of police in Millbrook, his bronzed face betrayed no sign of emotion as he looked down at his royal flush.

But his luck was out that evening. Just as he was about to call the bluff of that liverish oaf who ran the city's most profitable restaurant, there was a knock on the door. With an apologetic cough, a uniformed sergeant poked his head into the smoke–filled room.

"Chief, forgive me, please... but something urgent..."

"Hold on," the police chief snapped. A pot of almost three months' salary was at stake. *Why did he have to be interrupted now?* "What is it, Olsen? It had better be worth the disturbance, man."

The young sergeant looked nervous. "Uh... if we could speak in private, sir?"

With a heavy sigh, Hugo Martinez lifted an apologetic shoulder to his waiting companions. Placing his precious cards down carefully on the blanket–covered table, he lifted his powerfully built form out of the chair. "Just a moment please, gentlemen."

He shut the door sharply behind him, his bad temper obvious. The hallway outside the exclusive restaurant's private banquet room where the regular weekly card game took place was deserted. Still the nervous sergeant felt compelled to whisper the message despite the isolation.

As he listened to the details, the police chief's face grew paler, even behind his skin tones. *No... Surely not... It was impossible...* Then he spat out a vicious tirade of insults against the Lord, His mother and even some of the saints.

For Hugo Martinez knew without a doubt that he had just lost all chance of playing his winning hand that night.

*****

"Christ, Angie... I've only had a couple of hours' sleep in three goddamn days!"

Through bleary, bloodshot eyes, the cinematographer blinked awake to see Angela Ryan's face staring down into his own. At almost the same instant, he realized that the pain he could feel in his ribs was being caused by the toe of his tormentor's thick, leather boot.

"Wakey, wakey, Ray. We didn't come here to sleep through the damned crime wave. Grab that camera and move it – the Chief of Police wants to give a statement. Lee's already downstairs."

Grumbling and swearing under his breath, Ray Jensen struggled out from under the covers and in the weak light from the solitary exposed bulb felt for his fur–lined boots under the bed. He was still wearing the clothes he'd gone to sleep in a short time before, and his fleshy face was shadowed by thick stubble.

"You have no idea what I'd give for a coffee right now." He groaned again as he heaved his heavy equipment onto his shoulders and followed the impatient journalist out of the hotel room. They were on the fourth floor and were forced to enter the icy, malodorous darkness of the stairwell to make their way to ground level. The elevator had stopped working ten days ago and no one had bothered to fix it. But by now, they'd all spent enough time in the sleepy town to know that was par for the course.

"Talk to me nicely and I might save your life." Torch in hand, Angela was clattering down the steep stairs ahead of him. "I've still got a pound of pure Arabica left. Soon as this is in the can I'll give you enough for a cup." Her voice echoed in the confined space.

"Hey, anyone ever tell you you're all heart, Ange?"

They were nearing street level and through the thick concrete walls, they could hear the swelling noise outside. Angela grinned in the dim light. "Nope, and if they did I'd think I was getting soft."

Ray Jensen was sure she wasn't joking. By 6 a.m., the crowd outside the gates of Millbrook House had swelled to half of the community's population. Film and television crews from around the country, with a couple of international crews, were jockeying for the best vantage points as they filmed the activity in the home of the once mighty family. Surrounded by the buzzing, tugging mass, Angie began arguing loudly with a French camera crew who were trying to move her on so they could place their own presenter in the prime location she had assumed.

But Angela Ryan had had plenty of practice in standing her ground. Her French was limited, but fortunately it consisted mostly of insults, and with black looks and plentiful swearing protests, the French were forced to move on.

"Okay, Ray, let's go." As her sound technician adjusted his controls, Ryan reached into the pocket of her green, fur–lined anorak and pulled out a comb, which she ran quickly through her thick, dark red hair. It was her only concession to grooming for on–air presentation. Ray held up two fingers and Angie took the proffered microphone. In a moment the camera was rolling.

"Over the last few hours the situation here in Millbrook House has grown even more disturbing. Estimates now put the crowd at close to five thousand but no one is yet sure if the authorities have made any progress with the investigation into the fire at the ancestral home of Janet Kennedy, a descendent of the original owners of the home, Catherine Hart and her husband, Dr. Alfred Tredway, and the shooting of her husband, Duncan.

"EMTs have taken Mr. Kennedy to Vassar Brothers Medical Center. Police haven't been able to speak with Mrs. Kennedy or the Kennedys' daughter, Kristie, as of about half an hour ago. They're not sure at this point if they were home or of their current whereabouts. As you can see, the grounds are now swarming with officers not only from the New York State Police's forensic team but also from the Dutchess County Sheriff's Office, the Millbrook Police Department and a number of fire departments. The Chief of the Millbrook Police Department is coming out shortly to give us a statement..."

It was a three–minute grab, shot direct by satellite to a national, and possibly worldwide, audience of millions. Most would be barely able to believe what they were seeing. But American viewers would be reassured to find Angela Ryan once again in the thick of the action. The slightly built redhead was a familiar sight wherever in the nation a hot spot caught fire. Casually dressed, face bereft of makeup, the thirty–four–year–old correspondent had filed a long list of tough crime stories. Those who worked with her sometimes felt driven beyond the limits of personal safety, but the male ego ensured there was never any official complaint. If Angela Ryan could handle it, so could they.

*****

As Martinez approached the media scrum, with Olsen in tow, the sound of what seemed like a world of voices started screaming at him. "Ladies and gentlemen," Martinez paused as he waited for the screaming reporters to quiet.

"Ladies and gentlemen, please." Martinez paused again as the din died down. "We'll be making a short statement and will only take a couple of questions. Millbrook Police Department will be taking command of the investigation. Sergeant Tim Olsen will be the lead investigator under my supervision and he will tell you all that we know at the moment." Martinez stepped back to give his junior the limelight.

"Th–th–thanks, Chief," Olsen stuttered momentarily at being forced to give his first media statement. He coughed, to appear to clear his throat. "At eleven minutes past midnight this morning, Millbrook Police Department received a nine–one–one call that a fire had started at Millbrook House. Duncan Kennedy was found outside the home with a gunshot wound and has been taken to Vassar. At this point, we have not been able to contact Mr. Kennedy's wife, Janet Kennedy, or their daughter Kristie.

"The Millbrook Police Department and fire crews are anxious to inspect the home, but it has been difficult to access because of the severity of the fire and wooden boards covering its doors and windows. The fire caused the home's roof to collapse, making the building too unstable to enter, and completely destroyed a nearby stables block and garages.

"An abandoned horse float with flat tires also blocked the property's front gates, which were padlocked. Bullet cartridges and pools of blood have been found at the property.

"Once we can get access to the inside of the house, we will be looking to inspect the home's CCTV system in the hope that it might provide some clues about how the fire started and whether intruders were involved. The house, a garage and stable block and another outbuilding were severely damaged. As soon as the house is deemed to be safe by the Fire Department, we'll carry out a search to establish if anybody was inside. Forensic investigators have been at the scene to make an initial sweep to collect evidence and officers will be making a house–to–house investigation. That's what we know at the moment."

Initially relieved to have completed his initial media briefing, Olsen was taken aback at the reporters screaming questions at him and he turned to Martinez. Martinez, stepping back towards Olsen and slapping him on the back, turned back to the crowd.

"Alright, alright, just one question at this time." The crowd hushed. "You," he paused as he pointed, "Angela Ryan, yes, your question?"

"Is this related to Kennedy's current business strife? Or does it go back to the blackmail attempt a couple of years ago?"

"Look, we just don't have enough information yet. As I said at the beginning, Millbrook Police Department will be taking charge of the investigation and I'll be supervising it personally. I'll be calling another press conference as soon as we have more information. Thank you." Martinez turned to Olsen and they walked away as the reporters started screaming again from behind the crime scene tape.

Chapter 2

Suspicion Abounds

It took three days for Millbrook Fire Department to secure Millbrook House before the Fire Chief would permit police access to the site of the gutted house for the first time. Extensive debris in the main building meant a proper search could take several days and possibly weeks.

The large horse box which had been left by the gates of the property and the animal carcasses found at the scene had been removed almost immediately for forensic tests. Officers would be waiting for some time for the results of the necropsies. By the time officers had completed a complete search of the outbuildings, a cursory search of the annex part of the main building and started removing the remaining vehicles from the site, Duncan Kennedy had regained consciousness from surgery and was recovering slowly at Vassar. But his wife and daughter had still not been located.

Millbrook's Chief of Police arrived at the scene just as his lead investigating officer authorized entry to the main part of the house for forensic specialists to begin the lengthy, painstaking process of sifting and examining all the contents. Since Millbrook Police Department was small, the Governor had authorized the New York State Police to assist Martinez because of the notoriety of the incident. Olsen had nearly a hundred officers and support staff working directly under his command at the scene. The officers on the investigation were checking "every possible line of inquiry," developing profiles on each family member, speaking to friends and relatives, and alerting ports and airports in their efforts to find out what happened to the family.

Correspondents had offered conjecture not about the cause, but about the motive behind the cause: was it that Kennedy's business was close into bankruptcy with debts in the millions, or was it further extortion from a disgruntled client? But investigators could not convince them that the speculation about the family was "unhelpful," as it had upset friends and relatives and could only hinder the scrutiny of possible suspects.

*****

It had taken the forensic detectives, with large quantities of heavy machinery, several days to remove the larger pieces of debris. The cranes brought in to lift out the destroyed structural framing pieces and huge sandstones, and the trucks brought in to haul them away, had finally departed.

The officers had just started the painstaking process of sifting through the extensive smaller pieces of the wreckage. Olsen exited the temporary structure housing the communications equipment with his mug refreshed with coffee, which had become grimy after being brewed within an inch of its life; a sip, a grimace and a shake of the head. He had taken to standing between the command post and the rubble with a portable two–way radio: it allowed him the luxury of seeing progress and being close to the fixed radio if he needed it. It would take time for them to complete the sorting process and for all the contents to be examined; it would be a process that could continue for weeks. Hugo Martinez had made his way through the mass of correspondents for his daily briefing from Tim Olsen on the progress. He liked Angela Ryan and had taken to exchanging pleasantries with her on his way past the media scrum; she was professional, and attractive, which only assisted her cause to get first comment.

"Good morning Ms. Ryan." Martinez adjusted his belt and his two–way radio.

"Morning, Chief. How many today?" She referred to the amount of coffee he'd already had – the question had become almost a daily ritual. He chuckled.

"Stopped counting after five." His ritual answer. They exchanged knowing looks and laughed.

"Anything new?" The second ritual question, this time from Ray Jensen.

"Hi Ray. Don't know yet. Just about to find out." Another stock answer. Their heads all then turned towards the rubble as two groups of the specialist searchers hollered to Olsen.

"Looks like we got something." Ray hoisted the camera back on to his shoulder, took stills of the two groups of the specialist searchers and then tracked Olsen's progress. Martinez sighed, waited for the transmission. Ryan said nothing, intently focused on the young sergeant.

Olsen approached the closer group and caught the Chief out of the corner of his eye. He took a thin, metallic container from the extended arm and examined it. They watched him gingerly climb over the rubble to the second, further group and bend over to gingerly shift a few pieces of the ruins. Martinez's radio crackled.

Post, Bravo 1. Switch to Channel 7, over, the Chief and the news crew heard Olsen's voice crackle over the portable.

Shit. Martinez's thoughts sauntered; he grimaced and started to fiddle with the equipment on his belt as they watched Olsen's animated conversation with the command post. He suddenly stopped his fiddling. *No, brainy.* His frown turned upward slightly. He would keep his impatience in check for the moment.

"Well, it looks like I need to get a report."

"Thanks, Chief," both newsies chimed towards the Police Chief's back as he sauntered to meet Olsen at the edge of the debris. They watched the two men for about ten minutes before short bursts of siren parted the on looking media crowd. The two morgue transport vehicles were closely followed by a van, white, decaled with the logo of a security company. While the few other crew cameras followed and took background shots of the hearses, Ray and Angela tracked the security company van against instinct.

"Wonder what that's about?" Ray asked.

"Don't know. Hugo'll tell us." Angela had taken to first naming the official in his absence.

"Yeah, good one. Knew your legs would come in handy some day," Ray mocked her. She rolled her eyes at him and she blew a raspberry at him. He laughed back.

Both were disappointed that day as the Millbrook County Police Chief scurried past them as he left for the day, without his customary friendly post–action briefing.

*****

It was almost three weeks after they had attended the initial press conference at the burnt out house. The cameras caught the backs of Martinez and Olsen returning to the inside Millbrook County Police Headquarters and the sounds of the reporters screaming more questions at them.

"That was Millbrook County's Police Chief, Hugo Martinez, and the lead investigating officer, Sergeant Tim Olsen," Angela Ryan intoned as she turned back to the camera. "Sergeant Olsen has just confirmed that the two charred bodies found inside the burned–out Millbrook House a week ago were those of Duncan Kennedy's wife, Janet, and daughter, Kristie. The flames that gutted the mansion caused its internal walls and floors to collapse. The badly damaged house was too unstable for officers to enter for several days, but when they did, detectives discovered two bodies inside. Due to the position of the bodies, officers working the scene had to remove a ton of collapsed internal walls and floors to move the bodies and a .22 rim fire rifle was found lying near the corpses. It took some time to remove the bodies and the rifle from the scene for transport to the State Police Headquarters Laboratory in Albany.

"It then took several days for the pathologists to conclude the autopsies and determine that the corpses were those of Janet and Kristie Kennedy, who had not been seen since a fire gutted their house two weeks ago, and that they'd been shot. Mrs. Kennedy's body was so badly burned she could only be identified using dental records. We don't yet know if the rifle was legally owned by Mr. Kennedy or someone else brought it in and the Laboratory will need to conduct further tests to establish if it was the one used to shoot the Kennedys and to kill the animals.

"Three horses and three dogs were also found dead at the estate and Chief Martinez has also informed us that the necropsies determined that the horses were shot but the dogs died in the fire. Forensic officers continued to search for evidence at the property today, as special prayers were said for the family at a nearby church.

"Police are also looking into Kennedy's financial dealings as well as those of his business partners. The company is close to going into liquidation, and Kennedy and his partners were facing large bills from creditors and tax authorities. Kennedy is apparently recovering well from the gunshot wounds he received at the scene, but his doctors have said that he's not yet well enough to speak with police. Police have said they think the sprawling property was set alight in an arson attack but they'll need to speak to the financially troubled Kennedy to find out if he can tell them anything about what happened or why.

"Now, last time we were at the scene, we saw a van belonging to a security company leave shortly after the medical vans that took the bodies away. The forensic team has recovered what appear to be film reels from inside the burnt out shell. Kennedy's company had a security system using closed circuit television at his office and he'd recently had the house fitted out with a similar system. Somehow, the cameras and the film survived the fire but police won't tell us just yet whether they can use the film. That's all Martinez has told us today.

"I'm Angela Ryan, reporting from the Millbrook County Police Headquarters. Back to you in the studio."

"Cut," Ray said, "Good take. It's in the can."

"Thanks." She paused. "Damn." Another pause. "Shit!" she whispered, her eyes went blank. He knew that look. He had studied her for too long not to know that look.

"What?"

Nothing.

"Ange, wakey wakey."

Still nothing. He shoved her, awakening her from her trance.

"Ange, what?!"

"The cameras. The van picked up the cameras!" Angela guffawed with joy.

"What? Whaaat? Whadaya mean the van picked up the cameras?" Ray's mind was slow today; he had gone without his second cup of Arabica this morning. His eyes narrowed, his lips turned upward. "Yeah, the cameras. Shit, what a shot!" He got it.

Angela watched, inanely humming, as Ray packed up his gear. They shook their heads as they debunked to their vehicle, to depart Millbrook County Police Headquarters.

Wish we could try and salvage the images from the video for them! Their minds were again synchronous, as they often were.

CHAPTER 3

UNWANTED ATTENTION

To bag an interview with the mother of the millionaire businessman who survived gunshot wounds in an arson attack on his home, and whose wife and daughter were murdered during the attack, would seem like the pinnacle of her career. It would be the first time the anguished woman would speak of her grief to the world. It would be the first time in her career that she would conduct an interview in the newsroom rather than in the field.

Angela had surprised even herself with her career progression in the eight years after the Jane Roe saga had ended. After a brief period as a publicist with a celebrated agency and a job as a writer at a major network, she joined one of the morning shows as a writer and researcher the year the Roe decision became public. She moved up to become that show's regular "Today Girl," handling lighter assignments. Within a year she had become a reporter–at–large, developing, writing, and editing her own reports and interviews. When a stubborn pig–headed man of the old guard was offered the host role, he refused to take it unless he was named sole host, without Ryan as co–host. That had sealed it for her: the other major network had been making approaches, promising to give her a prime time on–air gig, particularly after the early work she had done on this case. She took her bargaining power and brought Ray along on her coattails. She would be officially designated as the program's, and the network's, first female host. What neither she nor Jensen knew was how their careers would pan out after that first in–studio interview. Of course she would have no other cameraman than Ray Jensen. His directorial debut would also be an original experience for him.

"Hey, Ray," Angela Ryan called to the newly titled "director" as he walked across the floor of the studio. She had just finished having makeup and hairspray applied.

"Ange, what were you thinking when you agreed to this?" He was exasperated by the tightness of a tie around his neck. He wasn't used to working in the formality of a newsroom and much preferred the field.

"I have no fuckin' idea!" Ryan was also incensed by the idea of wearing something other than her usual casual field attire. "But what, you wanna miss this?"

"Pulling the interview of the century, no, the millennium? Hell no! When's she get here? You met her yet?"

"She's in makeup now. Yeah, just for a minute when I was getting my hair done. Me! Getting my hair done! And makeup! What a laugh." Jensen couldn't hold in the chortle. "Hey, come on! You look like you got your makeup done too!"

"Yeah, yeah, alright!" Ray moaned.

"You all set?"

"Yeah. How 'bout you?"

"No."

"Oh, come on! You forced me into this; you're not going to get out of it now! At least I won't have to worry about the wind blowing your hair in your face!"

"Yeah, alright, alright!" Angela moaned. "I'll cop that. How long we got before we're on?"

"About ten. Time to get on the set. Better get her out here."

"Yeah, it's time to get settled in the chair." Ryan turned about, moved towards makeup, looking for an assistant, someone, to ask about getting settled in front of the camera. Angela found a dowdy, slightly chubby girl, who looked like she hadn't left school yet; she'd seen her around the newsroom before. "Sarah?"

"Y–yes?" The girl jumped on hearing the crack reporter's voice and stumbled into a camera.

"Could you find Mrs. Kennedy, please? Ray and I'd like to get her on the set."

"Y–yes, s–sure, I'll get her!" The plain teenager, a little overwhelmed, was more that pleased to run off on an errand for a woman the caliber of the semi–famous Angela Ryan. Angela wandered back to Ray's position in front of the set, saw him with a hand over his mouth, desperately trying to hold in his laughter.

"What are you snickering at?"

"That poor child!" Ray moved his hand away from his face. "You know she thinks a lot of you, right?"

"I know," Angela rolled her eyes. "She'd be quite pretty, if she paid more attention to herself. She's got potential though." They considered that thought in silence until they saw the young girl slowly walking the elderly interviewee from behind the framing towards the set, supporting her elbow with her hand free of the clipboard. Angela headed towards the women, one more aged than the other, a heel catching on a bundle of cables almost causing her to stumble but she quickly regained her footing.

"Hello again, Mrs. Kennedy," she said to the grief stricken woman. "You look wonderful! Are you ready?"

"Hello. Why thank you, dear." Enid Foster Kennedy tried to keep her sorrow in check, but the anguish could not escape her voice and, as they moved slowly to the chairs on the set, her misery was obvious to everyone on the set. "No, I'm not ready. I can understand outliving my husband but I don't think I'll ever accept that I've outlived a grandchild."

"No, I don't think I could accept it either. Let's go sit. We're almost ready to go." As she helped Mrs. Kennedy get settled before seating herself, Ryan unobtrusively glanced at Jensen and got the half minute signal. Again she had timed it to perfection.

"Okay, Mrs. Kennedy, we're just about ready," Angela said just as she turned towards the camera. It was strange to see Ray standing offset from the camera this time, rather than behind it. He gave her their usual silent code for "Go, we're rolling."

"I'm Angela Ryan. Welcome to *Twenty/Twenty* and thank you for joining me for my first special presentation. This will be the first in a number of presentations over the coming months. Tonight, I'm joined by Mrs. Enid Foster Kennedy, mother of Duncan Kennedy. Thank you for joining me, Mrs. Kennedy. How is your son?"

"Thank you, dear. Duncan is slowly improving, getting better."

Ryan asked Mrs. Kennedy about, and she spoke of, her grief but said nobody knew of her son's financial problems. The mother of Duncan Kennedy said she was driven with sadness and shock and found it hard to believe that her son was unable to face telling his family of his impending financial doom.

Mrs. Enid Foster Kennedy, who lived in the area where her son and his wife and fifteen–year–old daughter had lived, also said she could not ever believe that her son would ever take such reckless and fraudulent actions; it must have been those awful partners of his. Mrs. Foster, who was reported to be seventy–eight, described her young granddaughter, Kristie, as "beautiful" and spoke of her struggle to understand what some hideous monster had done to his family because of her son's partners.

"I can't condone what his partners have done." Her eyes welled up with a tears and she let out a little sob as Angela leant forward and patted her hand. She drew a breath and continued. "Duncan talked to nobody, we knew nothing about his financial situation and it's come as a tremendous shock. So many of his friends have told me that, had they known, they would have helped him however they could. They were a very close, loving family unit and I don't think he could face telling them he thought they were going to lose everything, but it wasn't his fault."

Mrs. Foster said her granddaughter had been an accomplished horsewoman and "absolutely loved" her horses. Kristie attended a private school; her father loved clay pigeon shooting and liked playing the country squire, even wearing tweeds to meetings. "Kristie was just a lovely girl," she said. "Kristie was in a local horse show only the weekend before and placed first in a championship."

Prior to going to air, Angela and Ray had taped an interview with the last person to see the family before the fire and at that point, Angela cut to the taped portion. John Hughes was a neighbor and host of the weekend horse show in which Kristie had participated, and he could not fathom the tragedy: "Duncan was fine, just his normal self – they all were. They are very nice and a very close family. Duncan is very much a family man who loved his animals almost as much as he loved his daughter."

As Ray cut back to Angela after the tape concluded, she wiped a tear from her cheek and turned back to Mrs. Kennedy.

"It must be hard."

"It's very hard. I've lost a daughter–in–law and beautiful granddaughter and I've nearly lost my son. Life will never be the same without them. I'm finding it very difficult to come to terms with." At that point, the mature woman pulled a photograph out. It was a classic happy snap. A little out of focus and badly framed but nevertheless a record of one of the myriad joyful moments that punctuate family life: a long weekend, Mom and Dad in the background, a teenager with them, and all smiling contentedly at the camera.

"Thank you Mrs. Kennedy."

"No, thank *you*, dear."

"Ladies and gentlemen, that concludes my first program. See you again next week. Thank you, good luck and good night."

As the studio lights dimmed and the end–credit music began, Angela turned back to Mrs. Kennedy to see the picture again. Her son, his wife and daughter's innocent smiles in that photo – or the women's last thoughts – simply did not bear thinking about. Little did she know that the thought of the women's innocent smiles, their last thoughts, again would come back to bother her.

CHAPTER 4

UNDUE NOTICE

For Lydia Kennedy, the morning of her eleventh wedding anniversary began like any other summer's day.

It was just before six when she stepped out onto the deck of her cliff side home, her perfectly maintained thirty–nine–year–old body wrapped in a brilliantly patterned silk sarong.

Heaven... Pure heaven... Lydia smiled to herself as she took in the glittering ocean lapping lazily onto the outrageously expensive curve of sand that was Montauk's Gin Beach.

This long–established summer retreat of New York's rich and powerful was less than a two hour's drive north of the city, but for Lydia it was a lifetime away from the damp and dingy Manchester slum where she had spent her childhood.

On mornings like this, with the ocean sparkling diamond bright in the early sunshine and the rhythmic murmur of the breakers in her ears, the former Lydia Tobin would remember to bless the patron saint of ambitious women who had surely brought Duncan Kennedy into her life.

That miracle had occurred in London almost a dozen years ago, just when Lydia was beginning to feel the first stirrings of real panic about the future. It wasn't as if she hadn't done the groundwork – she worked hard on getting the right wardrobe, accent, address – and although she had spent her last penny in the process, her ultimate goal still remained frustratingly out of reach.

By the time of her fortuitous meeting with the American entrepreneur thirteen years her senior, Lydia had slept with an indefinite number of men – quite a few of whom hadn't even minded paying for the privilege. Yet time and time again the barrier of class had thwarted her ambitions. It was as if some indefinable hovering stench invariably alerted her prospective prey to the lowliness of her background.

But on that late June evening her luck had changed. A hard–won invitation to a smart dinner party at the honorable Arthur Neeson's Knightsbridge flat had provided the key to the door of her future.

Widowed just eight months, Duncan Kennedy had been on a business trip to London when he had accepted that fateful dinner invitation. For the forty–year–old businessman it was love at first sight when he was introduced to the fetching brunette in the low–cut dress which so perfectly matched her green eyes. They were seated across from each other at the long candle–lit table, and it didn't take Lydia long to sense the difference in this approach. Americans it seemed were much less concerned about class than her fellow countrymen.

She could see the warm light of appreciation and desire in Duncan Kennedy's dark eyes but something bothered her... The light was slightly dimmer than she was used to. He had tried to keep the details of his predicaments, both past and present, from her but, with all her classless cunning, Lydia had found out what went wrong and she would not let anyone destroy her promotion in life or thwart her ambitions again. It had not been hard for her to discover the circumstances surrounding his first dilemma: the extensive media coverage at the time had made it easy. It was the murder of his wife and daughter, and the police's inability to identify and capture their executioner, that had really wound up the media exposure: he had extracted much public sympathy for that.

But the media coverage of Duncan Kennedy's second financial predicament has not been as extensive and it had been harder to scrape together the details of the quandary he faced with his current business partner, Lydia Price, whom she had taken to calling "the other Lydia". He lost almost all of his dead wife's family money, but not his own fortune – the Manhattan residence and an astounding, to a girl from the slums of Manchester it was astounding, amount of cash – it had been his – in the breakup with his and the other Lydia's business partner. It was why he had moved from Millbrook to Montauk and he had been able to bring only Robertson with him;

Lydia had tried to win Robertson over with their common birthright, but the "southerner" had never been able to win the "northerner" over. She supposed it was his loyalty to his former mistress; she also supposed he knew more about Duncan's predicament but Lydia couldn't drag the more intimate detail out of him.

Such a bad stain, in fact, was something that her privileged man almost couldn't bear to face the future on top of the loss of his first wife. Lydia had convinced her namesake in the business partnership to let her fight back on their behalf to prove their "innocence" and expose their charlatan partner. They had come away with their reputations relatively unscathed. It was not quite their fault: it had almost certainly been caused by their former partner's fraud and their failure to see it early enough. And in less time than it later took her to find Montauk on the map, she landed her prize.

The marriage took place a mere six months later beneath the arches of St Patrick's parish church, rather than the Cathedral of the same name, in Manhattan. It was then the blushing bride got her first inkling that her husband's fellow citizens might not be quite as egalitarian as she had first surmised. Not all of the female guests were thrilled with the eligible widower's choice of wife. No doubt, Lydia told herself, they resented the fact that an outsider, and a Pom at that, had beaten them to such a desirable catch.

Yet she had seen no reason to let their antagonism worry her. Not with the gold and diamond ring on her left hand that proclaimed her Mrs. Duncan Kennedy of Manhattan and Montauk. Slowly acceptance had come, and Lydia had settled into her adopted country with the ease of one who has found her spiritual home. Even the feeling of being in the shadow of his first wife had diminished and she had eclipsed Janet at her job of being the prominent mate of a prominent man. Lydia wasn't sure if Duncan had noticed, but she had taken on a slight variation of one of the dead woman's axioms. *You attend to the firm, beloved, and leave the rest to me.*

She loved the summers at the beach. With Duncan busy in Jersey with the "other" Lydia all week, she had the house to herself and enjoyed her solitude. She was never bored – she was too grateful for the ease and pleasure of her life.

Turning away from the view, Lydia went inside and prepared for her usual morning walk. At her heels her peach–colored poodle,

Dominique, pranced excitedly as she picked up her broad–brimmed raffia hat. She had seen what damage the sun could do in the complexions of her American contemporaries.

"Come on, then, Dommie."

As they left the house Lydia followed the excited animal down the path through the trees that led to the beach. The sun on her arms felt like a sensual caress. Later it would grow fiercer, but by that time, she told herself, she would be safely ensconced inside with the latest magazines.

The sand was still cool beneath her bare feet as she headed towards the jutting headland with its unused lighthouse. Apart from a handful of surfboard riders far from the beach there were few people around at this hour. The real summer crowds – the holidaymakers who filled the apartments and inns of the Long Island beaches – wouldn't be descending for another few days.

Lydia Kennedy frowned at the thought. She'd grown as intolerant as her long–time neighbors to the intrusion of outsiders onto the strip of sand which she had grown to regard as her own. Why couldn't the hordes find somewhere else to go with their litter and ice boxes and raucous stereos?

"Dommie! Come back here!" Lost in thought, she had allowed the little dog to wander too far away. Now she called again as she watched him scrambling over the rocks. He was still at the silly stage, she thought fondly. Just fourteen months old. Her sweet baby.

"Dommie!" She called again and clapped her hands until finally the dog bounded down the hills of sand towards her. As he came closer Lydia could see he was carrying something in his mouth. *Now what...?*

Then her mouth tightened. "Dommie! Drop it! Drop it at once!"

Perhaps it was the rare sharpness of his mistress's tone that caused the dog to do as he was told. And with a look of disgust Lydia kicked sand over the used... well, they'd called them French letters in her youth. You'd think people would at least have the decency to dispose of the damn things properly. Kids, no doubt. In this climate, unlike Britain's, they could do it outside.

Lydia walked on with a frown. It was a wonder any local girls were still game enough for that sort of mischief after the vicious attack that had happened at South Lake, a couple of beaches down the coast. Twice now. And still the police hadn't come up with any likely suspects. Remembering the headlines, Lydia shivered despite the warmth of the sun.

But the shiver she felt at the thought of the attacks was nothing to her reaction ten minutes later, when she arrived at the base of the headland. She was picking her way through the sharp rocks when she saw it, a splash of color floating gently in one of the tidal pools.

A lost towel, she guessed.

Until she got closer...

I knew he knew more!!! her mind screamed.

*****

The 911 dispatcher patched the call through to Long Island at precisely seven minutes past seven that morning.

A young sergeant was the duty sergeant at the station that morning. He was twenty–three years old, the same age as Tim Olsen had been when he had taken a similar call, and to him the details meant nothing. As far as the officer was concerned, it was just another Hamptons socialite having a conniption.

"So that's near the Montauk Lighthouse, right? Okay, we'll get a car there right away."

Only after he passed on the information did the young sergeant discover that this was no ordinary 10–53, particularly for the Chief.

Oh, God... I have to interrupt the Chief's breakfast...

*****

Both policemen saw the irony.

Hugo Martinez had been on losing streak after being dealt lousy hand after lousy hand at an evening poker game when Tim Olsen had brought him the news.

Both men had come a long way since Millbrook. Now the Deputy Superintendent of the New York State Police, the first Hispanic chief of police to make it so far, and the Chief of the Long Island Police Force, it was another young sergeant who knocked on the door to bring them the news. This young sergeant looked as nervous as Olsen had been back then when he had brought similar news of another body to Martinez.

Again, the nervous sergeant felt compelled to whisper the message.

As both men listened to the details, both their faces grew paler. *No... Surely not again... It was unimaginable...* For more than a decade, they had not been able to solve the death of his first wife by garroting before she was shot, a detail that had been withheld from the media. The police wanted them to think she had died of gunshot wounds; it was not uncommon for the police to withhold "minor" details, Martinez had learnt the small trick to enable him to weed out true leads from pranksters hoping for reward from his mentor. They did not need the vicious invective of slurs this time: they just looked at each other. For each knew without a doubt that they had just lost all chance of finishing their breakfast that morning and that their careers were in the balance if they did not solve this and the previous crime.

*****

"Christ, Angie... I've only had a couple of hours' sleep in three goddamn days!"

It was almost déjà vu. Through bleary, bloodshot eyes, the cinematographer blinked awake to see Ryan's face staring into his own through the van's window. This time, the pain he could feel in his ribs was being caused by his tormentor's elbow.

"Wakey, wakey, Ray. We didn't come here to sleep through the damned crime wave. Grab that camera and move it."

Angela Ryan paused, and laughed. She also recognized it was almost déjà vu. The players were almost the same but it was Long Island instead of Millbrook. Again, the crowd outside the gates of Duncan Kennedy's residence had swelled to half of the community's population. Again, film and television crews from around the country were jockeying for the best vantage points as they filmed the activity in the home of the once mighty family. This time, it was a Hollywood camera crew who were trying to move Angie on so they could place their own presenter in the prime location she had assumed. But given her rise and rise within her profession over the last twelve years, she had earned the right to keep them out. She hated the jockeying for position and had not missed it one iota;

but both she and Jensen remembered their younger days and their enthusiasm for field work.

"Okay, Ray, let's go." As her sound technician adjusted his controls, Angie reached and took the proffered microphone from Ray. In a moment the camera was rolling.

"Death has put Duncan Kennedy in the spotlight again. The unsolved murder of his heiress wife, Janet, and their daughter Kristie, over thirteen years ago and his hasty marriage to his British born second wife, Lydia Tobin, first brought him to national notoriety. Now, the second Mrs. Kennedy has found the body of his butler on the beach outside their Hamptons beach house..."

CHAPTER 5

INAUSPICIOUS PROGRESS

The door seemed impenetrable – it slid with some difficulty; it seemed as if there was something impeding its progress as Alyssa tugged at the handle. The small shop front was at the end of the single–floor building row, which contained a mix of professional, retail and eatery businesses across the road from Hoboken's largest shopping mall.

This can't be good... No, don't panic, she thought. It had taken her over two hours and her last hundred dollar bill to get through the Holland Tunnel: the cab had been caught behind the overturned truck. She had thanked the powers that be for her foresight to have removed her jacket while waiting to pass through the tunnel: the early–August summer heat permeated the taxi, even with the windows down. It was an unusually long, hot summer.

Save for her never–ending desire to be early and, luckily, the cabbie knew the building where her interview was as his daughter worked in it, she would never have made it on time. As she pushed the door closed behind her, she turned away from the reception desk to take a gasp of air without the receptionist seeing.

"Hi, I'm Alyssa Giordano. I have an appointment with Mr. Kennedy and Ms. Price."

"I'll let them know you're here," the girl who looked like she should still have been in school responded with a nod. Alyssa hoped that the run in her pantyhose wasn't visible as she sunk into the low settee and adjusted her skirt. She had bought the most expensive suit she could afford, hoping to show at least an air of professionalism.

It was her twelfth interview after passing her final examinations at Albany Law School. She had heard of Kennedy's notoriety from news reports from the year before and her parents had cautioned her against taking an interview with him; but she was past caring about that given her pressing financial concerns.

She had not yet attempted the Bar Examinations in either Albany or Trenton, as she knew the student loans officer would soon be knocking and the examination fees could wait a little. Alyssa had lost track of the number of résumés she'd sent out, to firms in Albany, Manhattan, Jersey, to as many State and County Judges as her – really her parents' – resources would allow.

The results on her transcript were adequate, better than passing grades, but they were not outstanding. Alyssa was in the middle of her class and she had made the Dean's List twice; but her grade point average was not what the big firms, or the more senior judicial officers, were looking for. Although she had not studied as hard as she could or should have, Alyssa seemed to float through effortlessly; the liking the Dean had taken to her did not trigger the connection that the Dean had with her past in Alyssa's memory, but it had bemused her.

Although the firm was an inconsequential one in Hoboken, Alyssa was tired of the abundant rebuffs from the Judges and the hundreds of firms she'd applied to. All she wanted was a job. *Stop squirming! You look fine.*

She wrangled herself out of the couch, hoping she didn't look too undignified, as the tallish, pot–bellied man approached. "Hi, I'm Duncan Kennedy," he said, offering his hand.

"Alyssa Giordano." Her hand tingled as she let go of his solid shake.

"Follow me." She caught a glimpse of the chubby woman sitting at the table from behind Kennedy's girth as she followed behind him into the conference room. "This is Lydia Price, my partner. Take a seat."

"Thank you. Good morning Ms. Price." Alyssa pulled the chair out as she reached across the table to offer her hand. Price's grip wasn't as firm as Kennedy's was, as dainty as the generously proportioned hand could make it.

As both Alyssa and Kennedy took their seats, Kennedy next to Price and Alyssa across from them, the door at the other end of the room opened. The tall sinewy blonde sauntered in, brushing his hair off his glasses with his long fingers.

29

"Bill Morisette," he announced, offering his hand.

"Hi, Alyssa Giordano," she muttered, shivering as she gripped his strong hand, halfway out of her chair. "No, no, sit," he said, motioning for her to return to her seat. He turned his chair towards her as he sat down next to her.

"Bill is our senior Associate," Lydia said. "So let's get started."

Alyssa hoped they took her instant attraction to Bill, and subsequent skittishness, as job interview nerves. The previous interviews had given her some confidence in the process itself, but Bill's charisma and magnetism had rocked that slightly. Alyssa remembered to smile, the tips she had learnt in her client interviewing class and tried to maintain eye contact with all of them as they fired questions at her. She also dredged up the questions – the start date and her availability, the firm pecking order, the type of work she'd be doing – she had forgotten at the other meetings. She'd be working with Bill and his clerk, Connie, assisting them with the housing development sales for one of the firm's major clients: it pleased her to no end that Bill would be her supervisor – real estate law had been one of her better subjects, but she hoped her attraction didn't show too much.

"When will you be taking the Bar Exams?" Kennedy asked.

"I–I'm not sure. I–It really depends on where I get a job," Alyssa stuttered. "I'll take the first Exam I can after I start work. If I got the job here, I'm hoping I can take the Exam in Trenton in February."

"Have you thought about taking a Bar review course?" This time it was Price, smiling, who begged the question.

"I'm looking at some Bar Review courses at the moment," Alyssa smiled back. "And I've got some materials about a number of them here in New Jersey and some in New York. Again, it'll depend on where I get a job as to which one I choose."

"I think that about does it. Any more questions, Lydia?" Duncan asked. Price just shook her head. They all stood as the encounter concluded and Duncan opened the conference room door for Alyssa.

"Thanks for coming," he said, as he ushered her towards the exit, "We'll let you know about the job in a couple of days."

"I'd appreciate that, Duncan," she started as she shook his hand. "I look forward to hearing from you." She turned towards the pretty front–desk girl, smiled and nodded before walking back to the door. It slid open effortlessly this time; Alyssa wondered if it was a sign as she stepped out and slid it back into place, breathed deeply before stepping off the portico to find her way home.

*****

Compared with the last graduation ceremony she had attended, Alyssa's Commencement Day started gloriously.

Neither the dark grey clouds nor the early winds that had overshadowed the start of her parents' Commencement Day arrived for hers. The fact that this ceremony was occurring at the opposite end of summer rather than in late spring may have had something to do with it. Justice Susan McCoy, of the New York State Supreme Court, looked stunning during the Commencement address despite the heat; the unusually high temperatures had not abated.

Alyssa had wondered how she would get the six extra tickets she needed; the Law School had limited ticket numbers to four for those graduating and both sets of grandparents as well as her parents and siblings wanted to attend. At least Uncle Bobby had begged off attending, relieving Alyssa of the need to ask for more tickets; his mother–in–law had dictated that his wife and Alyssa's cousins visit that day. Somehow, the extra tickets had ended up in her envelope when she collected them. Alyssa wondered how it had happened, but she had not made the connection with her Boston heritage; but the Dean had and remembered her maternal great–grandfather, the Senator, with fondness and was just a little disappointed that he could not attend. The Commencement ceremony and Law School reception passed quickly and Alyssa had just enough time to have a few words in private and a congratulatory hug with Peggy Cooper, a classmate, before she was dragged home for the late lunch with her family.

The trip back to the house had again taken several vehicles, but they passed the traffic more easily. Alyssa's mother and grandmothers had put lunch in the oven while she was dressing, before they had left the house early that morning. Unlike her parents' Commencement, this was just a family affair: only her grandparents, parents, four sisters and her sole brother, as her classmates had their own families to contend with. It had become a tradition to cook enough food for what seemed like an army for a month, as their family had become: it made it only too easy to refrain from portion control, but who cared today?

"I remember watching your parents graduate with you on my lap," Alyssa's maternal grandfather intoned as they all sat down, plates piled high.

"Oh, come on Poppy Ian! Don't start!" Alyssa rolled her eyes.

"Ah, yes. That was a good day. You remember when you got married, Gino, Moira?" It was her paternal grandfather, Paolo, reminiscing this time.

"Stop! Please, not you too, Nonno." Alyssa begged, fork halfway to her mouth, as she almost spilt the mouthful of food over her almost clean shirt.

"Oh, come on boys, that's enough" Nonna Maria interjected.

"Just get back to your food!" It was Nanna Caitlin who interrupted this time. Her parents started to laugh, and the laughter echoed around the room as the meal continued late into the night.

CHAPTER 6

COMMENCEMENT

It was the day after graduation, a week after her meeting with Kennedy Price. The Albany summer weather had remained constant.

Alyssa, relieved that Commencement day had passed as uneventfully as her family would allow, was even happier that her mother had turned off her alarm and allowed her to sleep late. As she folded away the cap and gown her parents, and now she, had worn at their graduation, her cell phone's ringing startled her. She jumped, bumping the bed, knocking the phone to the floor.

"Hello?" she answered it after kicking it almost across the room.

"Hello. Alyssa?"

"Yes?"

"Hi, it's Bill Morisette. Congratulations, Duncan and Lydia asked me to call to offer you the job. When can you start?"

"Wow! Thanks," Alyssa exclaimed, pausing, not wanting to sound too excited. "Look, I'll need to quit my job here," – she didn't let on she was working for her parents – "find a place to live over there. Is August thirty–first okay?"

"Hmmm," Bill uttered, "Yes, that's good. I'm starting holidays for my honeymoon on Friday that week."

"You're getting married?" Alyssa hoped the disappointment in her voice wasn't too obvious. "Congratulations. When's the wedding?"

"Thanks, it's the next Sunday, September 6. Again, well done on the job. We'll see you on the thirty–first. You'd better get working on your review for the Jersey Bar Exams." The phone disconnected before she could thank him again for the announcement.

"Mom! Mom!" Alyssa almost fell down the stairs as she ran searching for her mother. "I got the job with Kennedy Price, in Hoboken!"

"That wonderful, darling! When do you go?"

"I start on the thirty–first." Her mother embraced her and squeezed hard.

*****

The fortnight before starting the post at Kennedy Price had been hectic: packing up, getting a hold on an apartment close to work. The first week of her first real job in the law was nerve wracking: re–introducing herself to Duncan, Lydia and Bill, meeting the secretaries, learning how real estate transactions worked in actuality.

She walked to work that first morning. Although the weather was turning, Alyssa felt exhilarated enough about her perceived change in fortune and needed to work a bit of her excitement off. This time, as she approached the offices of Kennedy Price, she had no trouble sliding the front door open.

The same girl who had been on the front desk when she arrived for her interview was still there. "Hi, I'm Alyssa Giordano; I'm starting work here today." At least she'd been able to obtain a different suit so she wouldn't be remembered from the first meeting as only having one outfit.

"Hi, I'm Gayle," the girl answered pleasantly enough. "I remember you from the interview." She got up and came around the high desk and offered her hand, which Alyssa took. She was taller than Alyssa had first thought and almost waif–like, her long sun–bleached curls setting off her tanned face quite prettily. "Duncan and Lydia aren't here right now, but Bill's waiting for you. I'll show you into his office."

"Thanks," Alyssa responded to Gayle's back as she followed her into Bill's office.

*****

She sat at a desk in the secretarial pool in a space divided from the reception desk and Gayle by a thin partition, rather than in a formal office; space was limited. There were only enough offices for the partners and Bill and the conference room was more accurately the office lunchroom; but Alyssa did get to see clients by herself in there occasionally.

Alyssa was disappointed that Morisette was getting married; she was drawn to him, absorbed in his charisma. His charm had fascinated her at their first meeting and captivated her even further during that first week at her new job.

She tried to use her limited feminine charm, her voluptuous body – during a couple of meetings in his office, she'd pushed her chest forward onto his desk, allowing the buttons on her shirt to "accidentally" fall open and show more cleavage – to catch his attention and make him realize it was her he wanted. But she couldn't catch his awareness sufficiently for him to call off his wedding without just saying so; she didn't know him well enough, really wasn't confident enough in herself, to do that.

Bill came back from his honeymoon appearing well rested and, in the months that followed, Alyssa continued her attempts to captivate him, show her curves to him. He noticed it, her. Alyssa began to feel that Bill oft looked at her longingly, and regretfully, when he mentioned his wife. But he took no overt action. He couldn't completely suppress his growing craving for Alyssa but his self–control and willpower only allowed him the occasional explicit flirtation.

*****

As Veterans Day 1993 approached, the change in seasons had become more pronounced. Alyssa's mood had begun to turn in the same direction: she was feeling as if the weight of the world was on her with the load of work on her desk. Her days became longer, arriving at the office first and departing last, in the dark in both instances. Alyssa mostly kept her time at the office during what was supposed to be weekends to daylight hours.

The secretaries, especially Gayle and Connie, had not quite been able to keep their contempt for Alyssa under wraps. Duncan made her squirm and she got an uneasy feeling in the pit of her stomach every time he came to her desk: he always managed somehow to touch her suggestively but not quite sexually. He seemed to dump all his tax cases on Alyssa, piling her desk to just below boiling point, leaving him with almost naught to do so he could go off to the movies with his wife, whom Alyssa had never met. Lydia didn't seem to want to know her; she was buried in the burden of family law cases on her desk, not leaving her much time for a love life. Her appetite had diminished significantly under the strain; she had fainted a couple of times from low blood pressure rather than hunger.

Bill seemed to be her only ally; he tried his best to assist her with Duncan's tax cases, but that wasn't his area. He had taken her to the medical center after the second fainting turn – she figured his concern to be genuine that time rather than sexual – where the doctor had waxed and waned about the importance of nutrition.

"Alyssa," Gayle barked from the reception desk, with a mouthful of lunch, "phone, line three."

"Thanks, Gayle." Alyssa tried to appear pleasant and upbeat without asking who it was. She wanted to hide her discomfort from them; she thought to risk offending someone was to risk her job. She'd arrived at 6:30 a.m., having only had a piece of toast and nothing else since then.

She picked up the receiver and announced herself.

"Good afternoon, Ms. Giordano," she heard on the other end. "I'm Melissa, from Justice McCoy's Chambers in Manhattan. Her Honor wondered if you were still interested in a clerkship with her and wanted to interview with her."

Alyssa stopped herself short of audibly gasping. A clerkship, in the State Supreme Court in Foley Square! That would be a coup, but could she bring herself to move away from Bill? Wouldn't it be a failure if she had to run home with her tail between her legs to live with mommy and daddy again? She knew in her head he was married. She had met his wife, Theona, at the bank a couple of times and begun to form a friendship with of her. It was silly, to be regretted later – how much hurt it would cause her only time would reveal, but her profound yearning for Bill overruled her head.

"Thank you so much for calling, Melissa," Alyssa mused "but I started a job in Hoboken a couple of months ago which I consider I'm committed to. Could you thank Her Honor for me, but I don't want to waste her time, when she could offer the interview for the position to someone else."

"Alright, Ms. Giordano," the executive assistant replied. Alyssa sighed as she replaced the receiver on the hook.

"What was that all about?" Connie barked from behind her. Alyssa jumped slightly off her chair, startled.

"Nothing," Alyssa uttered as she swiveled her chair to face Connie, seeing Gayle standing with her head around the partition. "Justice McCoy's secretary, the Judge wanted to interview me for a clerkship with her. I'm happy to stay here, so I turned the interview down."

Gayle and Connie glanced at each other, rolled their eyes and turned back to the work on their computer terminals. Alyssa's face reddened, with fear rather than embarrassment, and her eyes welled with tears as she turned back to her own terminal and continued copy typing the contract documents Bill had dictated to her. She felt so alone, shunned, but to leave now would make her feel she had failed to make it on her own; she really didn't want Mom and Dad to think she couldn't live, and love, on her own.

Alyssa passed the rest of the afternoon in silence, only leaving her desk to get her sandwich from the kitchenette to nibble on. The phone rang at seven, the usual time of the evening for the security company to call if the office alarm had not been activated by then. She stood, shakily, and packed her desk readying her things to leave. She began her ritual to lock the office, ensuring the back door was locked before returning to her desk to collect her bag before turning on the alarm on the way out the front door.

"What are you still doing here?" the voice boomed, making Alyssa jump in fright and her face pale. It was Duncan Kennedy. "Did I startle you?" He moved closer, putting his arm around her to stroke her back.

"Yes, sorry," she mumbled, "I had to finish a few things, I'm just leaving now."

"It's so dark. Would you like me to walk you home?" Duncan enquired, suggestively.

"No, thank you, I drove in today," she replied shaking slightly, picking up her bag and moving towards the front door. Alyssa hoped he would take her rebuff for the hint it was supposed to be.

"Okay, I'll walk you to your car," he said walking behind her to the exit. As she slid the door open, she heard him punching in the code on the alarm pad and felt his hand rub his hand over the hooks holding the back of bra together. Alyssa hoped he hadn't felt her shudder at his touch.

They stepped into the car park together and Duncan and enquired about the offer by Justice McCoy. *Damn! They told him! Bitches!* she thought. He watched Alyssa as she climbed into her not quite broken down car, telling him of her rejection. *Don't feel bound to stay,* he told her, *I'd be disappointed if you decided not to stay, but it IS a good opportunity.* His insincerity was blindingly obvious even to someone as naïve as Alyssa thought she was. She made her excuses about it, saying she was happy where she was: it wasn't a complete lie, she was happy to have moved out of her parents' home and be living on her own but she wasn't going to tell him how nervous he made her.

"Are you going back to Albany for the weekend?" He held the door open and leant down, bringing his face close to hers.

"Yes, Mom and Dad are picking me up in about half an hour."

"I'd better let you go then." Duncan moved out of the door well and closed the door for Alyssa.

She waved goodbye to him after closing the door and drove off, barely making it up the stairs to her front door and to the kitchen sink to vomit and wash it out before her parents arrived.

CHAPTER 7

UNDER PRESSURE

She was stressed. The Bar review course had been eating into time at the office: she was arriving barely before, and was leaving the office at the same time as, the secretaries to make the night classes and Lydia Price had indicated her disapproval with scathing glares. And she needed more time away from the office, to actually take the Exams. She was tired. The self–study time and assignments had been cutting into her sleep: she had been getting only a couple of hours a night, slumped over her study notes most of the time.

And now she was anxious, panicky. They hadn't signed off on her request to take the time out of the office to sit the Exams, despite the fact that she had submitted it to them more than a month ago. And the last thing Alyssa wanted on a Friday afternoon, after being the victim of not only Lydia's derisive glares but also those from the secretaries, before the anticipated sleepless weekend of study ahead of her, was to have the conversation she needed to have with someone. But, since she'd submitted her request to the partners at the same time as the application to the New Jersey Board of Bar Examiners, she presumed she'd given them enough notice for them to say yes.

She'd expected Duncan to be in by mid–morning, as was his practice, so she could press him to sign the form; but when he hadn't arrived by the time she got back from lunch, Alyssa elected to stop procrastinating and ask Lydia sign it on his behalf.

"Here goes nothing," Alyssa mumbled as she approached Lydia's office.

"What is it!" Lydia snapped as she heard the mumbling. That didn't bode well, Alyssa perceived.

"Lydia, you got a moment?" she asked as she reached, and stuck her head in the barely open door.

"Just a moment," she snapped again.

"I just wanted to talk about the Bar Exam."

"What for? You should be ready by now."

"I am. Well, at least I think I am. But I wanted to ask about the approval for my leave, for me to go to Trenton for the Exam."

"Have you got all the forms ready?"

"Yep," Alyssa replied. "The forms had to be in by December fifteen, well over a month ago. I filed them with the Board of Bar Examiners in plenty of time. You signed the check, remember? And I put in my leave request a month ago." She sensed that Lydia was holding back, but Alyssa couldn't understand why.

"Ooohh, yes. When is it? The Exam?" It had been so long since she herself had taken the Exams that Lydia had "forgotten" that it was always held on the last Tuesdays and Wednesdays in February and July.

"It's two and a half weeks away. February twenty three and twenty four, but I'd like to be in Trenton the night before. And I'd stay over the night of the twenty fourth and drive back early the next morning."

"What the hell for? We need you here, at least the day after! You'll have plenty of time to get there!"

"I don't want to run the risk of getting stuck in traffic. I won't be allowed in if I'm late." Another thing Lydia seemed to have forgotten.

"Look, I don't have the time for this now. You'll have to ask Duncan."

"But Duncan's not in!"

"Too damn bad. You'll have to ask Duncan." Lydia stood up from her desk and forced Alyssa out the door.

"When's he going to be here?"

"I don't know. Ask Connie, or Gayle," she snarled as she slammed the door behind Alyssa; she was stunned and stared at the door for what seemed an eternity before returning to her desk and, as she sat down, saw Connie and Gayle whispering over some papers.

"Connie, Gayle, do either of you know when Duncan will be in?"

"No," Connie retorted.

"Tomorrow, I think," Gayle barked.

"Okay, thank you," Alyssa replied meekly. *Jeez, what is with everyone today?* she thought as she turned back to her desk to keep working on the figures she had to prepare by the end of the day for the closings due next week.

It wasn't until the secretaries were getting ready to head out the door at the end of the last business day of the week that Kennedy arrived. Alyssa jumped as she heard the front door slide open: she'd been disturbed by her lunch–time conversation with Lydia about taking time to sit the Bar Exams and had been caught up in thought, planning how to approach Duncan on the subject, and had finalized barely half the figures for next week's closings.

"Hello ladies!" he announced, directed to the secretaries rather than to Alyssa, as he slid the front door closed behind him and made his way down the corridor between the offices and secretarial pool towards his partner's office.

"Hello Duncan," Gayle and Connie chimed in chorus, fawning over him. They seemed to enjoy the flirtatious attention that he bestowed upon them, that Alyssa so loathed.

"Hi Duncan. Got a minute? Can I talk to you?" Alyssa asked as he stopped outside Bill's office.

"Not right now; I need to talk to Bill. Can you give me ten minutes," Duncan cut her off as he turned and entered Bill's office and closed the door behind him; it wasn't a question, really, but a statement.

"Sure," Alyssa responded as the door slammed behind him, not quite sure if he heard. Ten minutes turned into an hour and the senior partner made several trips between his junior partner's and senior associate's offices. Alyssa tried to work but she was distracted by Duncan's travels between Lydia and Bill's offices. Finally, after a nerve–wracking hour and a half, Alyssa heard Lydia's door open again.

"Alyssa, can you please come in." This time it was Lydia who posed the question as a statement.

"Sh–sh–sure," Alyssa stuttered as she stood and walked over to the office in the back corner of the office space. As she entered the room, she saw that Lydia had seated herself behind her desk and Bill was sitting in one of the two chairs on the other side of the desk;

Duncan remained standing and motioned for her to sit in the empty chair next to Bill.

"Duncan, Bill and I have been discussing the conversation you and I had at lunchtime," Lydia started as Alyssa lowered herself onto the edge of the empty chair. "We're not going to be able to approve your leave application for the Bar Exams, we can't give you time off at this point."

"What? Why?" Alyssa was stunned.

"I'll be away. Lydia and I are going to England that week," Duncan said. Alyssa understood him to mean his wife, rather than his business partner, since she had met, and now knew, the second Mrs. Kennedy and had heard her accent. She had some sympathy for the "accident prone" woman; Alyssa's instinct told her that Mrs. Lydia Kennedy, whom everyone in the office called "the other Lydia" was not "accident prone".

"And we need you here to look after Duncan's tax cases while he's away," Lydia interrupted. "You can take the Exams next time they're scheduled."

"But that won't be till July!" Alyssa's voice started to crack under the mounting strain; it meant that they wouldn't increase her pay packet until she'd taken, and passed, the Bar Exams. "And the tax cases are ready!" She moved her gaze from Duncan to stare at Bill, hoping for some sign of support from him; Bill, who had been silent throughout the heated exchange, unable to bring himself to contradict the people currently holding his career in their hands, he shifted his gaze from Alyssa's pleading, begging eyes to look at his shuffling feet.

"You'll just have to wait," Duncan retorted. "And you'll have to reimburse the firm for the Exam fees: we'll be taking it out of your pay packet." At this point, Alyssa slumped into the back of the chair and burst into tears. She'd never be able to pay them back and pay the Exam fees on her own. If she asked her parents for yet more money, they would want to know why and, with the truth, the Senator would be told and stick his kind, great–grandfatherly nose in; she sobbed a little harder knowing, if she wanted to stand on her own two feet, there was no other option but not to ask. Bill, remaining silent, simply stretched out his hand and stroked Alyssa's shoulder.

"Oh, pull yourself together!" Lydia snapped as she turned her stare from Alyssa to Duncan, who merely nodded his head once.

"We're not heartless, we won't take it all out at once, the money for the fees; we'll deduct it over a few pay packets." Alyssa nodded as she heard a softening in Lydia's tone, and a small amount of compassion which she did not expect given her previous callousness, as she stopped sobbing and took a tissue from Lydia's pudgy outstretched hand.

"You can get yourself sorted to take to the July Exams first thing Monday morning," Duncan, his tone still strident, indicated. "And we'll agree to let you take the time off now, without pay of course. When are they?"

"July twenty six and twenty seven," Alyssa uttered barely above a whisper as she wiped her face. But she wasn't going to let them off so easily now; they had pushed her around enough today and the urge she felt to punish them overwhelmed her self–doubt and diminishing confidence. As her strength grew, she said "I want the whole week off, and I want it off with pay."

"No, not the–" Duncan started.

"Yes, that's okay," Lydia interrupted him as she changed the dates on the form and signed it. She pushed across her desk towards Duncan and held the pen out for him.

"But–" Duncan tried again.

"But nothing, Duncan." She stabbed the pen at him; he took it and signed the form begrudgingly. "Now go and get some rest over the weekend. Are you right to get home by yourself?" Lydia asked Alyssa, her tone still sympathetic.

"You didn't bring your car today, did you?" Bill inquired as he shifted his head to look into Alyssa's eyes.

"No, I didn't," Alyssa sighed. She couldn't bring herself to look at him.

"I'll take her home." Bill indicated as he looked at Lydia.

"Alright," Duncan said, "off you go then."

Bill rose from his chair slightly before Alyssa did and opened the junior partner's room office door for her. She went out ahead of him and the door slammed behind them. As they proceeded down the corridor, he stopping at his office door to watch her collect her handbag from her desk, they could hear the raised voices of their employers.

What the fuck did you do that for! Kennedy yelled.

Don't yell at me! Price screamed back. *Now what the fuck did I do what for?!*

Tell her she could have all that time off in July. The volume of Kennedy's voice lowered ever so slightly. *We're not going to be able to tell her she can't go then!*

We shouldn't be telling her she can't go now! Price's voice pitched higher. *We'll lose her, just like we lost the last one! Again! And we can't afford that right now!*

That wasn't my fault! She was useless. And just remember whose money it is that funded this joint starting.

No she wasn't useless; she just refused to put up with you and your antics! You remember who keeps this place running, keeps the money rolling in. And keeps you in your playboy lifestyle!

Oh, don't give me that bullshit! You know you wouldn't be here without me! Without my money!

What! Your money? Don't you mean your dead wife's money?

Having heard enough, Morisette started down the corridor to the front door at the same time Giordano moved away from her desk in the same direction after collecting her bag. Alyssa reached the door first, barely ahead of Bill. As she tugged at the handle, as it happened on the day she arrived for her interview for the job with the firm, it seemed as if there was again something getting in the way of the door from sliding open with any ease. He reached for the door from behind her, putting his hand over hers on the handle, and, her spine tingling as she felt his hand on hers and his taut form skimming against her back, they worked together to slide the door open.

CHAPTER 8

INHIBITIONS

They walked to his car, got in and drove to her apartment in silence. The silence remained as he parked when they arrived. He exited the small car first, and opened the door for her. She fumbled in her handbag for her keys as they walked speechlessly to her front door and dropped them as she tugged them out. He was able to stop himself from running into her as she bent to pick them up; but he wasn't able to stop himself from looking at her sensual form as she did so. She dropped them again at the door as she fumbled to get a key into its lock and, again, he wasn't able to stop himself from looking at her voluptuous figure as she picked the keys up for a second time.

After finally unlocking and pushing open the door, she didn't remove the keys or close the door as she raced into the bathroom and slammed that door behind her. He stood at the front door, dazed, unsure what to do. As he heard her begin to dry–retch, he pulled the keys out of the door and closed it behind him as he entered the apartment. He stopped after barely taking three steps inside the accommodations: he was stunned, just as much at how small and decrepit the surroundings in which she lived were as he was at the sounds he heard emanating from the bathroom. The room in which he was standing, really only a living room with a daybed and small kitchenette, was dingy, paint peeling, and the small room without a door purporting to be a bedroom, a drape attempting to cover the opening without success, really wasn't big enough for a bed.

I can't leave her alone tonight, can I? He pondered as he tried to block out the sounds of her continuing to gag behind the closed bathroom door. *At least the bathroom has a door.* He sighed. *Wait! Yes! No! Theona!* His mind scalded as his back straightened in fear. *No, hang on a minute! She's at her mother's!* He smiled at that thought. He shook his head as he heard the vomiting stop and faucets start and sat himself on the daybed. It was another minute before the faucets stopped running and she walked out of the bathroom to see him sitting on the daybed.

"Sorry," she said.

"That's okay. Nothing to be sorry about. Are you alright?" She could hear genuine concern in his voice as she saw him pat the space beside him.

"Yes, I'm fine," she lied. He knew it was a lie, she knew, somehow sensed, he knew it was a lie; the ever so subtle changes in her appearance and demeanor, too subtle for the others to notice but not him, belied the notion that she was fine. She inhaled, then exhaled, deeply before walking towards him to obey his gestured instruction. He lifted his arm as she sat, put it around her shoulders. She leant in slightly and put her arms around his waist. He discerned that, at this moment, she just felt comforted by his touch, his presence, but not the sexual energy he was exuding for her. In her inexperience, she had been unable to hide her feelings for him but he had hoped he had been careful enough to hide his own feelings. "Theona?"

"At her mother's. For the weekend."

"You mind staying a bit? I don't want to be alone at the moment."

"Not at all. Of course I'll stay, I don't mind at all," he babbled. He drew her head to his chest as leant back against the armrest. He smelt her hair as he felt her breasts, her beautiful wonderful breasts, rub against his chest. "I'm sorry."

"What for?" She was surprised at the regret in his voice.

"What they did, the Bar Exams." He breathed in the scent of her hair again. "I begged them not to."

"Why?"

"It's not fair to make you wait until July."

"No, why did they—"

"Oh, okay. It was him, the lazy misogynist pig. He just wants to swan around in his own importance, on the blood sweat and tears of others."

46

"But surely she had something to say about it."

"She tried, but she can't really do much."

"Huh? They're partners!"

"He's got the money; and she can't afford to buy him out right now. He likes watching people bow to his will."

"Oh. I see. That makes sense now."

He could see it didn't, but he didn't contradict her second lie. He yawned.

"You're tired," she said. "I should let you go."

"No, I'm right." He yawned again.

"No, you're tired," she giggled.

"Yes, I could use a bit of kip."

"Here, let me up so you can lie down."

"No, you're right. This is big enough for the both of us, isn't it?" She just nodded at the statement. He used his free arm, so he wouldn't have to remove the other from her shoulders or her head from his chest, to lift her legs onto the daybed so he could extend himself along its length; she matched his maneuverings and extended the length of her body against his.

"Isn't Theona expecting you?"

"No, not this weekend. This is a secret mother daughter business weekend."

"Ah, yes. The secret mother daughter business weekend."

They laughed and yawned and slipped into an easy silence, not needing to speak. He wanted to offer her more than just friendship, support, but didn't; she would have accepted what he wanted to offer, but decided that all she really wanted at the moment was a little bit of comforting. The meeting with the bosses had drained them both. Despite the early hour, they fell asleep in each other's arms.

The touch of his arms around her, rather than the bright sunlight pouring through the small window, woke her. She didn't open her eyes immediately, but when she did she saw he was still in the clothes he wore to the office yesterday. She adjusted her head to see that she was also still in the clothes she wore to the office yesterday, but both their shoes were off; she didn't know how, and didn't care, how he got them off without waking her.

"Hello, sleepyhead." His voice was low, gentle.

"Hello, sleepyhead." She matched her voice to his.

"Sleep well?"

47

"Yep. You? How long have you been awake?"

"Yep. Since sunup. Hungry?"

"Mmmm. Yes!"

"Alright then." With that, he sat up, forcing her to raise herself up with him, and swung his legs over the edge of the bed. "Let's go get something to eat."

"My teeth are fuzzy, my face is dirty."

"You jump in the shower while I grab a change of clothes from the car."

"Huh?" She looked at him inquisitively as he grabbed her keys and opened the front door. She wondered, *Why would he have a change of clothes in his car?*

"Theona makes me keep an overnight bag in my car." He rolled his eyes. "Just in case she wants to take a spontaneous weekend away."

"Oh." She rolled her eyes back. "That's spontaneous." He laughed as the door slipped shut behind him.

As she left the bathroom in a towel, she saw, as expected, he had returned before she had finished her routine and was sitting back on the daybed.

"There's a clean towel in there," she said as she pulled the towel tighter.

"Righto," he said as he stood and picked up his bag.

His arm grazed hers as they passed each other, him into the bathroom, her to the doorless bedroom. The smallness of the apartment meant that she could hear all that happened within it; she listened to the shower running as she dressed and fixed her hair in a loose plait. It was his turn to see her sitting on the daybed as he exited the bathroom, fully dressed, bag in hand, hair still wet.

"You ready?" he asked as he stopped outside the bathroom door.

"Yep."

"Where's a good place to eat around here?"

"Around here?" She chuckled. "I don't know. I normally don't go out to eat around here."

"Right." He chuckled. "I don't think I'd go out to eat around here either." He pulled open the front door and let her out first. "I know a place."

They fell back into the easy silence of the previous evening as they approached his car. The hush continued until they were seated in the café he'd chosen. The banter at the café was basic, limited to ordering, checking the fare was satisfactory, banal mindless chatter until it came time to pay the check; she wanted to contribute, he wouldn't let her and a small but friendly argument ensued. He refused to let her hand over any of her cash and she eventually accepted his graciousness, at which point the silence resumed and remained until he pulled up outside her apartment block. He turned off the engine and they sat silently for what seemed an eternity but, in reality, was scarcely a minute.

"Thanks for breakfast," she said, remaining motionless.

"That's okay," he replied, also remaining still.

"What you up to for the rest of the weekend?"

"Dunno yet. You?"

"Well, I was going to study. But now? I'll probably do some laundry."

"Laundry. I gotta do some laundry too. Take the weekend off from study." He stroked her forearm; she felt a shiver electrify her spine.

"I'd better go." She put her hand over his, holding it on her.

"Yeah, you'd better go." They sat, his hand on her arm and her hand on his, for another eternity before she removed her hand from his to open the door. He stared at her back as she got out of the car. He waved at her as she closed the door behind her before driving off; she stood on the sidewalk as he drove off, watching until she could no longer see the car.

*****

"Thanks so much," Alyssa said into the telephone. She'd spent the first half of the working week splitting her time, and her mind, talking to the Clerk of the New Jersey Supreme Court about transferring to, and paying for, the July sitting of the Bar Exams. "So you'll send me a letter?" She listened a moment. "Yes, that's the address. Thanks again." She breathed a sigh of relief as she put the hand piece back to its position.

"What was that?" She jumped at the male voice behind her and swiveled the chair around to see Morisette behind her, leaning against the partition.

"The Clerk of the Court." Her eyes moved to look at Connie, sitting with her back to them and her attention directed to her computer but she sensed that her ears were pricked. "I'm set for the July Exams. And they've agreed to carry over the fees till then."

"So my affidavit worked?" Bill smiled as he turned his eyes towards Connie to see her shake her head. Alyssa, still looking at Connie, also saw it. She turned to a case file and rifled through it; they both decided to ignore her feigned lack of inquisitiveness. "You won't have to pay the fee again? I thought they weren't refundable."

"No, they're normally not refundable, or even transferable. But the clerk said that the Court agreed my circumstances were extenuating enough to transfer the fees."

"That must be a relief."

"It is."

"You wanted to talk to me about some files?" He pushed himself off the partition. "Bring them in," he said as he headed back to his office.

"Sure." She swiveled back to her desk and picked up the files for the cases she wanted to discuss. As she stood and followed him into his office, out of the corner of her eye she caught Gayle sitting on Connie's desk as they whispered to each other. She knew they were whispering about her, again. She pretended not to notice; she knew of no other way to deal with it.

CHAPTER 9

DOWNWARD SPIRAL

Spring was building to another hot summer.

Her parents had tried to put a stop Alyssa's weekend working habits by picking her up – they didn't trust the rundown car she'd bought for herself – on Friday nights for trips to Albany and only returning her mostly on Sunday afternoons, sometimes Monday mornings. However, it wasn't that she didn't want to spend the weekends in Albany, but her parents' expectations only loaded more pressure on. But at least they had replaced her dilapidated car with a decent one her father considered reliable, but only after he had examined it. It allowed her to make her own way to Albany and back again, so at least she could take her own sweet time about when she left. And, not only did the travel time cut into her study time for the Bar, so too did the time her parents wanted to spend with her, taking her to galleries, to visit her grandparents or just simply talking to her.

Alyssa had been able to build a wall around herself to block out Gayle and Connie's scathing looks. Gayle, who got the mail ready addressing and stuffing the envelopes for the Post Office in the afternoon, didn't mind doing it for the others, especially Bill – Alyssa imagined that Gayle also had a crush on him, but hid it better – but loathed doing so for Alyssa.

Bill's imposed routine of meeting her mid–mornings for coffee to discuss her work had helped, but it hadn't helped Gayle's attitude as it cut into the secretary's time with Bill. Alyssa would miss the daily interludes over Easter, but at least it was late this year. She'd continued her flirtations, showing him her cleavage as often as she could; Bill hadn't stopped her, he seemed to enjoy ogling her.

This time, she wouldn't be able to avoid the trip back to Albany, but she had come to accept the inevitable. Alyssa had been able to avoid it for some months, making excuses about studying for the Bar Exams, but Easter was not an occasion where any excuse would hold with her staunchly Roman Catholic mother. The drive from Hoboken to Albany was not as difficult as she expected before the long weekend; Duncan and Lydia had decided to close the office at lunchtime and it was either too late or too early for Alyssa to be caught in traffic. She had gone home to change from her work wear and collect her one piece of luggage for the weekend and still missed the traffic which had already come and gone and the workers would not start the drive until the usual workday end. *Thank you for making Duncan so lazy,* she prayed silently as she pulled into the driveway in time for dinner.

"Hello, anyone home? I'm here," Alyssa called as she fumbled with her keys in the door, the rucksack almost falling from her shoulder.

"Hello. In the kitchen," Moira answered. "How was the drive?"

"Good, pretty easy for today. Anyone else home?" she called out from halfway up the hall to her room to deposit her bag.

"No, just me at the moment," her mother yelled.

"Where's Dad?" Alyssa's voice lowered as she retraced her steps to the kitchen.

"Golf." As she returned to the kitchen with her half–finished novel, Alyssa saw Moira roll her eyes as she put the casserole dish in the oven. "Where else? Can you watch the oven while I go change?"

"Sure." Alyssa sat at the kitchen table and took to the page where she had left off the night before.

Alyssa looked up as she heard the door thump shut. She had been so engrossed in the book that she had not heard the keys turning in the lock or the door open.

"Ciao, Moira? Alyssa?" the male voice intoned; he had seen Alyssa's car in the driveway.

"Hi Dad. In the kitchen." Gino hugged her as they kissed each other's cheeks.

"Where's Mom?"

"Changing. She went in about half an hour ago."

"Hello darling," her mother, now dressed for dinner, declared as she wandered into the kitchen and hugged her father. "Have you told her?"

"Not yet. I've just got in."

"Told me what?" Alyssa demanded, looking askance from one to the other.

"Shall you tell her or shall I?" Moira asked Gino.

Gino said nothing, but put his hand in his pocket, fished out a set of keys and handed them to Alyssa.

"What are these?" This time, Alyssa's tone was a little less demanding.

"The keys to your new co–op," Gino announced, beaming. Moira drew her hands to her mouth to cover her smirk, but could not hide her excitement.

"What? I don't understand!" Alyssa exclaimed.

"Well," Moira started, "We were a bit uncomfortable with where you're living now, and it's just not safe for a young lady."

"We'll come up next weekend to show you around and help you move in," Gino interjected. This time, Alyssa would allow them to help; it would only be a few bags.

Alyssa jumped up; knocking over the chair she had been sitting on, and threw her arms around her parents without saying a word. The rest of the weekend passed as uneventfully as Easter could in the Giordano household apart from the gift her parents gave her; attending the Vigil Mass and the traditional Giordano Easter Sunday feast, it was the most uneventful, and eventful, Easter that she had spent with her family.

At least she would not have to move as far to her new home this time. And she would have more time, and seclusion, for studying for the Bar.

*****

The "party," if you could call it that, celebrated not only Alyssa's first year at Kennedy Price but also her having completed the Bar Exams. It was only a few small cakes and pastries over morning coffee in the conference room the Friday after her actual anniversary, but she was surprised and pleased that Bill had remembered and organized it for her. The secretaries made some small effort to hide their disdain for Alyssa from the partners, which seemed to go over their heads.

Alyssa prayed silently that Lydia and Duncan couldn't feel the sexual tension which had been mounting between her and Bill. There were a few general conversations going on around her as Alyssa stood watching against the external wall.

"So," Duncan turned and said to her, "I finally got the IRS to give the Ruiz's an extension on paying their overdue taxes."

"Great!" Alyssa said, trying to sound excited but knowing that it would mean he was throwing more work at her. "What has to be done?"

"It's almost done." Duncan sighed. "They've sold their house in Suffolk, it closes at the end of November, but they should be able to buy a new smaller one, with what's left over after the taxes are paid."

"So what has to be done?" Alyssa repeated, trying desperately not to cringe.

"They've signed a contract for a new place on Long Island. But they'll need bridging finance as the escrow's shorter, end of October. Can I leave that with you?" Duncan replied.

"Sure, I'll get on it straight after lunch." As she said it, Alyssa could see Bill eyeing her, then looking at his feet, while he was half listening to Lydia as he watched Duncan about to sink Alyssa's planned early evening.

"Before would be better."

*****

The month and a half since the anniversary of her appointment had been rougher than usual.

It was the day the Ruiz's needed to have the bridging finance for the Long Island property, otherwise they'd lose it. The finance broker had been able to find all bar the last ten percent and they needed to decide if they wanted to pull the money out of their 401(k) plan.

Alyssa's heart was in her throat all day that Friday, waiting for Mrs. Ruiz to call with the answer; she'd already left several messages for Mrs. Ruiz before lunch and lost track of the number of times she had spoken to their bank manager. If she didn't get an answer to the vendor's attorney by close of business, then the whole deal would be off and they would lose their deposit as a penalty.

"Alyssa, Mrs. Ruiz, line four this time."

She was now so used to Gayle barking at her from the reception desk about her phone calls that she did not hear the snarl in her voice. Anyway, it was almost time for the weekend and Alyssa didn't care this close to closing time.

"Thanks so much Gayle," she said picking up the phone. "Hi Mrs. Ruiz, what's happening?" She listened. "Yes? You could pull the funds out?" Another pause, more listening. "I'll let everyone know. Thanks for letting me know." Again a pause, further listening. "Yes; yes it'll be okay now. I better get this letter done; it's got to go today." Alyssa started typing the letter before she had hung up the phone.

"What's happening?" Bill enquired. Alyssa swung her chair around to see him peering through the floor to ceiling trellis overlooking Connie's desk, dividing it from the internal passage.

"That was Mrs. Ruiz." The relief in Alyssa's voice was obvious. "She was able to get the funds out of their 401(k) plan without any penalties and the bank's already said they've got the rest."

"Good," Bill smiled, "Let Garrick Westman know."

"I'm on that now," Alyssa said as she was turning back to her computer.

The letter finished printing with minutes to spare; she just hoped she could get it faxed before Gayle left with the mail.

"Gayle, could I please have an envelope?" Alyssa asked as she started to copy the number from the letter to the keypad on the fax machine.

"Here, I'll do that," Gayle snarled, snatching the letter from her hand. Bill saw Alyssa's downcast face flush as he exited Duncan's office for his own. Alyssa's eyes barely caught his pause and glance at her as she turned back to her own desk, but she understood his meaning.

Alyssa heard the fax machine warble as she reorganized her handbag. *Why do I keep so much in here?* She saw the transmission report on the reception desk as she walked to the exit but did not stop to check if her letter had transmitted satisfactorily.

Gayle almost slammed the door on Alyssa's wrist as she ran out with the mail, the handbag wedging it open just enough to allow Bill to catch it before it went any further. She trembled as she felt his touch in the small of her back and hoped that he did not feel it. She angled her head slightly, to see him beaming at her, and she beamed back. As they strolled out together, they said nothing, nothing needing to be said.

*****

The week since the Ruiz's' finance had been approved had been a blur; almost as normal as Alyssa had become used to, but it was odd she hadn't heard from Garrick Westman about it. There were always things that needed to be organized and other closings that would not stand still, so she had ignored the strangeness of it.

She turned, glancing at her watch. As she heard the door slide open. It was the first time she'd seen Duncan walk into the office on a Saturday; it baffled her. She was glad she'd had a couple of hours in silence before he arrived. Oh well, who was she to question the great mysteries of the world?

"What are you doing here?" He looked at Alyssa in bewilderment, slightly stand–offish. That wasn't a first, him not being suggestive, since the Ruiz's purchase had gone off the rails almost two weeks ago; he had toned it down for some reason unknown to Alyssa and she was glad for it.

"Just updating the loose bound Tax Codes. It's the only time I've had to do it this week." She indicated to the pile of ring binders and replacement pages.

"Oh. Oh, okay." He paused, looked at her in a strange way momentarily and headed into his office.

Alyssa's head came up as heard the keys on the fax machine at the front desk beeping, annoyed at his intrusion on her quiet time in the office. She was almost finished her filing, which had taken her the whole Saturday morning.

Not much more to go... she thought, so she kept her head down.

The machine squawked to sound that the transmission was going through and Alyssa turned her head to see Duncan start punching away at the keypad again. She hadn't heard him come out of his office; as she finished her filing on the Tax Code, she wondered why he was being so secretive.

"Don't stay too long," Duncan called from the front door as the noises on the fax machine stopped.

"Just a second, I'm coming now. I'll walk out with you," Alyssa rejoined as she grabbed her bag and ran to the door. Duncan slid the door open silently, let her out as he turned on the alarm and followed her out. He walked in front of her without a word and drove off. Alyssa stood for a moment, shaking her head, thinking it strange, but put it out of her mind and didn't give it any further thought.

CHAPTER 10

DANGER ABOUNDS

The Wednesday morning after Duncan's strange weekend appearance in the office was odd, strained, but different from the usual tensions that Alyssa felt in the office. Gayle had barreled into Bill's office with some papers; it was not her usual flutter or fluster.

As she exited, arms crossed, she had shot a glare at Alyssa as she walked past. It was a different glare, not her usual contempt, stronger, angrier. Alyssa shook her head at it and did not understand it. Bill also exited, close on Gayle's heals, and headed into Duncan's office. A few minutes later, both Bill and Duncan walked out of his office, Bill retracing his steps, both passing Bill's office towards Lydia's. Alyssa frowned as she saw it, leaving the kitchen for her desk with her mug refilled with coffee. Gayle was called into the junior partner's office, the door closed behind her, not leaving for over an hour.

"Alyssa, could you come in?" Bill called as he poked his head out of Lydia's office behind Gayle as she left and returned to the front desk. His voice was strained, which surprised her.

Alyssa nodded as she stood, grabbing a legal pad and the closest pen, and walked in. Bill ushered her to the warm seat next to Duncan, across from Lydia at her desk. Bill remained standing; the seat must have been his.

"The Ruiz's purchase has been rescinded," Lydia pronounced, her voice stern and unfriendly.

"What? Why?" Alyssa was taken aback. She did not know what went wrong, what to think. Duncan handed her some paper. It was a letter, obviously faxed, from Garrick Westman advising that the vendor was pulling out because they had not heard about the Ruiz's' finance by the deadline over a week ago. It also went on to describe how their fax machine had printed a blank page, indicating it had come from Kennedy Price, the previous Saturday, the day Alyssa had seen Duncan at the office. Alyssa sat there, reading and rereading the letter, still not understanding.

"But the letter went out a week ago!" Alyssa went on to describe Gayle's actions the day Mrs. Ruiz had called her with the news about withdrawing the funds from their 401(k) plan.

"But they didn't get it! The transmission report on the file was forged! Can't you read?" Duncan demanded as he stood and paced behind her. He let the chair topple and hit the wall behind it. His anger terrified Alyssa.

"Do you understand what they are saying?" Bill asked as soothingly as he could, "That the fax they got on Saturday was sent to dummy up the transmission report on the file, to cover up the fact that it didn't go out when it should have."

"I get that," Alyssa replied stridently. "But I didn't, wouldn't, couldn't do that. I told you what happened with Gayle. Duncan, you saw me here Saturday, I didn't go anywhere near the fax machine!" She pleaded with him, her voice cracking.

"Don't you dare accuse me of this!" Duncan screamed; making Alyssa jump back, almost but not quite fall off the chair.

"We will deal with this. Go back to work, *now*." Lydia's voice was angry, scaring Alyssa. She left her office, stunned, frightened. Embarrassed at the tears streaming down her face, Alyssa went back to work. Or tried to; she achieved little that afternoon.

*****

Alyssa didn't absolutely know which day it would be, but the day before Veterans Day 1994 would be her last day at Kennedy Price.

The impending sense of dread inside had kept growing in the two weeks beforehand, since the meeting in Lydia's office. The property purchase file associated with the Ruiz tax case file had been disappearing from her desk on a regular basis. She'd seen it on Bill's desk a couple of times since it fell over, when she'd gone in to have a check signed or to talk to him about something or other. She'd frowned at it the first time but said nothing. Duncan and Lydia had been in deep exchanges behind closed doors with him for about a month; there had to be more to it, but Alyssa knew without being told that they were talking about her and about it as well.

They'd even dragged Bill out of the office one morning, not returning until well after lunch; that had exasperated Alyssa, even infuriated her, she missed her daily meeting with Bill because of it. The disintegration of the Ruiz's purchase had not been her fault, but Alyssa still felt guilty about it.

She knew that they were talking about her, deciding whether to keep her or to give her a pink slip. Duncan had turned sour, the strange incident on an earlier Saturday recurring in her mind, Lydia even more surly, angrier than usual. The secretaries spoke in whispers behind her back with their hands over their mouths, staring at her. What upset her even more was that the closeness she had felt with Bill was dissipating.

Since her "anniversary party," Alyssa had heard rumors that Bill had been offered a full partnership at Garrick Westman.

Maybe that was why he was backing off, not because of what had happened to the Ruiz's deal.

The meeting with Duncan and Lydia in her office went as expected. They had made a report to and sought, and received, advice from the Bar Association and the Board of Bar Examiners. Her employment would be terminated unless she admitted her wrongdoing and apologized: they would accept that, as would the Board of Bar Examiners, and allow her to continue working for them, even keep helping her study for the Multi–State Professional Responsibility Examination, the final part of the Bar Examinations she needed to take for her admission to the Bar. But they would not tolerate it otherwise. They let her leave to consider the proposition, but only allowed her until after her lunch break to make her decision. She pleaded with them, begged them to understand she had done nothing wrong, tears in her eyes but desperately holding back from sobbing. They refused to listen.

Alyssa left Lydia's room without stopping, not even to gather her handbag, and departed the office. She wandered, neither knowing where she was nor aware of her surroundings. Her mind churned, not knowing what action to take, not understanding how it had turned so badly against her.

She tossed up the idea of giving into them, meeting their demands: but she could not accept responsibility for it. As clarity returned to her, she stopped meandering, got her bearings, and returned to tell them her decision. Before returning to Lydia's room, Alyssa tidied her desk and collected her belongings in a box, which she took with her into Lydia's office. Duncan and Lydia's disappointment, disillusionment, in her was clear but it could not hide their relief. It only hardened her belief that she was right and her resolve not to give in to them. They gave her a pink slip and some additional cash in lieu of notice. She gave them back her key, turned on her heels and headed out.

As she walked the hall, feeling as if she was walking the gauntlet, Bill stood in the doorway of his office. Alyssa stopped, moving the box from both hands to under her left arm, staring at him for what seemed like infinity but in reality was only a few seconds.

"Where are you going with that box," he queried, but it was really a statement rather than a question.

"I'm leaving." The tremor in Alyssa's voice had left the instant her resolve had returned.

"I know. Look, can I..." Bill started, but stopped as he saw Alyssa's face harden and her jaw become hard–edged. She said nothing, turned away from him and left the offices of Kennedy Price for the last time, the first time in daylight in over a year. As the car's disc player kicked in after Alyssa had turned the key, the words to Alanis Morisette's *Ironic* rang out.

*****

It had been two weeks since she handed her keys in and she had barely left the chair in front of the television, let alone her home.

Veterans Day 1994 was the first day she hadn't been at work in over a year. Bill's last day at Kennedy Price had been the day before Veterans Day; he had taken the partnership at Garrick Westman. Alyssa felt some small satisfaction that they considered he had deserted them. It had certainly been a memorable day, but Alyssa couldn't remember much in the days that had since passed.

Her stare lifted from the television and Alyssa shook her head. What was that? Was it really a knock at the door? Alyssa had been in a downward spiral: the constant hum of the television had barely distracted her from her melancholy. At least she had dragged herself into the bathroom this morning, completed some ablutions and put on a clean shirt, shorts, again dispensing with a bra.

There was another knock. She stumbled out of the chair and headed for the door in a state of confusion.

"Hello," he said. Alyssa remained motionless just inside the door, bewildered. "Hello," he repeated, "can I come in?" Alyssa pulled the door back enough to let him in and stood out of his way as he passed into the hallway.

"I just wanted to see how you're doing," Morisette said.

"I don't know."

"When's that from?" he asked as he moved in, pointing to the plate of scraps sitting on the floor in front of the television.

"I don't know; maybe this morning, maybe yesterday. I've been a bit disorientated," Alyssa mumbled. "What day is it?"

"Thursday, Thanksgiving." He paused to watch Alyssa shake the cobwebs from her mind, briefly, to recognize the significance of the day. "So this is the place you bought. When did you move in?"

"After Easter. Mom and Dad bought it for me."

"You got your Bar Exam results?" She looked down, the tears welling in her eyes. "You failed?" Just a couple of nods. "When did you get the results?"

"The day I left." It was a whisper Bill could barely hear.

"You should get them reviewed."

"I asked about that. They're too low." She paused, and sighed. "Do you want a tour?" she offered as she wiped the tears from her face, hoping he would say no and leave, praying he would take her in his arms and just hold her.

"Sure," Bill replied, as he walked past her into the co-op to survey the large, open-plan room. Alyssa remained still, silent. "So, this is the living room, kitchen there." He paused, turning back towards her. "Have you told your parents?" Bill inquired in a low voice.

"I told my mom I quit on Veterans Day," she started to ramble, "but she rang the office yesterday to speak to me and Duncan told her I was on leave and she rang here and made me tell everything... I suppose she told Dad."

"What are you going to do?" he asked.

"I don't know. I've applied for a couple of jobs but no luck yet. They want me to go back to Albany. They know I've been unhappy here, but I think it was just the job: I hated it so much, like I was being crushed. I suppose you understand that, that's why you left too. I don't want to go back just yet; I don't know what to do."

Bill fixed his eyes on her, putting his hands in his pockets. Alyssa's eyes followed his hands down, catching the bulge which the position of his hands in his pockets couldn't entirely cover; her eyes continued to the floor and stared into the distance of it.

"Great view!" he exclaimed as moved towards the dining room windows and onto the balcony overlooking the Hudson. Bill wandered back into the kitchen, poked around the cupboards and approached where Alyssa stood.

"So, what's back there?" he asked, standing close, in Alyssa's space. She could feel his erection.

"Bedrooms, bathroom, laundry," Alyssa muttered breathlessly. Bill headed down the hall, Alyssa following unsteadily; he stuck his head in the bathroom and the bedrooms as she followed him.

Alyssa leaned against the bathroom doorjamb to steady herself as Bill exited the main suite. He stood in Alyssa's space again, but this time the span between them was gone. He drew the palm of his left hand against her left cheek.

"I'm sorry. I didn't know what else to do. I couldn't leave you alone there with them," he whispered. Again, Alyssa remained motionless, silent, against the doorjamb.

As his left hand continued to stroke her cheek, Bill moved his right hand to her belly, inside her shorts. Alyssa shuddered as Bill touched her, making her wet, and she bumped her head against the wall's edge as he moved in to kiss her.

"Are you sure? Theona," she murmured as she put her hands to his chest and pushed him back ever so slightly. He pushed forward, as she rubbed her left thigh against his hip, and he pressed his lips to hers, parted them with his tongue and explored her mouth for what seemed like an eternity.

Bill, withdrawing his tongue from her mouth, licked her lips, gently biting the bottom one. "Yes, I'm sure," he breathed.

He clutched her wrists, dragging her to the main bedroom. Alyssa stood frozen in front of the bed where he put her, stunned, and watched Bill undress himself, unsure of what else to do. She looked down to his hardness as he moved his hands under her shirt, closing her eyes to feel him pull it over her head. Alyssa ran her hands over Bill's head, through his hair, groaning, as he seized her breasts and attached his lips to one of her nipples and began to first lick it and then suck the other.

Bill detached himself, sat on the edge of bed and slipped his fingers down the back of her shorts and inside her panties; he ran his hands down her buttocks, thighs and finished undressing her. He grabbed Alyssa's hips and pulled her over him as he leant back on the steel framed bed.

She straddled him, stirred her hips back and forward, rubbing herself over his hardness as his fingers clenched over her hips. He pushed her hips back slightly and guided himself towards her, she mounted him; the sense of him breaking her throbbing faintly but also gratifying her. Bill thrust his hips inside her, harder, rhythmically, steadily.

As she moved with him, Alyssa fell forward and supported her writhing torso on her extended arms and began to whisper encouragement to him. He watched her face as moved one hand to her wetness, the other to her breast and felt her without slowing his thrusting. She arched her back as she felt the burning in her groin pass through her womb and she could no longer contain the scream within her.

Bill moved his hands to her ribcage, sat up and threw her over without breaking the rhythm of his driving force. Alyssa quivered again as he began plunging even harder, deeper inside her. She wrapped her arms around his shoulders, hooked her heels between his buttocks, his panting almost deafening her. He broke her grip around his shoulders as he pushed himself up, grabbed her wrists again, this time pinning them behind her head, kissing her again wildly.

As Bill pulled his tongue out of Alyssa's mouth, her eyes rolled back, her eyelids fluttered, she almost passed out. Alyssa opened her mouth to scream again but this time she could not make the sound come out.

His momentum became harsh, almost brutal. Bill's drive did not seem to want to end; despite the pain of having her virginity broken, Alyssa did not want the ecstasy riddling her body to leave her.

It was Bill's turn to wail. He peaked, convulsing.

Bill sighed as he stopped moving, laying on top of Alyssa without withdrawing from inside her for what seemed an eternity and she could feel his tension release. He finally rolled onto his back and pulled Alyssa over him to hold her.

Thinking about it as she lay in his arms, her first sexual encounter, just seven weeks before her twenty–second birthday, had been less than enchanting. She was happy to have lost her virginity to the man she had a silly school–girl crush on, but having an affair a man barely into his second year of marriage wasn't an ideal circumstance for Alyssa. In spite of everything, she was not displeased that it had happened, but she was unsure whether she should be giving thanks for it.

"I have to get back to work. I've got a settlement conference tomorrow," Bill said, withdrawing his shoulder from under her head and sitting up, dragging Alyssa up with him. "I need a shower, to get your smell off me."

"Okay," she mused, "the clean towels are in the cupboard under the sink." Alyssa leaned back on the bed, wrapping arms behind her head, as he walked into the bathroom. She listened to the running water, to him shower, eyes closed. Her eyes opened as he walked out from his shower and she watched him dry his glistening wet body and dress.

As he finished buckling his belt, Bill reached down, sat on the edge of the bed and kneaded her breasts with both hands, put his tongue in her mouth and kissed her hard.

"I've got to go," he said as he pulled back from her mouth and got up.

"See you later," Alyssa said as she closed her eyes and listened to him leave, the front door almost slamming behind him.

CHAPTER 11

TIDES TURNING

"If you just go down the stairs, his office is the second on the left. He'll be waiting for you outside," said the receptionist, this time an older woman.

"Thank you." Alyssa turned towards the stairs, not remembering the woman's name, her mind blocked by her apprehension.

The offices of Garrick Westman were plush, more lavish than Kennedy Price. Alyssa had spent hours adjusting the corset under her filmy chemise, making herself sit just so. It had taken half an hour to get the stockings under her skirt turned the right way. She knew it was wrong to turn up at his office, to want to see Bill, but she couldn't not see him one last time. As Alyssa walked down the stairs, looking down at each one as she took a step, she held the rail as tightly as she could without looking unfeminine, hoping she wouldn't catch her heel and stumble.

As she hit the last step and looked up, Alyssa saw Bill staring up at her. The longing had not left him, but it was tinged with a little guilt.

"Come in." He put his arm lightly around her back, Alyssa shivered, only slightly but enough for him to feel it pulsate through his hand as it rested on her, as he ushered her into his office. She remained standing as he walked to his chair. As they both sat, opposite each other across his desk, she examined his new office.

"I just wanted to thank you, for yesterday." Alyssa leant forward, her cleavage pulling at her shirt, as she crossed her legs.

"No need to thank me." He paused for a beat. "It was wrong." Alyssa could see him hunger for her as he said it, unable to unfix his gaze from her chest.

"I know. But…" Alyssa halted briefly, grimaced slightly, not knowing how to finish the sentence.

"Are you a virgin?" Bill posed, slightly embarrassed, finally lifting his gaze up and locking his eyes with hers.

"Not anymore." Alyssa smiled, pensive as she said it. This time, Bill's gaze did drop and he fixed it on the edge of his desk. Alyssa let him sit there, just to give herself the opportunity to explore his face one last time. "I just wanted to say goodbye before I left." That comment brought his eyes, but not his head, back up to lock on hers.

"When do you go?"

"Mom and Dad are coming to pick me up tomorrow; there are too many bags for my car. I didn't get much sleep last night, packing."

"What about your car?"

"Dad had it towed yesterday." Bill silently raised his eyebrows; Alyssa rolled her eyes, shook her head. "He said the motor sounded strange and he didn't want me driving it till he could take a look at it."

He stood, walked around to Alyssa's side of the desk and pulled her up from her chair by her wrists. Bill saw her tremble as he ran his hands slowly up her arms; his palms moved to her back as he pulled her to him. Alyssa nestled her head in Bill's shoulder as she moved her arms around him. He nuzzled his lips against her cheek, began kissing it, moving his lips slowly to hers. His kiss became fervent as he began exploring her mouth.

He stopped as quickly as he started, but not as quickly as he should, moving his hands from around her back to her shoulders and down her arms. He grabbed her hands and closed his eyes.

"You should go." Bill, eyes still closed, let go of only one of her hands and turned away from her, back towards his desk. Without releasing her hand from his, Alyssa stepped back towards the office door to leave. Bill squeezed her hand tightly as he felt Alyssa pull away from him; they stood, holding hands for what seemed an age, in the simplicity of the moment. Bill turned back towards her and opened his eyes, let go of her hand, finally, after they stared at each other for what seemed like an eternity but in reality was only an instant.

Alyssa walked out, head down, saying nothing.

*****

It had taken several trips to take her remaining belongings that would be returning to Albany with her to the entry alcove. She did not want to go; but she felt an overwhelming pressure in her chest to comply with her parents' wishes.

Alyssa had started her removal ahead of time; she knew Mom and Dad would be early. They just wanted her home; but she felt like she was going back to the place which she thought of as a mental prison. Although she loved her family, she felt she had finally broken free from the obligations imposed on her, some self–imposed, other imposed by her heritage, when she moved from the family home. To have moved to her own place indicated success and independence. To return "home" was to give up independence; it was failure. But now without a job, she couldn't support herself at the co–op and, although they wouldn't admit it, Mom and Dad refused to return her allowance as a bargaining tool to get her "home" to watch her. They had never really considered that the co–op was now her home, just a crash pad for her so that she wouldn't have to deal with a grueling daily commute from Albany to Hoboken and they wouldn't have to bear the costs thereof.

She had five bags and a couple of boxes, packed with novels, and it had taken her half an hour to get them from the apartment to the alcove. It wouldn't take long to get the gear outside to the car when they arrived, Dad would see to that. At this time of morning, nobody else would be up, so she felt comfortable enough to leave her gear in the alcove while she went back up to the apartment just to make sure the deadbolt was locked. She had timed it so she had time to have one last rummage around the apartment and be back down in the alcove just as her parents pulled up and parked at the front of the building. Alyssa pulled the security door open, securing it back with the boxes, as Gino or Moira exited the car and approached her.

"Hello darling," Moira said as she hugged Alyssa.

"Hi Mom," Alyssa said as she returned the squeeze, pulled back and turned to her father. "Hi Dad." They didn't bother to hug.

"Hi sweetheart. Is this it?" Gino asked.

"Yep, that's it."

Between the three of them, they were able to manage all the bags and the two boxes in one trip to the car and all piled in. The conversation on the three hour drive was mundane, banal and was limited to what her family and her parents' friends, and the children of parents' friends, were doing with themselves. Half an hour outside Albany, Alyssa felt the weight of the return to the city bear down upon her; she fell silent and pretended to nap. She pretended to wake herself as she heard the sound of the car stop.

The process of removing her belongings from the car and returning them to her childhood room was the reverse of putting them in the car. As she entered her old room, Alyssa felt her humiliation was complete as Gino and Moira left her in relative peace to return her possessions to what they saw as their rightful place.

*****

In the three weeks she had been living back in her parents' home in Albany, she had done little. At first, Alyssa felt a wave of relief pass over her at having left the stress and trauma of Kennedy Price, and Hoboken, behind her.

The first weekend had been spent unpacking and replacing her clothes in her old closet. Alyssa had hoped she had called the room in her parents' house in which she had "lived" her own for the last time when she moved to Hoboken.

But as the days passed, Alyssa contemplated her future, about what her parents thought, about Bill and what had happened between them. And she could not get Morisette out of her mind. His name reminded her of her favorite female singer, and the song about the irony of life. During the first week of her return to her parents' home, her relief passed and she started feeling guilty, as if she had failed her lineage and spent hours at a time crying. In between bouts of crying, Alyssa scoured the job advertisements and sent out applications; as she sent out letter after letter, the burden of the process tormented her and caused more weeping. Her mother had tried to console her, her father offering encouragement and assistance for her search for a new job, but their show of love only made Alyssa feel worse, more of a failure, more pressure, and more guilt; maybe they did not realize the pressure they were exerting on her, causing her to lose sleep over her perception that she had failed them. As her third weekend of unemployment approached, Alyssa made excuses that she thought she had forgotten some item in her Hoboken apartment and that she needed to return for a brief period. Her parents accepted her excuses; they understood, without saying so, that she needed to get away from their attentions and Alyssa spent her Friday afternoon returning to her now former home across the Hudson for the weekend.

Alyssa rose early on Saturday morning and showered leisurely, taking the time to wash her hair. She dressed casually in jeans, a taut t–shirt that exposed the fullness of her curves, and her well worn joggers, pulling her hair back into a ponytail. She had breakfast at her favorite café before heading to the supermarket; take–out on Friday night after her long drive and her breakfast would not strap her finances completely, but she could not eat out all weekend if she did not want to rely completely on her parents' generosity. Seeing Bill, dressed casually in jeans, a button down shirt and loafers, walking ahead of her as she turned down an aisle was a surprise; she stopped short and the woman behind her clipped Alyssa's basket with a shopping cart as she tried to pass around. Alyssa turned to the woman and apologized; out of the corner of her eye, Alyssa saw Bill stop, pausing to pull up his cart before he turned around. Staying in Hoboken into part of the working week crossed Alyssa's mind as he retraced his steps and approached her with his cart.

"Hello," Bill smiled, quirkily, at her.

"Hi," Alyssa said, returning the smile.

"What are you doing here? I thought you went back to Albany."

"I did. I came back to pick up a few things from the co–op."

"How long are you staying?"

"I'm not sure, maybe tomorrow afternoon. I might go back Monday afternoon, maybe evening." Alyssa paused, looking to the floor as she shuffled her feet, changed the basket between her hands. "Is Theona here with you?"

"No, she's gone to see her mother for the weekend. For a cousin's birthday, or something."

"Oh, another "secret women's business" trip. So you're a bachelor for the weekend?"

"Yeah, I'm free and easy." As he leaned on the push bar of his cart with his forearms, he smiled again as he ran his eyes over her body. "Maybe we could have... lunch. What are you doing this afternoon?"

"Nothing." Alyssa sensed that it was something other than lunch that he wanted.

"Well, I've got what I need. How about you?"

"Yes," she replied slowly, her thoughts racing.

"I'll come round after I've put this away," he uttered, indicating to his cart of groceries. He looked at his watch. "Hmmm, it'll take me about an hour. How about I meet you at your place at 1:30?"

"Sure," Alyssa replied, knowing what he really wanted was to have her again, but unsure of her own mind. As they proceeded to the checkout together, the banter turned to the mundane. Bill, after having his offer to drive her home rejected, paid for Alyssa's groceries over her weak protests. Bill walked with her to the mall's exit, where they parted ways, Bill heading for his car, Alyssa for home on foot.

CHAPTER 12

RETURNING HOME

It was only a short walk home for Alyssa; at least she could now feel there would be some fairness about their implied understanding. Although her grocery bags slowed her, Alyssa almost ran back to her building and up the stairs to her apartment. She would not have long to put her rations away, if she wanted to give herself time to change. As she moved the provisions from the bench to the cupboards, her mind churned with thoughts of seeing Bill naked again and guilt at having those thoughts. Her face reddened with embarrassment, at her own lustful thoughts, rather than with the exertion of running home. *Do I really want to?*

Alyssa stood still in the kitchen, after she had finished unpacking her groceries. Her eyes fixed to a point on a cabinet, but she stared past it; she let her mind go blank for a few minutes. Alyssa came out of her trance with a start, shaking her head and checking her watch. She looked at her clothing and wondered if she should change. Although she understood that his lust for her meant that it didn't really matter how she was dressed, something sexier could make him want her even more. She knew in her rational mind that to continue some semblance of a relationship with him would only lead to heartache. But her body wanted to re–experience the quivers of ecstasy he had sent through her on the last occasion they had made love, if it could be called that. Her face cooled, and she smiled, lost in the contemplation of her decision. Yes, she would let him have her again, knowing he was married, knowing it was wrong.

She checked her watch again; it was only a quarter of an hour before Alyssa anticipated Bill's knocking at the door. She hurried to her bedroom and pulled two negligees, one cream and the other black, from the dresser. Looking from one to the other, Alyssa decided that the black robe would look too severe against her alabaster skin in the afternoon light and returned it to the open drawer; the cream one was fitted so it would enhance her already voluptuous cleavage, and she would wear nothing else. After throwing the gown on her bed, she stripped down to nothing, tossing the clothes in the hamper and hid it in the closet. Returning to the bed, Alyssa removed her watch and the chain with the baptismal medal her grandmother had brought with her from Italy so many years ago, putting them on the dresser, and adjusted the bed linen; she picked up the gown, slipping it over head and adjusted herself to show her breasts at their fullest. After fussing over the bed linen again, she left the bedroom and entered the passage to the front door. Alyssa checked the clock just inside the door; it would only be a few minutes before he arrived, if he was his usual punctual self. She leant against the wall, sighing, letting her mind empty. The knocking startled her, bringing her out of trance; Bill was as punctual as he had ever been.

"Coming," Alyssa called out, waiting until the second hand passed a quarter of the way around the dial; she did not want Bill to think that she had been waiting just inside the door for him.

She pulled open the door and saw his left shoulder leaning against the corridor wall, a knapsack on his right shoulder, hands in his pockets; saying nothing, she simply smiled at him. Bill also remained silent, also smiled, and pulled himself from against the wall as he reviewed her body. As he stepped towards her, putting one hand on her belly, the other around her back, and pushing her against the passage wall, he let the door swing closed behind him. Alyssa reached out and slid the bolt into its latch to lock the door before putting her arms around his neck, pulling his head towards hers and ran her fingers through his sandy hair; their lips touched, gently, softly. Without letting his lips leave hers, Bill released his right arm from Alyssa's back, pulling back slightly to let his bag slip from his shoulder and fall against the inside of the door. Alyssa parted her lips, her tongue moving towards Bill's mouth. As he returned his arm around her back, Bill squeezed Alyssa hard against himself, compressing her ribs, and explored her mouth with his tongue with a force she could never have imagined.

73

"Hello," he whispered as he pulled back from the kiss, letting his lips rest on hers.

"Hello," Alyssa murmured. "What's with the knapsack?"

"A change of clothes. Is that okay?"

"Yes, yes." Alyssa pressed her lips back against Bill's, and it was her tongue which explored his mouth. Bill ran a hand down Alyssa's back, resting it momentarily on her buttock before bending slightly to run his arm down towards her knees. With her arms still around his neck, he scooped her up, kicked his shoes off and carried her to the room where he had first taken her.

"Undress me," he muttered, as he put her down, her back to the bed, her arms still around his neck, his arms moving to rest around her back.

"What?" Alyssa had not quite heard the low sound he had uttered.

"Undress me," he repeated, slightly louder.

Alyssa skimmed her arms around his shoulders to rest her hands on his chest. She began to shake as she unbuttoned his shirt. As she reached the last button, she put her hands on his rigid, well defined, abdomen, ran them up his chest, over his shoulders and down his arms to slip the shirt off his back; the shirt stopped at his elbows, he had not removed his hands from his back. Alyssa unbuckled his belt. She moved her hands to his fly, feeling his hardness as she unzipped his jeans, then back to his biceps to break his hold on her back. As he dropped his arms and his shirt slipped from his arms to the floor, she moved her hands inside his pants to his buttocks; Alyssa knelt as she ran her hands down the back of Bill's thighs, moving his denims to the floor. He grabbed her by the hair to steady himself as she moved his pants over his feet; he pulled her up after he had stepped out, moving his hands to the nape of her neck, drawing her head in to his to kiss her.

His left hand moved to the small of her back as he pulled her into him as his right moved down her left shoulder, slipping the strap over her upper arm, then to her breast; his lips moved across her cheek, to her neck, down her chest. Bill reached into the left cup of Alyssa's negligee, exposed her stiff nipple to the air, and explored her breast with his mouth, biting, sucking, and licking. As he continued to delve into her breast, he repositioned his hands under the robe and over her buttocks. He lifted her onto the bed and climbed over her; instead of entering her immediately, he slipped the remaining strap of the negligee off her right shoulder, exposing her other swollen breast and turned his attentions to it. He pushed himself up, straddled her and ran his hands down her sides, removing the gown. After he pulled it over her feet, he crawled back towards the wall against which the cast–iron bed frame rested; as he did so, he grabbed her wrists, crossed them and secured her hands over her head with the negligee he had just removed.

Bill lowered the length of his body over Alyssa and resumed kissing her, firstly her mouth. He continued to explore the length of her with his hands, his mouth and his tongue and she groaned uncontrollably; with her hands tied securely to the bed frame, Alyssa could do nothing to stop his lips moving down her breasts, her belly towards her groin. The rhythmic waves of ecstasy began to pulsate through her, and her groaning became louder, as he began sucking on the inside of her thighs; her groan changed to a scream as his mouth delved into her external sex organs. Bill's mouth began to retrace his path back up Alyssa's body, as her scream changed back to groaning; he stopped at her breasts for what seemed an eternity. Bill hoisted himself onto his elbows, hooking his hands around her shoulders, to watch her face as he entered her. Alyssa matched Bill's thrusts as best she could in the restraints as he moved slowly inside her. Through the haze of her bliss, Alyssa sensed that Bill was more in control of himself this time, more at ease with taking her this time; he was taking his time to gratify her in ways she could never have imagined this time. Finally, more than an hour after he entered, his thrusting quickened as he felt her muscles tighten around him again, he'd lost count of the number of times, and he could control himself, hold himself back, no longer. Waves of quivering sensations pulsated through their bodies in chorus; they reached the climax of their sexual excitement simultaneously.

He lifted himself up, almost immediately this time, loosening Alyssa's wrists in one quick motion, and rolled onto his back. He again pulled Alyssa over him, wrapped his arms around her shoulders as she nestled her head into the cusp of his shoulder and put her arm over his taut, sinewy chest and intertwined her leg between his. They fell asleep, in a flash, in each other's arms.

*****

Bill awoke to see the early morning sun streaming in an unfamiliar window, not his own, feeling the weight of the head nestled in his shoulder, his arms around the not yet completely familiar shoulders of a woman.

He turned his head, his eyes, slightly. Even without his glasses, he could discern that the color of the hair was mousy brown rather than the black of his wife's southern Mediterranean ancestry; he was myopic, not colorblind. It took him a moment to recognize the face beneath the hair and realize who he was with. He adjusted himself, ever so slightly, hoping not to wake Alyssa just yet, to check the clock on the bedside table. They'd slept through the afternoon, through the night, and it was still too early on a Sunday morning to be awake; the mental, not the physical, exertion of the previous afternoon had tired him more than he had comprehended at the time. The movement, not slight enough, woke Alyssa and she yawned as her eyelids fluttered open. She too saw the morning sunlight streaming through the window.

"What time is it?" Alyssa intoned as she tried to lift herself up.

"Seven," Bill replied, not letting her rise, drawing his arms tighter around her back and pushing her body back against his.

"Really? It's morning?"

"Yep."

"You wore me out yesterday!"

"I wore you wore out? You wore me out; you're too young to be worn out. I'm an old man." He chuckled, at himself really.

"No you're not."

He rested his cheek against hers, bringing his lips almost, but not quite, to her lips.

"God you're beautiful," he sighed.

"No I'm not," she whispered back.

"Yes," he paused for emphasis, "you are. I love your breasts!"

"Thank you." Not knowing what else to say, she barely got the words out. "Why?" Alyssa had so little confidence in herself, her appearance, at this point that she did not know why anyone, let alone Bill, would want her. Knowing her parents', particularly her mother's, notions on infidelity, she was questioning her own conscience more than his.

"Why what?"

"Why this, us? Why are you still here? You're married."

"I'm still here because I just woke up. I know I'm married, it's a mistake."

"Huh?"

"Come on sleepyhead, wake up," he laughed. "I just woke up. My marriage, it's a mistake." That jolted Alyssa sufficiently to make her pull herself out of Bill's arms and sit bolt upright.

"What do you mean, your marriage is a mistake?" *Maybe that's what he meant, not us, when he said it was wrong? Or am I just too naïve?*

"It's a mistake, it was when I married Theona and it still is. I don't, didn't, love her. I shouldn't have married her."

"Then why did you go through with it?"

Bill was silent, turning his gaze away from Alyssa and stared at the ceiling. He'd been attracted to Alyssa the first moment he saw her and he'd seen her attraction for him, to him, grow in the time she'd been at Kennedy Price. His guilt at his involvement, albeit limited, in what Duncan and Lydia had done to her had grown exponentially since she was fired; he'd not done it to hurt her, his growing love for her had wanted to protect her from them, particularly Duncan. *Or was it lust? Hatred, loathing for the frightening sociopath who was his wife?* Bill knew a little of Duncan's past, and he'd seen his, Duncan's, licentious feelings for Alyssa. But he did not know enough about the incident to be sure of Duncan's perspicacity to completely trust him, and he wanted to keep her, Alyssa, as far from his true nature as possible. He did not see that Lydia would support Duncan; he thought he knew her better than that, but there must have been more she knew about Kennedy than he.

"Why did you go through with it?" Alyssa repeated, turning his face back to hers.

"I didn't know how to get out of it."

"Hmmm, okay. What are you going to do?" Alyssa was digging, trying to elicit the response that he felt for her the way she did for him.

"I don't know. She's turned out to be a completely different person now from the person I first met. I have to leave her; I have to figure out how to leave." He paused, Alyssa could see that he wanted to go further, perhaps to reveal her feelings, but left him to his own pace.

"When's she going to be home from her mother's?"

"Tomorrow. She'll be going straight to work. Enough thinking about her, I want to think about you."

"But…"

Before she could say any more, he sat up and put his arms around her. He drew her body to his, pinning her arms to her body, and squeezed her almost expelling all the air from her and kissed her, hard. He ran his hands down her back and grabbed her buttocks, lifting her so he could explore her neck, her breasts, with his tongue. He moved her over him and he entered her, he showed her how to control him from above. By the time he had finished with her, it was mid–morning and both were hungry. Bill refused to dress before he went to the kitchen to make them brunch of fruit, eggs, toast, and ample coffee and wouldn't allow Alyssa her clothes as she followed to watch him. They ate in at the kitchen table, in an almost civilized fashion at the dining table just outside the kitchen, Alyssa thought, except for the fact that they were naked.

She had barely finished her meal before he cleared the table and came back to ravish her again, on the kitchen table this time. He took his time in exploring her, so much so that she was so overwhelmed with gratification that she lost her ability to use her vocal chords when she tried to scream. He spent the rest of the day, into the night, exploring her in every other room of the co–op before returning her to the bedroom. Both were too exhausted by the day's activity to even consider more effort and they again fell asleep in each other's arms, before the sun had completely set.

Monday's morning sun awoke them simultaneously; both were famished, only having had one meal on Sunday. They had no need for words as they showered together, ate together and dressed in front of each other before walking out the front door together; they went their separate ways after a long kiss in the co–op alcove, Bill to work and Alyssa to Albany.

CHAPTER 13

GOING THE WRONG WAY

In the days before Christmas, after Alyssa had returned from Hoboken, Moira had tried to talk to her again several times and offer her counsel as gently as she could. Gino had kept his distance, at first, letting Moira force the issue.

Alyssa rebuffed her gently every time, feeling the pressure increasing on, rather than being lifted from, her shoulders. At least the weekend away had lifted some of the guilt Alyssa felt about her dismissal life and made it easier for her to talk to her mother. Gino had offered the pleasantries Alyssa remembered from her childhood as if she had never left home, but had not tried to raise the subject of the time she had spent living away from them. But the time came when they, really it was her father who by this point had had enough of being pushed away and, forced her hand; if she wasn't going to take advice from them, she was going to take it from someone else, someone they trusted.

The meeting with Jake Ritchie had crawled on all afternoon. Her parents had dragged her there, and sat in on the meeting Alyssa had with him. As her parents' attorney, he felt some obligation to see her, and not to refuse to allow them to sit in on the discussion. But she wished she could have refused; there were things she didn't really want them to know, things that they really didn't need them to know if she was going to be able to use it for her benefit, which she had to tell Ritchie if he was to be of any help to her.

"The best thing to do right now is to walk away," Ritchie said. "You don't really need him, or the stress. You don't need to take the

Exams in New Jersey again. You can take them anywhere you want, whenever you want."

"That's what I thought," Alyssa nodded as she breathed a sigh of relief.

"But what about him!" Gino yelled, frustrated. "We can't leave things as they are! We gotta show him he can't do this to people!"

"Oh, calm down Gino," Moira pleaded. "Please listen to what Jake has to say."

"Look Gino," Jake continued as he looked over the top of his reading glasses, "she really doesn't need it. We can't prove that he was wrong, we just don't have enough evidence right now."

"You need evidence? I'll get you evidence!" Gino's voice escalated as he jumped off his chair, Moira reaching for his arm to calm him.

"Bullshit Gino!" Jake yelled back, knowing the only way to deal with his client's, his friend's, fire was to give back in kind. "You do it your way and it'll only make it worse! There are ways to do things and there are ways to do things."

"Come on, Gino." Moira tugged on his arm, her husband taking the hint and sitting back down. "Just listen to what he has to say. That's why we're here."

"Alright, alright." Gino sighed and leaned against the back of the chair. Alyssa sat patiently, waiting to hear what she already knew to be the answer.

"Look," the worldly wise attorney sighed. "Now there's no limit on the number of times she can take the Exams here in New York. But what she doesn't need is him kicking up a fuss. She needs references and they do character checks, and he's agreed to let things lie, but only, ONLY, if she walks away."

"Whadda ya mean? You spoken to him? Who does character checks?" Gino was surprised, taken aback that something had been done without his knowledge.

"Yes, I've spoken to him, with Alyssa's permission." Jake was patient. "You called and asked me to fix it. To do that, I had to talk to him. As I said, Alyssa needs references and it's the State Supreme Court does character checks, all the Courts do. If she doesn't meet the standard, the fit and proper person standard, they'll reject her application."

"But Jake, but–" Gino couldn't get the words out.

"But nothing, Gino." Jake was exasperated now. "It's just the way it is, the way the rules of admission are, here in New York, there in New Jersey, everywhere in the country. Now Kennedy's said he won't put up an objection if she leaves well enough alone."

"But, but–" Again Gino couldn't get the words out.

"Look, Dad," Alyssa piped up as she whipped her head around to look at him. "Jake's right. The best thing I can do right now is to walk away, and I'll take the Exams again somewhere else." She turned back to Ritchie, smiled wryly and winked with the eye that her parents couldn't see. "Thanks Jake." Ritchie nodded, squinted, removed his glasses and rubbed the bridge of his nose; the sense he caught from Alyssa throughout the meeting, and which she seemed to be confirming with her wink, was that there was something she wasn't telling him, didn't want to tell him in front of her parents, but he didn't know what it could be and it confused him slightly.

"Alright, alright," Gino groaned. "So what do we do now?"

"Well, it's up to Alyssa, really." Ritchie put his confusion to one side for the moment, as it appeared that it had slipped past Gino and Moira's attention. "She needs to do a couple of things: decide when and where she wants to re–take the Bar Exams, or even if she wants to do that right now, and get a job. The job is probably more of a priority right now."

"Look, we can help with the job," Moira said. "She can come and work for us."

"No, Mom, I think–" Alyssa started.

"No," Ritchie interrupted. "I mean she needs to get a job in a law office. That's what she needs right now, to get some legal experience." *And to make sure she's able to get the paperwork for the Bar,* he thought to himself. *Should I? There's something she's not telling me.* He leant back in his chair, rubbing his jowls with one hand, tapping the armrest with the other. The three Giordanos waited patiently for him to continue until the head of the family could wait no more.

"But if you think she needs to be working," Moira said, "she can come and work for us while she looks for a job in another law office."

"No." Ritchie decided he needed to put the question to the younger Giordano in the absence of her parents before he could answer his own question. "Maybe I can offer her something. Gino and Moira, can you wait outside while Alyssa and I talk about what we can come up with." A command rather than a question. Alyssa blushed and bowed her head; Gino and Moira looked at each other, then nodded in unison at Ritchie and left the room.

It seemed like they were sitting in the reception waiting room for an age. They fidgeted in silence, flipping through the magazines left for those waiting to see the attorneys, watching the receptionist file her nails. At least Ritchie had the sense, unlike doctors, dentists, they thought, to keep the magazines current. But it was really barely any time at all, less than a quarter hour, before the buzzing of the phone startled Mr. and Mrs. Giordano into attention.

"Yes, Jake," the receptionist said into the handset he'd picked up. After a short pause to listen, he spoke again. "I'll let them know." He put the phone down and stood. "Mr. Ritchie's asked if you can go back in. Would you like me to show you the way?"

"Thanks Peyer, no, we know the way." Gino said, as he and Moira stood to return down the passage to the attorney's office. They saw Eddie Kann, Ritchie's partner, had joined Jake and their daughter while they were out of the room.

"Okay," Eddie Kann started as Gino and Moira seated themselves. "Jake and I have had a good chat with Alyssa. One of our staff, John Patterson, you know John, my paralegal?" They nodded at this and let him continue. "Well, John is going on leave in the new year, for at least a couple of months. Alyssa can fill in for him while he's away." Taken aback, her parents looked at their attorney, at each other and then at Alyssa before turning back to Ritchie.

"We can't ask you to do that!" Moira was firm in her opinion. Gino nodded in agreement; he knew who wore the pants in the family and when not to argue.

"You're not asking." Ritchie interjected as he stood, arched back and paced behind his desk; the meeting had taken long enough for his back to ache. "We're offering this to Alyssa, and she's happy with that. Now, depending on that goes, we can work it out with Alyssa if she wants to stay. Or she can look for another job. It's up to her."

"Are you sure, darling?" Alyssa just nodded at her mother.

"Thanks, Jake; thanks Eddie." Gino stood and offered his hand; Jake reached across the desk and shook it.

"That's fine," Kann said as he looked at his watch. "Oh, shit. Gotta get home. My wife's waiting to take me to the opera." He rolled his eyes and laughed, as did Gino; that earned him a deathly glare from his wife as they walked out of the attorney's office.

"We'll see you in the new year, Alyssa, the tenth," Ritchie said.

"Thanks again, Jake, Eddie." Alyssa shook their hands. "I'll see you on the tenth." The relief on her face wasn't obvious to her parents, with their backs to her, but it was obvious to her new, albeit temporary, employer. They left the attorneys to lock up the office and returned to the parking garage, and their car, in silence. Moira turned to her daughter as Gino pulled the car onto the street.

"You sure about this, darling? You know you can always come and work for us."

"Yes, Mom, I'm sure." She yawned, not wanting to talk, not wanting to explain why she wouldn't work for them again: it was their assumption that she would work for them, not with them to enhance their business, that really riled her. They didn't get that and she couldn't tell them, didn't have the guts yet.

"You look tired."

"I am."

"Why don't you rest your eyes till we get home?"

"Okay." Alyssa closed her weary eyelids and rested her head against the car window; she fell asleep almost instantly and didn't wake till she felt her father shaking her in the garage at home.

*****

It was not exactly the birthday gift she had been hoping for. Alyssa's twenty–second birthday occurred two days after she had started with her second new job in just over sixteen months. And it was a job in the office of her parents' attorneys: she had hoped she'd be able to get a bit further away, move out of her parents' sphere of control, and their house again. But she wanted, needed for her own peace of mind, more of her own money for that.

"Okay, so you've met everyone, and that's the office." After giving her the employee tour of the office, they entered Jake Ritchie's office and he slumped into the sofa pressed up against the wall opposite his desk behind the chairs facing the desk. "Grab a chair." She obeyed, turning it to face him before seating herself in it. "So, you got everything?"

"Yep." She paused. "Look Jake, I really appreciate this. I couldn't, I mean I just—"

"Yep, I get it." He laughed. "I hated working for my parents too." It was his turn to pause. "Look, as Eddie said before Christmas, John's going to be away for a bit. If you keep your nose down and do the job well, I could probably work it so you can stay on when he gets back."

"Thanks, Jake."

"But that's maybe not what you want. Is it? Ya gotta understand that your parents'll want me to keep them up-to-date."

"Yeah, I know. And I'm sorry about that. About putting this on you. I didn't want that. I don't know what I want. Can we just see how it goes? Maybe they'll let it be."

"No, yes, that's okay. Really, it's okay. Yeah, you're right, let's just see how it goes." He paused again, his brow furrowed in thought. "He's a fuckin' asshole. We're not all like him. We gotta keep people like that out, or get 'em out when they get in, if we can. When we find out about them."

"I know not everyone's like him. But I don't know if I have enough stuff. At least I don't think so. Yes I do, even I know I don't have enough. How do I, what do I—"

"I been thinkin' 'bout that. You're right, you've not got enough on the sexual harassment right now. Not with the card he's holding over you right now: you'd need to find the others he did it to, and get them to testify. The other stuff, you probably could get him investigated, but again with the card he's got, he can just brush you off as a disgruntled ex-employee trying to get back at him."

"But I'm not!"

"I know you're not. You're smart." She blushed at that: she'd never thought of herself as smart. "Smart enough to know what's enough and what's not. And when not to play it, and now's not the time to play it. People like him usually get their comeuppance in time, without any help from anyone else."

"I don't wanna hang around for the rest of my life waiting for him to get his just desserts. What can I do now?" Alyssa Giordano really wanted to hurt him NOW, the way he had hurt her or worse; Jake Ritchie saw it, sensed it and hoped that her mother's even temperament balanced her father's sense of wounded justice and the temper that came with it.

"Right now, nothing. Keep that information up your sleeve for now. Maybe you won't have to do anything. People like him usually bring themselves down. Shit follows them, people like him." Her gut flipped at that thought. She remembered the news stories about the incident with the body in the Hamptons.

"What does that mean?" Alyssa was confused.

"You heard of Angela Ryan, right?"

"The anchor for *Twenty/Twenty*? Who doesn't know her! Pop said she's the hottest news man in the business," Alyssa laughed. "Mom hates it when he says that!"

"Your mom knows your old man's joking when he says that."

Alyssa laughed. "Yeah, I know. Mom likes her too. She thinks it's a good thing that she's done something with her hair."

"She wants to come in and see you."

"Huh?"

"She wants to come in and see you. You're probably too young to remember this, but Angela Ryan interviewed him when his first wife died."

"What!" Alyssa was stunned. "He was married before Lydia?"

"Yeah, you would be too young. And then his butler died, when was that?"

"Yeah!" She closed her eyes, and grinned. "I remember that! It was about a year before I went to work for him!" The conversation she overheard the day they refused to let her take the Bar Exams was coming back to her: it finally made sense.

"See! Shit follows people like him."

"When does she want to see me?"

"Whenever."

"Okay. Whenever, can you set it up?"

"Sure. I'll let you know. Eddie and I wanna sit in on it."

"Right on. Okay, I better get to work then." The response appeared to take forever. Ritchie lifted his left hand to his glasses, in slow motion, and removed them. His right hand moved, in slower motion, to rub his left bicep. She stared at him, he didn't seem to notice.

Shit, he doesn't look too hot! "You need anything?"

"Yep." His speech slurred as he closed his eyes. "Nope, off you go."

She shook her head as she left his room and pulled the door behind her, wondering if he was alright, and if he was right, if assholes really got what was coming to them, hoping it wouldn't take too long for her to find out.

CHAPTER 14

ONE STEP FORWARD

As the woman exited the elevator into the plush office lobby, her heel caught the edge of the carpet and she stumbled. Her effort to remain upright caused her to drop the file she was carrying, flinging its contents over the floor. She stood still, bowed her head and chuckled.

"You alright, Lyssie?" Peter Parker asked as he giggled at her from behind his reception desk and headed towards her.

"Yes, Peter," she sighed. When she first met the man behind the desk, Alyssa Giordano thought it strange that a man would want to be a receptionist of all things. But she and the man with the comic book superhero name had become fast friends not long after Alyssa had started work at Kann Ritchie.

"Shit! What happened to you?!" he asked as he saw the large stain on her white shirt.

"I had a fight with a cup o' coffee!" She rolled her eyes as they both crouched to scoop up her papers.

"Oh crap," he giggled even harder, "you and coffee!"

"Yeah, me and coffee. Don't talk to me about me and coffee!"

"Lucky you, your dry–cleaning's come in. You'd better go change."

"Why?" Alyssa was puzzled. It wasn't the first time she'd returned to the office with coffee spilled down her shirt. Parker glanced slyly around the foyer.

"Angela Ryan is here." He whispered as he took another secretive look around the foyer again. "With a *policeman*!"

"What's she doing here? Where?"

"Shhhh!" he whispered. "They're in the conference room. They want to see you! But Jake said he wants to talk to you first."

"What the hell for?" She shook her head, confused. "Wait! A cop? Why'd a cop come with her?" The cogs of her mind started to race.

"That's what *I'd* like to know!"

"Oh, yeah!" Alyssa's mind turned to the conversation she'd had with Jake Ritchie the day she started working for him and Eddie.

"*What*, Lyssie? What?"

"You ever heard of Duncan Kennedy?"Alyssa looked around the reception area conspiratorially this time.

"Yes. I saw the reports Ms. Ryan did on him on her show. I've watched her show for years you know," he said as he leaned over his desk and handed Alyssa her clean shirts. Alyssa leaned over the reception desk.

"I used to work for him," she whispered in his ear.

"You didn't!" Parker gasped. "Did you?"

"Yep." Alyssa smiled and winked, leaving Peter to ponder what she might know. She pondered why a policeman would want to see her as headed towards the bathrooms to change her shirt.

*****

"You wanted to see me, Jake?" Alyssa asked one of her father's best friends from high school as she stood at his office door. Why did he take it out of the safe room? She was surprised to see the file she had kept on Kennedy in Ritchie's hands.

"Yes, Lyssie." Jake Ritchie, facing his office door as he perched on the windowsill, watched her wonder for a moment before he waved her into the room. "Come in. Weren't you wearing a different shirt before you went to Court?"

"Yeah," she sighed. "I had a fight with a cup o' coffee!"

"Bloody hell! Not again!" He laughed. "I better ban you from coffee!"

"You better *not* ban you from coffee! Not unless you want me to be useless." She laughed. "You know I'm no good to anyone without my caffeine fixes!" They laughed simultaneously at her mild "addiction" to the beverage, both knowing that she worked better with it than without.

"Yeah, I know, I know. I'm the same. How'd you go with Paul Rivera's case this morning?"

"Good," she replied as she crossed to his desk and took a seat. She knew she'd have to wait until after she'd reported on her outing to the courthouse before she asked about the journalist in the conference room. "I got the additional discovery motion filed. Abbie Carmichael was in the Clerk's office when I filed it, so I gave it to her while I was there. Saved myself a trip to One Hogan Place." She was quite pleased that she'd been able to avoid the necessity of taking the short detour via the New York County District Attorney's Office on her way back to the office.

"Abbie Carmichael? Who's she? Where've I heard that name before?"

"Ever watched *Law and Order* on NBC?" Alyssa already knew that her favorite police procedural show was also one of Jake's favorites. "They've just replaced the Jamie Ross character on the show with a new A.D.A. called Abbie Carmichael."

"Oh yeah, I remember now," Jake laughed as he rose from his perch on the windowsill. He flicked the file onto his desk and took his seat behind it. "Why'd they write her out?"

"Something about a bitter divorce and her leaving the D.A.'s Office to get married again and spending more time with her family. Anyway, there's a real A.D.A. called Abbie Carmichael. She's been assigned to the Rivera case."

"Okay, back to that. So what's happening?"

"We've been assigned to Part 72, Judge Caruso."

"Oh, good. I know him."

"Our first calendar day next is next Wednesday. Abbie told me they won't be ready on the discovery motion before then, so they'll be asking for an adjournment."

"Even better! Caruso'll just love that!"

"Huh?"

"You don't know Caruso?"

"No, we haven't had any criminal cases in his Part before."

"Oh, right. Well, with him, if the People aren't ready, he blames them for the delay when he does the speedy trial calculation." Jake paused, unsure how to explain why the senior policeman had come in with the veteran reporter. "Peter told you Angela Ryan's here?"

"Yes." Alyssa looked quizzically at Jake as he massaged his left shoulder, wondering why he didn't mention the man who'd come with her. "Didn't we talk about me meeting her the day I started work here? That was three years ago."

"Yeah, we did. She asked me to wait till I heard back from her."

"Why?" Alyssa was confused.

"She's been doing some background work on a follow–up story on him."

"What? It's taken her three years to research his background?" Alyssa scoffed, hoping Jake would tell her who the man who'd come in with Ryan was. "She's been reporting on him for years!"

"There's more to it than that. She wanted to do some more digging on him before she spoke to you."

"Like what? What digging?"

"She found some," he paused for a moment, looking for the right word, "irregularities with his finances. And she found another woman he'd bullied."

"That doesn't surprise me." Alyssa laughed and waited a moment before asking who the man was, hoping Jake would tell her without her prodding. "Peter said she came in with a cop. Why'd a policeman come with her? Who is he?"

"His name's Hugo Martinez. He's the Superintendent of the New York State Troopers," Jake smiled as he formally announced the man's rank.

"Yeah. So? Who is he?" Alyssa dredged the memory of the man's name from her subconscious, but did not quite make the connection with her former employer's past.

"I'll let him explain it to you." Jake winked slyly at her.

"Oh, come on Jake!" Alyssa exploded. "Who is he? I don't wanna go in there not knowing who he is! What if he asks how I got the stuff I kept on him?" It alarmed her that the State's most senior Trooper might wonder how she came to be in possession of the documents she'd kept in her current employers' safe.

"It's okay, Alyssa. You don't need to worry about that." He picked up her file on Kennedy as he rose from his chair and walked around his desk to Alyssa's seat. "I've squared it away with him. It's better if you hear it from him."

"Alright, Jake," Alyssa sighed, knowing he wouldn't give her the answer she wanted as she stood up. "If you say it's okay."

"Yes, I say it's okay." His face paled as he worked his left arm in circles.

"You okay, Jake?"

"Yeah. Old football injury playing up. I'm just getting old," he laughed as he escorted her to the conference room, suspecting but not quite knowing it wasn't age that was causing his discomfort.

*****

The woman with the thick, dark red hair was one of the most easily recognized women in the country, even with her back to the conference room door.

Alyssa Giordano had grown up seeing Angela Ryan on television, but she did not remember the journalist's early reports about Duncan Kennedy: Alyssa was barely eight at the time of his first wife's death. But she did remember the correspondent's commentary on her former employer's servant: it was hard to forget the reports, not just from Ryan, that had surfaced in the year before she began working for him and it had not taken Alyssa long to dig up the details of what happened in Millbrook more than a decade earlier.

Yet she did not quite recognize the Hispanic man standing next to her, looking out at the magnificent view of New York Harbor. *A cop, Jake said. Why would Angela Ryan bring a cop with her?* She stood motionless before the glass of the conference room door, watching them watch the view from the conference room windows, wondering who he was. Ryan and the policeman turned away from the view as they heard the door open.

"Ms. Ryan, Mr. Martinez, this is Alyssa Giordano," Ritchie introduced. "Alyssa, Ms. Ryan and Superintendent Martinez want to ask you a few questions about Duncan Kennedy, if that's okay with you."

"Hello, Ms. Giordano." Martinez extended his hand as he crossed the room towards Alyssa. "I'm the Superintendent of the New York State Police." Alyssa was still cautious as she shook his hand, still unsure why he would be interested in Kennedy.

"Yes, Superintendent. Jake told me who you are. Ms. Ryan," she said to the redhead, who had also crossed the room, as they too shook hands. Her circumspection was obvious as she did not move far beyond the door: although she and Ritchie had discussed her meeting with Ryan, she had never heard of this Martinez fellow. "Why?"

"Why what?" the reporter asked.

"Why do you want to know about him? Why do you want to talk to me?"

"Mr. Ritchie's told us you used to work for Duncan Kennedy, at Kennedy Price," the reporter stated. "He told me he didn't think you'd mind you talking to me. About what it was like to work for him."

"Yes, I worked for him. But that was five years ago. I'm... I'm just a little... cautious," she paused. "Look, Jake, what's this all about? I'm just a little nervous about saying anything about him."

"I told you it's okay, Lyssie," Jake nodded at her as he handed her the file. "Let's all take a seat. I think now's a good time to talk about it."

"I don't know if you heard about what happened to one of his domestic staff in Montauk," Angela started as they sat at the conference table, Ryan and Martinez on one side, Ritchie and Giordano on the other. "In August 1992?"

"Yes, I saw your coverage of it on your show," Alyssa answered. "That was the year before I started to work for him and Lydia Price. I was still in law school then."

"Do you know what happened to his first wife and their daughter?"

"I heard they were murdered, weren't they? I think you mentioned something about it when you reported what happened in Montauk, didn't you Ms. Ryan?"

"That's right. Call me Angela. Ms. Ryan makes me feel *old*!"

"Okay, Angela. I'm not quite sure how you fit into all this, Superintendent?" Giordano asked Martinez.

"It's Hugo. I don't want to feel old, either." Everyone laughed.

"Okay Hugo."

"I was the Chief of Police in Millbrook in 1980," Millbrook's former Chief of Police answered. "I was in charge of the investigation."

"Oh! I see!" The young woman finally recognized the face of the policeman sitting in front of her as her mind made the connection between him and her former employer. "Didn't it have something to do with his first business falling apart? The murders, I mean."

"Well, that's what I thought," Hugo sighed. "But we couldn't prove it. We never found the asshole who did it, who actually killed the first Mrs. Kennedy and their daughter. And I never figured out why he was allowed to live." His disappointment at the case still being unsolved, cold, after so many years was obvious. "And he and Price had another partner in their law practice when they set it up. Alexander Boland. He went to jail for securities fraud just after Kennedy met his second wife."

"*See*, Alyssa. I *told* you shit follows people like him around!" Jake exclaimed.

"Yeah, Jake," Alyssa laughed. "You told me so. But I still don't understand why you want to talk to me? And why now?" Alyssa looked at the policeman, at the journalist, at her boss. The journalist looked at the policeman; he nodded at her.

"There was a woman who worked at Kennedy Price before you did. She told me some things about him which weren't pleasant. Not pleasant at all." Ryan's voice hardened sharply.

"What do you mean?" Alyssa, remembering the conversation had heard that February day Kennedy and Price had told her they wouldn't let her take the Bar Exams, thought she knew the answer.

"She told me Kennedy assaulted her, raped her. More than once. And something funny was going on with the escrow account. And then Kennedy accused *her* of stealing funds from the escrow account and they fired her."

"Why didn't she go to the police?"

"Kennedy threatened her family if she reported it to the police. She felt safer talking to me anonymously."

"Hmmm. That doesn't surprise me one bit," Alyssa sniggered.

"What do you mean?" This question came from Ritchie; he was surprised by her apparent callousness after she told him what she had been through with Kennedy.

"Sorry, Jake," Alyssa sighed. "I don't mean to sound heartless. After what I went through with Duncan, it doesn't surprise me that he threatened her." *Fuckin' asshole*, her mind raged. *So it wasn't just me!* "You know his business partner and his wife have the same first name? His current wife. Lydia?" Alyssa started to ramble. "Everybody at the office called them "the two Lydias". They called Lydia Price "Lydia the First" and his wife "Lydia the Second". But I always thought his wife was "Lydia the First", since she was married to him. She was always nice to me. Lydia his wife, I mean. But Lydia Price was always a bitch to me." Alyssa, realizing she was rambling, shook her head clear. "Have you spoken to the two Lydias?"

"Yes, I've spoken with them," Angela announced.

"And?" Alyssa asked.

"Lydia Price wasn't helpful at all. When this woman told her about what Kennedy had done to her, she didn't believe it. Kennedy denied it and she believed him. I don't think she knows anything more about the rip off Boland went to jail for than what she said at his trial. Looks like Kennedy was able to hoodwink her on that one."

"Yeah," Alyssa interjected. "He's always been good at doing that."

"But Lydia his wife, she was *more* than helpful. She told me he'd abused her as well."

"I thought so!" Alyssa gasped.

"I did some more digging, spoke to a few other ex–employees. And to their ex–partner, Boland. From what he and Mrs. Kennedy told me, Kennedy was involved in the securities fraud as well."

"And?" Alyssa asked again.

"That's when Angela came to me about it," Hugo continued, "to see if I could investigate him without getting this woman or Mrs. Kennedy involved. To protect them. I got enough to indict him."

"I knew it!" Alyssa shouted as she jumped out of her chair; her delight was obvious as she hopped about. "He *is* a swindler! A crook! A louse! The dirty rotten rat! The misogynistic woman–hating pig!"

"Calm down Lyssie!" Jake ordered.

"Alright!" she laughed. "I had to get that out," she laughed again as she sat back down. "So what happens now?"

"As I said, I got enough to indict him with what Angela brought me. But we're hoping you might be able to confirm a couple of things that happened when you worked for him," the policeman answered.

"I dunno. Jake?" Alyssa's fear of facing Kennedy again grew. "Will I have to testify?"

"Look, Lyssie, it's okay," Jake answered. "From what Superintendent Martinez has told me and the paper trail he's shown me, he's got enough evidence and you won't need to testify. The file you have may just tie up the loose ends. That's all they want."

"Mr. Ritchie's right, Ms. Giordano," Martinez acknowledged.

"So, will you help?" the reporter asked. Alyssa looked at Jake, he nodded and smiled. Alyssa Giordano sighed as she closed her eyes and contemplated how life had upturned itself; she smiled and opened her eyes after a moment's thought.

"You bet your ass, baby!"

CHAPTER 15

CONNECTIONS SEVERED

The diagnosis that her employer had had a heart attack came as no surprise. Giordano, as had everyone who worked for Jake Ritchie, had seen it coming over the last three years: the long hours he worked, the greasy food he ate when he remembered to eat, the drinking binges when he knocked off on Fridays and ordered everyone into his office so he wouldn't have to drink alone. Only he had not seen it coming.

Eddie Kann took control the day he found Ritchie collapsed in his office. He barked orders; to Peter Parker to call 911, to Phillipa Watkins to help him attend to his partner as they waited for the ambulance before sending Alyssa to Part 72 take care of Ritchie's case before Judge Caruso. He continued barking orders to the other attorneys in the office after Alyssa raced out the door.

"Eddie, Alyssa's closing," Jake gasped, through the oxygen mask, to the man walking beside the stretcher. "In Hoboken. It's today, isn't it?" he asked as the paramedics pushed the stretcher against the rear of ambulance.

"Yeah, Jake. It's today," Eddie answered as the senior paramedic jumped through the open doors and started to pull the stretcher through. "It's all ready. I've got it under control," he continued from beside the ambulance door as the stretcher came to a stop at the other end of the emergency transport vehicle.

"Sir," the junior paramedic, still outside the back cabin, interrupted. "We gotta close the doors. We gotta get Mr. Ritchie to Downtown Hospital."

"Hang on a minute," the woman, having run from the Center Street Supreme Court building to Wall Street, wheezed as she walked around the back of the ambulance and peered through the still open doors. "You okay, Jake?"

"Yeah, I'm fine, Lyssie."

"No, he's not fine, ma'am," the junior paramedic interjected again. "He's had a heart attack. We gotta get him to Downtown Hospital, *now*."

"Hang on a minute," the patient cut the paramedic short. "Hang on just a minute! The Rivera trial. What happened in Court, Lyssie?"

"Hang on a minute nothing, Jake" Kann ordered. "We'll take care of everything."

"It's okay, Jake," Alyssa answered. "Caruso adjourned it for a week, so I can get someone else up to speed on it. And we won't get penalized on the speedy trial calculation."

"Eddie," Ritchie turned to his partner. "Lyssie's closing!"

"Don't worry. I'll take care of it."

"You gotta go, Eddie. Don't let Lyssie go." They barely heard Ritchie as the young fireman jumped in the back of the ambulance and slammed the doors behind him.

"Don't worry, Jake. I got it covered," Kann, knowing what Ritchie meant, shouted back through the doors as he and Giordano stepped back from the rear of the ambulance. They watched as it took off, sirens wailing, tires screeching, towards the Emergency Center.

"I *was* going to drive to Hoboken for the closing myself. You got a problem going?" Eddie asked Alyssa as they headed for the entrance to their office building. "For the closing?"

"Nope," she smiled, also having understood what Ritchie meant. "You gotta take care of things here, Eddie."

"You know he's going to be there, don't you?"

"Yep." Her smile grew as they crossed the lobby towards the doors of an opening elevator.

"Right," he scoffed as they entered the express elevator. "That's what worries me!"

"It's okay, Eddie. I've toughened up since then." She winked at him.

"Yeah," he laughed. "You have."

"What time's it on?" she asked as she looked at her watch. "three o'clock, isn't it? Shit! It's 2:30 now! I won't make it in this traffic!"

"No, it's at 3:30 now. I called Garrick Westman to push back the time."

"What about the bank?" Alyssa was worried that it would shut its doors before she arrived.

"No, they'll wait."

"Did you tell 'im I'm going?"

"No. Wasn't sure if you wanted to."

"How is he?" Phillipa and Peter chimed together as the elevator doors opened and Eddie entered the law office's reception. Alyssa remained in the elevator carriage, holding the doors open.

"He'll be fine," Eddie answered. "You got Alyssa's sale file, Peter?"

"Yes," the receptionist said as he picked it up from his desk and held it out for Kann.

"Right, off you go," Kann directed Giordano as he exchanged it through the elevator doors for the file she was holding. "Call me when you're done."

"Will do," Alyssa called through the elevator doors as they closed.

*****

It was 3:45 p.m. by the time Alyssa pulled her car into the parking lot outside the bank holding the mortgage over the Hoboken co–op. Alyssa was tired from the mid–week traffic snarl she had encountered, again, in the Holland Tunnel; it had taken an hour for her to drive the nine miles from her East 90th Street condominium to Hoboken's largest shopping mall, across the road from the small shop front where she used to work.

Although he had hoped Alyssa would turn up, the attorney handling the closing for the couple purchasing her old residence expected that she wouldn't; he was surprised to see her when she hurried through the bank's doors. Pleasantries were quickly exchanged with her opposing attorney and the bank's manager, but the formalities of the transaction that would rid her of her last material tie to Hoboken took an hour. The branch administrator remembered her fondly even though he hadn't seen her since she'd so hastily departed, so he took it upon himself to direct them to the front door while he deposited the checks into the account she'd nominated. She had time to take a call from Eddie Kann while they waited.

"Who was that?" the attorney asked as they waited for the manager to open the bank's doors.

"My boss, well one of my bosses."

"Do you have to go straight back to work?"

"Nah, it's after five. He told me I got the afternoon off." The quip gave them both a laugh.

"I called your branch manager in Manhattan to tell them I've deposited those checks. He'll make sure they clear tomorrow," the bank manager said to Alyssa as he unlocked the door for them.

"That's great! Thanks, Matt," Alyssa smiled at her former bank manager, relieved that she'd made a large dent in her other, newer mortgage.

"Again, thank you both. That was effortless," the bank manager said as they exited.

"Thanks, Matt," the attorney said to the bank manager's back as he returned to his duties before turning to Alyssa. "So. That's that."

"Yep. That's that."

"The keys?"

"Oh, yeah, just a sec." Alyssa rifled through her hand bag: it took her a moment to drag them from the bottom before she stretched her arm out. "Here." He didn't immediately take the jangling key ring she offered him.

"I don't suppose you have time for a post–closing inspection?"

"Yes." She understood what he really meant. "I suppose I do have time for a post–closing inspection. Your car or mine?"

"My car's at the mechanic's," he smiled at her. "So we'd better take your car."

They walked to her car in silence, they rode to her former co–op in silence, he followed her up the stairs to the front door in silence. As she pulled the keys out of her bag and put one in the top lock, she felt him put his arms around her and press himself against her. He didn't let go until she'd finished unlocking the door and pushed it inwards. As they entered the apartment, Alyssa felt Bill Morisette stroke her hair as she dropped her handbag just inside the door. He grabbed her and pushed her against the wall; he wrapped his arms around her and kissed the nape of her neck.

He spun her around and picked her up; he pressed his lips to hers and pushed his tongue into her mouth as he carried her to the bedroom. As they undressed each other as quickly as they could,

Alyssa sensed the urgency of Bill's desire for her. He pushed her back onto the bed, straddled her and kneaded her breasts ferociously. With her own sense of urgency increasing, she grabbed his head, pulled him down over herself; she explored his mouth with her tongue as he plunged himself into her more aggressively than he'd ever done so before. After they peaked together, Bill turned onto his back and pulled Alyssa over him, wrapping his arms around her.

****

"So, what made you sell this place?" Bill Morisette asked as he stroked the bare back of the woman whose head was nestled in the cusp of his shoulder.

"Mom and Dad. They wanted me to cut my connection with Hoboken," Alyssa replied as she ran her outstretched fingers over his chest, down his abdomen and towards his groin. "And money. Living in New York and paying the mortgage on this place as well was getting too tough."

"New York? I thought you went back to Albany. How long've you been in New York?" he asked.

"I did go back to Albany." she replied. "But I got a job in Manhattan about a month after I went back. So I've been there just over three years now."

"You in Manhattan? There's trouble," Bill teased. Alyssa laughed. "You have any problems finding an apartment?"

"No, Dad helped me with that. He found me a nice one bedroom condo on the East Side that'd been fixed up just before I moved in."

"The East Side? How'd he swing that?"

"He worked a deal with the owners. He finished the restoration work on it just before I moved to Manhattan. They needed a new tenant and I needed a place to live."

"Cool. So where are you working now?"

"I'm clerking at Kann Ritchie."

"That's a great firm!" Bill was surprised that she'd scored a position at such a prestigious firm. "Their real estate department's got a great rep. The corporate securities department's good as well."

"Eddie Kann heads those departments up. He's shit hot at that stuff."

"Yeah, I know him. I've worked on some deals where he's represented the developers. Don't they do criminal defense work as well? Eddie doesn't do that sort of work, does he?"

"Yeah, mostly white collar defense stuff, corporate fraud, securities violations. Jake Ritchie looks after that. That's the department I mostly work in."

"You just do criminal work now?"

"Nah. Jake does some corporate litigation as well. And I do a bit in real estate with Eddie. He thinks I need to be "rounded". But I mostly work with Jake."

"So, how'd you swing the job there?"

"Dad went to high school with Jake 'n' Eddie," she sighed as he laughed.

"So what are you going to do with the money left over from this place?" Alyssa lifted her head from Bill's shoulder at his question and looked into his eyes, considering whether, or how, she should answer. "What?"

"I'm not sure I should tell you."

"Why?" He lifted his head and kissed her, parted her lips with his tongue.

"Nah, you don't wanna know," she answered as she pulled her lips from his.

"Oh, come on!" He kissed her again. "Tell me," he pleaded.

"I paid off my condo in Manhattan."

"Shit! You got enough to buy a condo on the East Side? How'd you swing that?"

"Prices aren't as bad as you think." He heard the caginess in her voice.

"Come on! You know I know what prices are like! How'd you swing it?"

"Dad. Again. That was part of the deal he did with 'em. He put up the deposit; I picked up a great deal on a bridging mortgage on it till this place closed, so the money from here went straight into the mortgage."

"You really got it made with him swinging things for you, don't you?"

"Yeah, I really got it made," she sighed as she rolled her eyes, the frustration dripping from her voice. "First he gets me a job, he finds me a condo, and then he helps me buy it. It pisses me off sometimes that he thinks I can't make it without his help."

"I'm sure he doesn't mean it that way."

"Yeah, yeah, I know. But sometimes I just wanna do things on my own."

"But he sure can swing a deal!" Bill laughed.

"Yeah, lucky me." Alyssa laughed. "Yeah, he's good at deals."

"Hmmm. God, you're beautiful!" He stroked her hair, pulling her head back into his shoulder as she ran her hand back up his stomach, caressed his chest. *I should tell her I'm leaving.* His mind wandered. *I wonder if she knows. Shit, she'd have to know. Ryan's all over him again.* He sighed. *If she works with Jake Ritchie, she'd be in the Supreme Court all the time. It'd have to be all over Criminal Term.*

She felt the slight change in him, in his mood. *He has to know about Duncan. If they came to me, they woulda gone to him as well.* She lifted her head, pressed her lips to his, ran her hand back down to his groin.

"We're not going to do this again, are we?"

"No. At least not for a while." He sighed. She said nothing, waited for him to say more. "I'm going to Europe for a couple of months." He left it at that; she didn't need to know he thought he might not return just yet, since he hadn't quite decided yet.

"Good for you! You look like you need a vacation." She saw the relief on his face, as she already knew it would be the last instance that she would let him take her for some time, but sensed there was more to it. "What is it?"

"Whadaya mean?" He knew what she meant, that she thought he must know about their former employer.

"There's something else, isn't there?"

"I don't know if you wanna know."

"Oh, come on!" She pressed her lips against his again, ran her tongue around them. "It's your turn, out with it." She laughed as he sighed.

"You hear about Duncan?"

"That he'd been arrested?" Her eyes hardened, ever so slightly, as she grinned, ever so slightly.

"Yeah."

"Yeah, I heard." She paused again, looked deeply into his eyes, again waited for him to say more. "The cops asked me about him."

"Yeah. Me too."

"The trial's scheduled to start next month."

"Oh? I hadn't heard that."

"That's the good thing, well one of the good things, about what I'm doing now," she sighed as her eyes, her smile, softened. "I get to hear all the gossip going round the Criminal Term."

"How do you feel?" He could see the relief on her face.

"Great! It's a relief, you know." She sighed.

"I know."

"There's one thing you can do for me, though."

"What?"

"Fuck me again."

His answer was simple. He raised his lips to hers, licked them, their tongues exploring each other's mouths. His free hand seized her breast, rubbed it, he rolled Alyssa onto her back as he suckled her neck. As he moved the length of his body over hers, she felt him grow harder; he moved down her voluptuous curves, his mouth explored her breasts, her belly, her supple thighs. After working his way back to her swollen nipples, he entered her and took his time in having his way with her, until they could no longer hold themselves back. He stayed on top of her without withdrawing from inside her for what seemed an eternity and she could feel his tension release.

"I have to get back," Alyssa said, pushing him onto his back as she got up. "I need a shower, to get your smell off me."

"Okay," Bill mused as he rolled onto his back and watched her walk into the bathroom.

He listened to the running water, to her shower, eyes closed. He opened his eyes as he heard the running water stop, watched her dry her glistening wet body and dress. As she finished buttoning her shirt, Alyssa reached down, sat on the edge of the bed and kissed him hard as ran her hand over his chest.

"I've got to go," she said as she pulled back from his mouth and got up.

"See you later," Bill said, imagining it unlikely that he would ever see her, let alone touch her, again. He closed his eyes and listened to her leave, the front door almost slamming behind her.

CHAPTER 16

TWO STEPS BACKWARDS

Depression was inevitable. But Giordano, like her inscrutable mentor, had not seen it coming: it hit her hard. Giordano, like Ritchie, had not seen her own crisis coming as others thought they had, but nobody bothered to tell her as they had told Ritchie; but it was for two reasons. The problems of the mind were harder to see, and nobody who saw her every day saw this one coming. Except perhaps her inscrutable mentor.

Jake had refused to spend any more than a month in hospital after his heart attack, had ignored his partner's refusals to allow him back to work even though he couldn't make it through a full day, let alone a full week, in the office. But at least he'd accepted his doctor's advice and eased back on his schedule, coming into Kann Ritchie's Wall Street offices only a couple of days a week. At least also he'd accepted Eddie's imposition of the conditions of his return: that they hire another attorney to help Alyssa with his Court appearances, and Alyssa would help him audit and catalogue the documents they held in their security room for their clients.

The first sign he'd seen, the day of Ritchie's return to work, of Alyssa's looming depression was her anguish at the fact that the trial she had so long awaited did not start on time. Kennedy had hired some hot shot as his defense attorney. The discovery motion he filed on what was supposed to be the first day of jury selection had tied up a bevy of assistant district attorneys for a month. Her boredom with her new task, which became very old very fast, added to the torment. Her mind was quick, her intellect sharp; but the ritualistic tasks of pulling documents from the security room anesthetized her thought processes.

She paled as the delays became exponential, as Kennedy sacked one attorney after another, or they withdrew for one specious reason after another. As the multitude of assistant district attorneys fending off the motion grew, as Kennedy came up with one spurious omnibus motion after another, so did Giordano's torment. Jake pulled her from her work in the Criminal Term as Kennedy's fast footwork made Alyssa thinner. Her moods swung: angry one moment, bawling the next. But that did not stop her from keeping abreast of developments in the case; Martinez couldn't refuse her calls.

It took a year for Alyssa's faith in justice to return, for the ever–growing assembly of assistant district attorneys to dispose of his delaying tactics; the trial judge finally decided to countenance no further delays, tolerate no further motions. She began to believe she might finally be rid of the cruel menace who had almost destroyed her.

The trial date had finally been set and she wanted to watch the jury selection; she wouldn't believe it was really happening unless she saw it for herself. Her grandmothers cried as Mom and Dad begged her not to go. Poppy Ian and Paul ordered her not to go. Eddie and Jake implored her not to go. But her obstinacy was dogged and she would not listen. Jake finally caved, convinced them to let her watch the jury selection on condition that he would go with her.

It annoyed Alyssa that Jake had sent her ahead, to Part 72 first, for some tedious, meaningless adjournment; she did not want to miss a moment of Duncan Kennedy's descent into the bowels of the justice system. It surprised her that the Part 38 courtroom was empty when she got there. She had expected it to be full, with the panel of men and women to be interrogated on voir dire before being sworn on the jury and a horde of journalists to record, and give an account of, every glorious moment for their viewers.

"Hi Billy," she caught the Court Officer's attention. "Where is everybody?"

"Um, hi Alyssa." His face reddened as he turned to see Alyssa approach the Bar table, where the attorneys were supposed to be sitting. "Judge McCoy's gone off the Bench temporarily."

"Why?" She knew the Court Officer well and was surprised at his timidity.

"Hang on a tick, Mr. Ritchie asked me to call him when you got here." He picked up a telephone handset and dialed a telephone number. "Hello? Mr. Ritchie? It's Billy from Part 38." He listened for a moment. "Ms. Giordano's here." He listened again. "Okay, I'll let her know." He hung up as he turned back to Alyssa. "Mr. Ritchie's on his way back He'll only be a minute."

"Oh, come on, Billy! What's going on?"

"You'd better wait for Mr. Ritchie."

"Lyssie?" the familiar voice echoed from behind her. She turned to see Jake, standing next to her parents, at the courtroom door.

"What's going on, Jake," Alyssa's voice was strident.

"Sit down, Alyssa," Moira sighed as the three of them approached her.

"Come on, Jake. What's going on," Alyssa repeated, refusing to sit, her voice cracked. "Why hasn't voir dire started?"

"He's gone." From Gino.

"*What?!* What do you mean, he's *gone?*" It was a whisper, but the urgency in Alyssa's voice was still clear.

"He's not coming. He's gone." Her father again.

"Jake? Gone where?"

"It appears he's skipped bail. His U.S. passport was scanned at Customs at La Guardia just before the last flight left last night."

"*Where*, Jake?"

"Don't worry, Alyssa. McCoy's already issued a bench warrant for him."

"*Where*, Jake?"

"Costa Rica."

"Hugo! What's Hugo say?"

"I'm sorry Alyssa." He stroked her arm. "He didn't clear Customs in Costa Rica."

"*What!*" Alyssa gasped. "How can *that* be?!"

"They can't find him. His passport wasn't scanned in Costa Rica."

When depression finally took hold of her, it was severe and it was remorseless. It hit her as harder than the edge of the Bar table hit her as, eyes rolling back in her head, she fainted.

*****

It wasn't the sound of the keys in the door that woke her. Alyssa's eyelids flickered as the smell of the pizza wafting into her nostrils as it entered the door that did. They way Mimi's Pizza Kitchen combined the sausage, pepperoni, mushrooms and peppers on the special always smelt magnificent. With anchovies added, Alyssa thought she was in heaven every time she smelt a hint of it, let alone ate it. *I must be dreaming.*

"No, sweetheart, you're not dreaming," the old man said.

"What?" Startled, Alyssa opened her eyes, sat bolt upright and swung her legs off the couch.

"You're not dreaming, sweetheart," the old man repeated as he crossed the room.

"Grampa Ted!" Alyssa exclaimed, shaking her head. "Did I say that out loud?"

"Yes, you did say that out loud." Ted Kavanagh answered.

"I must be going crazy," Alyssa laughed.

"Yes, you must be going crazy," the old man laughed.

"What're you doing here?"

"Moira said you needed a Mimi's Special."

"Mom always thinks I need a Mimi's Special."

"I thought you needed a Mimi's Special, then."

"Come on Grampa! What are you really doing here?"

"I'm worried about you, darling."

"Didn't you have a vote on the Floor this morning?" She referred to the Floor of the United States Senate.

"Pushed it through last night. Thought I might drive down and bring you your favorite pizza."

"You *drove?!*" Alyssa was stunned, not only that her ninety–four–year–old great–grandfather still had his driver's license but also that he had survived the drive from Capitol Hill to Manhattan.

"Yes, dear, I *drove!* I can still drive, you know!"

"And you drove all the way from Washington D.C. to Manhattan to bring me a pizza?" she scoffed. "Yeah right." She looked at the box longingly.

"Yeah. I drove all the way from Washington D.C. to Manhattan to bring you a pizza!" He didn't bother removing his jacket as he groaned and eased himself down next to her. "Crap! I'm stiff from sitting on my ass for so long."

"Here, gimme!" She snatched the box from his hand, opened it and shoved a piece of the pie almost all the way in. The senior United States Senator from Massachusetts laughed as he put the briefcase on the coffee table in front of her makeshift bed and took a small bite of the piece he'd picked up.

"So what are you really doing here, Grampa?"

"Moira and Gino wanted me to check up on you. They're worried about you, even more worried about you than I am. And you won't listen to them."

"Oh, come on, Grampa. I'm okay." Her ashen color and almost emaciated frame, and that he found her sleeping on the sofa, belied her statement. "I keep tellin' 'em that."

"You don't look okay."

"Really, Grampa. I'm okay."

The pair sat and ate in silence until the pizza was almost finished.

"So what are you going to do with your career? Have you thought about taking the Bar again?"

"I dunno. I don't think I'm ready to try again."

"You have to do something. It's been months since the trial was aborted. You have to get out of the mood you're in," he pleaded.

"Yeah. I know. Mom 'n' Dad've been bugging me about it. They've been harassing me about it at work too. Constantly."

"So, do you really want to be a lawyer?"

"I don't know. What's happened has really turned me off."

"I understand that. But you shouldn't let him take it away from you, what you've achieved already."

"I know, I know. But I'm just so disillusioned! I thought it was about justice." She sighed. "And the *fucker* didn't get what's coming to him."

"You know Lady Justice is blind, sweetheart." The old man didn't take offence at her foul mouth. He understood her cynicism. "Don't think about him anymore. He'll get what he deserves, all in good time."

"Whadda ya mean, Grampa?" She wondered whether he'd used his connections he'd made in the fifty–odd years in the United States Senate to impose his will in the search for Kennedy, hoping he hadn't.

"He'll get what what's coming to him, when the time comes." He winked at his great–granddaughter. "I still have some influence, you know."

"Oh, Grampa! *Please* tell me you haven't interfered!"

"No, no, Lyssie. I'm just keeping an eye on things." He smiled before took the final bite of the last piece of pizza. "Look. Why don't you take the Bar Exams in D.C.? You can get admitted and then do something else if you want. You don't have to work as an attorney to use what you've learnt. Just don't waste it."

"But I don't have the time to take time off to do a Bar Review Course. Or the money." She rebuffed him as gently as she could as she picked up a napkin to wipe her hands. She hadn't decided what she wanted to do with her life.

"You don't have to take time off to do a Bar Review Course. And I'll pay for it."

"Huh?" She was confused. "Whadda ya mean? Bar Review Courses are all full time study."

"Not anymore. BAR/BRI in D.C. is trialing a "home study" version of the Bar Review course. You get all the handouts and written materials you'd get if you went to a course."

"Really?"

"*And* you get the lectures on one of those iPod thingamies. And you get something called a "Paced Program". It's a study schedule customized for each student doing the course themselves."

"*Really?*"

"And it'd shut your mother up." He smiled at her as she laughed raucously at the thought that something could shut her mother up.

"Yeah. It'd shut everyone up!" She sighed. "I'll look into it."

"You don't have to. Already done." He opened his briefcase, pulled out a large envelope and handed it to her. "Here's the application form." She wasn't astonished that he'd brought the forms with him.

"Got a pen?" Alyssa chuckled as her Grampa Ted reached into his jacket and pulled out the pen he'd brought with him for her to fill out the forms. "You've really got it covered, haven't you?"

"You better believe it! I gotta get your mom off my back too!"

Their raucous laughter that the thought of getting the nagging woman off both their backs caused echoed simultaneously throughout the condo.

CHAPTER 17

ENDING PROCRASTINATION

"Crap, I hate forms," Alyssa mumbled to herself as she signed the last of the forms to be completed.

The information package, which she had spread out over the infuriatingly small table, had indicated that the forms could have been mailed to her and she could have mailed them back after she'd completed them. It was the first Friday of the year that the Committee on Admissions office was open and she decided to collect the package in person; Mom and Dad had told her it was a waste of time but she decided to spend the day in the national capital anyway to try and convince the Committee Clerk to waive the late fee and let her sit the February Exams. Her parents had been right: she failed dismally in her efforts with the Clerk. It annoyed her that her parents always seemed to be right. But she was here now, and she could get the forms filed a good two months before they were due. In her mind it would have been a waste of time to fly in from New York, collect the forms and head straight back to the airport and New York; she would just spend the day in D.C. completing the forms, take them back to the courthouse in person anyway and be guaranteed a place in the July Exams.

"Me too." Alyssa almost jumped out of her seat, not recognizing the male voice. Nor did she recognize the man to whom the voice belonged when she looked at him.

"Do I know you?" The envelope he was holding in the hand not holding his coffee looked familiar to Alyssa.

"We ran into each other at the courthouse. Literally. You nearly knocked me down as you walked out."

"I'm sorry!" Alyssa was mortified as she recalled seeing the owner of the voice, the man she'd bumped into, at the courthouse.

"That's okay." He laughed. He put his coffee mug on Alyssa's table and stuck his hand out. "Andrew Jackson. May I join you?" She looked around and saw that the only spare seat was at her table. She studied him for a moment: *This must be a career change for him.* His hair, longer than hers, was pulled into a tight ponytail as hers was. He was older than her by at least fifteen years, possibly more. Although he looked as if he was well defined, his thinness gave the appearance that he'd lived a tough life.

"Sure." Alyssa shook the outstretched hand and he sat. "Alyssa Giordano. Andrew Jackson: what a name!"

"Tell me about it! You doin' the Bar Exams too? February or July?"

"Yep, I'm going for July. I can't afford the late fee to take the February Exams. You?"

"Same here, July. Jeez those late fees really are a bit of a gouge!"

"Yeah, they get you where you can!"

"This your first time?"

"Yes. Well, yes and no. It's the first time I'm taking them here in D.C. I took the New Jersey Exams five years ago, but I missed out on passing by a couple of points on the first day's part and they wouldn't remark my papers. You?"

"Same here. I took my first round in Massachusetts last July and failed by a couple of marks. If ya don't mind me asking, why'd'ya wait so long? Why now, in D.C.?"

"Long story short, I was too lazy to try again." She didn't want to explain the long story to someone she'd just met. "Now my mom's bugging me," she rolled her eyes, "and I just wanna get her off my back." Another small white lie. Well it really wasn't a lie: Mom and Dad had been nagging; but so too had Eddie and Jake. Their obvious motive was money: they could make more money out of her if she was an attorney they could charge the billable hour for, but her gut, and the sly and surreptitious hints he had dropped, told her that his motive wasn't obvious. She did not have the inclination to inquire, she just wanted them to shut the hell up and leave her alone. "One of my great–grandfathers worked in D.C. and my old man seems to like the idea that I can make a difference if I get a job in Washington." She knew he would not make the connection with her surname and she really didn't want to tell him who he, her mother's father's father, the indubitable Senator Teddy Kavanagh, was just yet: she had tried to avoid the special attention his name drew whenever it was mentioned. "How 'bout you? D.C., I mean."

"I'm bored in Boston. I've been doing some union organizing and my Union offered me a lobbying job here if I passed the Exams. And D.C. is the first place BAR/BRI is doing the distance–learning format for Bar Review."

"Hey, yeah! I'm doing that one too!" They both laughed.

"Coz ya can't get time off work, right? They won't pay more till ya pass the Bar, but ya can't get time off for Bar Review. Assholes." He shook his head and laughed.

"Yeah. Assholes!" She nodded and returned the laugh.

"So how did you get the day off today?"

"The office I work for hasn't reopened yet. It's always closed till the second Monday after New Year's. The bosses like their skiing." A simple white lie wouldn't hurt; he didn't need to know that Eddie Kann and Jake Ritchie had ordered her here, given her the day off with pay and paid for the trip.

"Jeez! Some people have all the luck!" he rolled his eyes in mock frustration. "I had to call in "sick" yesterday and today, just so the boss wouldn't think I was taking today for a long weekend. Doing what?"

"Contract job with a corporate law office in New York, cataloguing the documents they hold in security for their clients, you know, mortgages, title deeds, wills. How 'bout you?"

"Jeez, sounds like fun!" His sarcasm was thick and obvious.

"Having teeth pulled is more fun. But it's a job. Whadda you do in Boston?" He looked at her sideways, seemingly unsure whether he should tell her the truth. "Come on," she pushed him, "tell me."

"I'm a surgical nurse practitioner at UMass Medical." He looked at her quizzically as she nodded, accepted it as if it was nothing strange at all. "You're not surprised?"

"No, not at all. I've met my fair share of male nurses. Nothin' wrong with that!" She shrugged. "So what made you decide to go into law?"

"Boredom with blood 'n' guts. And the union work I been doing seems like much more fun." He wasn't sure whether to believe she was so accepting just yet, having met more than his fair share of women who couldn't accept men as nurses, so he turned the conversation back to the task at hand. "So, where you up to with your forms?"

"Done," she sighed. "Just signed the last one."

"I'm done too." He looked at his watch: it was one–thirty. "I'm going back to the courthouse to file the forms. Wanna walk back over with me? You got time?"

"Yeah, sure. I don't have to be at *Ronald Reagan* till six. How 'bout you?"

"I'm going from *Ronald Reagan* too, but not till nine!" He groaned. She chuckled.

"But I gotta eat first," Alyssa said over the growling of her stomach. "I haven't eaten since some ridiculous hour this morning. Wanna have some lunch first?"

"I'm right for food. Another coffee'll do me. But you get something."

Oh, he doesn't eat, that's why he's so thin, she thought as he ordered another coffee. He watched her while she scoffed a burger, but he did pinch some of her fries, before she ordered another coffee, and also some water, and he a cola.

"Do you drink anything without caffeine in it?"

"Nope."

"Okay," she looked at her watch, "it's two–thirty. We should probably go if we wanna make it back to the Committee office. Maybe we can get 'em to process it straight away."

"Yeah, should be enough time before they close. Make 'em work for our money."

"I'll be heading straight to the airport after. Wanna share a cab?"

"Good plan. Maybe I can get an earlier flight if we hurry." He waved his hand at her as she started to pull her purse from her hand bag. "No, no, I'll get this check. You can get the cab fare."

"No, I'll get—"

"Oh bullshit. I'll get it. I don't understand this women's liberated bullshit. You *can*," he emphasized, hoping she didn't see the *God, she's hot!* look in his eyes, "let men get the check occasionally, you know."

"Okay, okay." She laughed. Recognizing the look on his face, she decided to ignore it; she realized that some men found her, and her developing inner strength, sexually attractive, but wasn't at the point in her life where she was confident enough in herself to exploit it. She didn't understand why she could never get a man, well most of the ones she knew anyway, to understand that she wanted them to let her be independent, pay her own way some of the time.

They meandered the short distance back to the courthouse and walked into the Committee on Admissions' offices, within the District of Columbia's Court of Appeals building, an hour before the office, and the building, was due to close to the public. There was only one other person who wasn't employed by the Committee in its offices when they arrived, but he had just finished his business and was leaving. The Committee Clerk gave them the due attention that he thought they deserved, which was less particular than his usual officiousness as he really didn't want to be there, but they were still done with the process within the hour and out the front door of the courthouse just as Security was locking it.

A cab appeared from seemingly nowhere as they walked down the steps to the curb and they made it to the airport named for the fortieth President in record time. They laughed at the coincidence as they approached the same airline check–in counter to get their boarding passes for their flights going in almost the same but slightly different directions. She had more than enough time to check in for her flight, as did he, and it cost him a pittance to get himself checked in on a flight leaving only a few minutes after hers. But they still had to wait for their flights to be called: the decision to wait together seemed inevitable, as predestined as their decision to exchange phone numbers and keep in touch during Bar Review and until, at least until, the Bar Exams.

*****

The old man's eyes fluttered as the light level was raised ever so slightly. He hadn't slept well: the wounds where the skin lesions had been were aching. But he had become accustomed to the effect of the painkillers were beginning to wear off after his two previous operations. And he quite enjoyed flirting with the pretty young nurses at the University of Massachusetts Memorial Medical Center.

"Good evening, sir," the nurse said, back to the door of the private room, as Senator Ted Kavanagh's eyes squinted, adjusting to the dim light.

"Good evening, young man. Time for "observations" again? Be gentle!"

113

"Yes, sir. And I'm not so young," the nurse laughed as he took the man's temperature. "How are you feeling this evening?" he asked as he checked Kavanagh's blood pressure.

"Little groggy, but not bad for an old man. You're named after a President, aren't you? How long you been at this game?" Kavanagh asked as Jackson slipped on his reading glasses and wrote on his chart, recognizing him from his shift the previous day.

"Yes, Andrew Jackson." Jackson wasn't surprised that the nonagenarian had forgotten his name under the lingering effects of the general anesthetic. But he was surprised that the ninety–five year old man's mind was sharper than a tack so soon after surgery under a general anesthetic. He'd seen much fitter patients many years his junior have trouble with the aftereffects of surgery under local anesthetic. "I've been in this game for quite a while now. Too long. Fifteen years now."

"I've seen you here before, during the week."

"Yeah, I normally work weekday shifts."

"You don't work weekends?"

"No, not normally. Been around long enough to get my pick of the shifts. But I need the extra cash."

"What for?"

"Law school loans, Bar Exam fees."

"Hmmm, the Bar Exam is tough work. They don't teach you a lot of things in law school."

"Yeah, it is. Working full time doesn't help either," he said as he continued to poke and prod the elderly gentleman. Andrew didn't bother to turn around when Kavanagh looked past him towards the door, thinking he was just casting his eyes over some pretty female nurse walking past.

"So what's the score?" he asked, as the nurse hung the chart back on the end of bed.

"Your temperature's a little high, ninety–nine point two. Your blood pressure's normal, pretty good actually: one–twenty–eight over seventy." Jackson checked the bandages and saw blood staining one on the United States Senator's arm. "How do your wounds feel?"

"Scratchy, aching. That one in my arm is really throbbing."

"That one took a little longer to close than the others, the incision there was deeper than the others."

"You were in theatre?"

114

"Yes, sir. I'll need to take the bandage off and check the stitches on this one."

"Aw crap, do you have to?"

"Oh, stop complaining, Grampa Ted!" Jackson jumped, startled, and turned towards the door as he heard the familiar voice.

"What are you doing here?" Kavanagh and Jackson chimed together as Alyssa Giordano walked to the bed.

"Hey, Dick. Mom sent me to check on you, Grampa," she said as she kissed him on the cheek.

"What'd your Mom do that for?" he asked. Jackson looked at her, confused.

"She knows how much trouble you are!"

"Come on, Lyssie, why are you really here?" Her book bag looked heavy as she slid it off her shoulder.

"I want to pick your brain about some constitutional law questions on the Bar Exam."

"I knew it! You've just come to use me!" Alyssa and her great-grandfather laughed.

"He's your grandfather?" Jackson asked Giordano, stunned at the connection between the influential man and his friend.

"My mom's grandfather. Is he behaving himself?"

"Yeah, Dick, he's behaving. He's one of my best patients."

"Dick? Dick?" Now it was Kavanagh's turn to be confused. "I thought your name was Andrew?"

"Yes, it is Andrew, Grampa," Alyssa answered for him. "But we call each other Dick. Just a bit of fun."

"How do you two know each other?" the Senator asked.

"We're doing the same BAR/BRI course," Andrew said.

"Ah, right." The old man smiled knowingly.

"You sure he's behaving himself, Dick?" Alyssa asked. "He's not flirting with the female nurses?"

"Well, maybe just a little flirting. But they don't mind. And he behaves himself most of the time."

"How's he doing?"

"Good, just gotta check this wound and change the bandage, give him some pain meds and we're done."

"Okay, I'll go get some coffee." She turned to leave her great-grandfather to the care of his nurse.

"No, no, Lyssie, stay. I don't mind," the old man insisted.

115

"You sure?"

"I wouldn't say so if I wasn't!" he pretended to scowl. "You can talk to your mom and give her a good report card for me."

"Don't be so grumpy!" she imitated his mock scowl as she sat in the overstuffed hospital chair beside his bed and pulled a textbook and legal pad from her book bag.

"Alright, darling," Kavanagh laughed. "Alright, Nurse Jackson, go to it."

"Yes, sir." It took the experienced nurse scarcely any time to remove the bandage and replace it after cleaning the wound. "Okay, that's it. I'll leave you two to it," Andrew said as he checked his watch.

"Back to the rest of your old codgers, hey?" Kavanagh asked.

"No, sir."

"Please, call me Ted."

"I'd be honored, sir. Ted. No, my shift's finished. I've gotta go home and study."

"Well, since my great–granddaughter's come to pick my brain, you can too."

"You sure, sir? I don't want to get in the way." He looked at Alyssa, who simply nodded.

"I wouldn't say so if I wasn't!" he said again. "And please, call me Ted!"

"Okay Ted. I'll go sign off."

"He's a good young man," Ted said to Alyssa after Andrew had left the room.

"Yeah, he is."

"Moira told me you were always on the phone to some man in Boston."

"Oh, Grampa! Don't tell me she asked you to check him out!"

"Yes, she did. But I told her you're big enough and ugly enough to look after yourself." Alyssa laughed. "So, where's it going?"

"What do you mean?" Alyssa blushed, knowing exactly what the old man meant.

"You know what I mean. Are you serious about him? He is quite a bit older than you."

"Oh, come on!" Alyssa was embarrassed by the question, and did not yet know her own mind. "I dunno."

"Well, I like him. He's my kind of people. I'd give Moira a good report card on him any day!"

"Thanks! That'll shut her up!" Alyssa smiled as she started to pepper him with questions. Twenty minutes into the veteran lawmaker's discourse on the workings of the institution of which he had been a member for more than half a century, he paused, mid–sentence. Alyssa turned to see that Jackson had returned, out of uniform, with a parade of men and women in white laboratory coats following him.

"Are you waxing lyrical again, Senator?" the senior dermatologist joked. The two men had first met each other when Kavanagh was a junior Senator and the doctor was a Resident at Boston Medical Center.

"Of course, Professor. And I suppose you've come to wax lyrical about me!" Kavanagh joked back. "You're early!"

"Of course, Senator. Nurse Jackson told me you had a visitor. How are you, Alyssa? Not tiring him out, I hope."

"Well, thanks Doctor Rosenberg. He's tiring me out!"

"So what's with the crowd you brought with you to prod and poke me?" United States Senator Ted Kavanagh asked.

"These are my interns, Senator," Adam Rosenberg, M.D., Boston University School of Medicine graduate, answered. "I thought it might expand their minds to listen to you ranting about the Constitution."

"Good. They need to learn about the foundations of our great nation! They don't teach enough of that in school these days. And you young bucks need to have it knocked into your thick skulls." The junior doctors laughed at the old man's sermonizing.

"But first they need to learn a little about medicine. Nurse Jackson, could you present Senator Kavanagh's chart," he directed his scrub nurse.

"Of course, Professor." Jackson put his glasses on again as he picked up the chart.

"Now just a minute, Adam," Kavanagh interjected matter–of–factly. "Young Andrew is off duty now. He's here to pick what's left of my brain." Alyssa and the old doctor laughed simultaneously; the young doctors and the nurse caught the teasing in his voice, but left to those closer to him to chuckle.

"No, no, Ted. I don't mind," Andrew started before he was cut off by Rosenberg.

"Now come on, Ted. This is a teaching hospital. And my students have just as much to learn from my nurses as they do from me. If not more, for that matter." The Senator looked quizzically at his old friend, his mind still a little slow on the uptake. "Ongoing patient care," the Professor of Clinical Medicine and Dermatology continued, "especially the care you get from my nurses after surgery, is just as important for their education. And Nurse Jackson is one of my best teachers!"

"Ah, yes!" Kavanagh remembered the lessons he learnt from the Assistant Sergeant at Arms in his early days in the United States Senate. "Yes, ladies and gentlemen," the Senator started his lesson for the junior medicos. "Listen carefully to Nurse Jackson. You never know what you can learn!"

It took twenty minutes for Jackson to present his patient to the class and for them to grill him on how to work with other medical professionals to maximize the benefit to their mutual patients. Both professor and patient were impressed with his teaching abilities. *He'll make an impressive advocate,* Kavanagh thought as Jackson repeated the prodding and poking ritual that he'd undertaken not long before. As the doctors left to continue their rounds, Jackson opened his own bag of texts and joined Giordano in her interrogation of the veteran lawmaker.

*****

"So, how's it all going?" Eddie Kann asked as he flipped the document back onto the conference room table. Neither his nor his partner's office was big enough for the four of them. Jake Ritchie had paid attention and was reviewing the notes Philippa had made in the margins of his copy during her verbal review of her monthly report; but, as had been her experience of him ever since she'd worked for her father's classmates, Eddie was still the big picture man and seemed less interested in the finer detail of the report and just wanted the short version.

"I'm more than three—quarters of the way through now. I've been through about thirty—four of the forty file cabinets now." It had been a mind numbing job for Alyssa to get as far as she had in cataloguing the documents the men were holding in security for their clients, and the only thought that kept her going was that they seemed willing to keep paying her for it.

"Only thirty–four! Surely you gotta be able to get through it faster than that," Eddie balked. "You've been at it for over a year now! How much longer until you finish?" It aggravated him that she'd spent so much time away from the shrine of work that could be associated with the billable hour that all managing partners in private law offices worshiped at.

"Eighteen months to be exact. Hmmm, depends on how long it takes me to find the packet owners. Some take longer, because I find they're dead and I have to find their next of kin, or they've moved."

"Come on, how much longer?" Kann goaded. *The faster she gets back to billable hours the better,* he thought.

"Six months."

"Six months! Bullshit!"

"Look, Ed. No bullshit." Her voice was firm, but she did not let herself raise it to the level of indignation to which he had raised his. "It's a fucking big job. I can only give you an estimate based on how long it's taken me so far."

"Come on Ed, give it a rest!" Jake intervened. "Alyssa told us six months ago it's a much bigger job than we first thought."

"But we can't have that many security documents!" Kann was surprised at the thought that he had had so many clients, developed such a large client base since he and Ritchie had first opened their office together.

"Get serious, Eddie." Jake sounded frustrated. "How long we been together? Almost twenty–five years now? We gotta get a handle on this. I've been saying that for years."

"Alright, Jake, alright." Eddie turned back to Alyssa. "So, six months, hey? And you need time off now?!"

"Yes, Eddie."

"What for?"

"God, you got a bad memory," Philippa laughed as she chimed in. "Review practice, the Bar Exams. She told us about that six months ago too, when she signed up for them."

"Maybe you need a brain scan, Eddie." Alyssa covered her mouth as she tried not to laugh at Philippa's facetiousness.

"Yeah, yeah, alright," he groaned as he stood to leave the room. The three remaining at the table also stood. "I'll get a brain scan. Break a leg with the Exams, Alyssa."

"Thanks, Eddie," she said to his back as he left the room.

CHAPTER 18

TESTS PROLIFERATE

The last Tuesday in July was a tense one for two hundred and twenty-eight prospective members of the Bar. The Committee on Admissions' records would indicate that a hundred and fifty of them had been to "this place" before and failed. She wasn't sure which category they classified her, or Andrew Jackson for that matter, having already taken the Bar Exams, but maybe they didn't count Exams taken in other states when classifying someone as either a "first–timer" or a "repeater".

In the six months since they had met at the Court of Appeals, they had become fast friends and her parents had complained of the phone bills from discussing assignments and the late night cram sessions for the Bar Review Course in which they were both enrolled. *Okay, you can send me to Boston on the weekends to study, Grampa Ted won't mind putting me up,* she'd jokingly said to them. *No, you won't bother Grampa Ted and we'd rather pay the phone bills,* they balked back until they realized she was toying with them. They did not quite understand how she could become associated with the unruly looking punk who they'd found a bit too shady, they didn't know anyone else like him, but they let her have the friendship so as not to distract her from her preparations for what they saw as the most important test of her life to date. She and Andrew had met twice more in person in the nation's capital since they first met there. The first face–to–face was for a practice run of the Bar Exams on a weekend in mid–June, about a month before the Exams and second was for a review of the results they'd achieved on the practice run. Jackson and Giordano never seemed to run out of conversation when they weren't talking about the Bar; but their friendship enjoyed comfortable silences as well. But, in the end, neither she nor Jackson cared whether they classified them as repeaters, neither intended to fail this time.

Many had arrived more than two hours early to have their names marked off the roll. Andrew, late again as she had come to know him to be, had knocked on Alyssa's hotel room door at 8:15 a.m.

"Hi, Dick," he said after she opened the door to see him leaning against the frame.

"Hi, Dick," she retorted as she turned back into the room. "You're late. Again. How long does it take to get from the twelfth floor to the fifth floor!"

"I know, I know." He followed her in. "An hour 'n' a half. Fuckin' alarm clock."

"I'll buy you a new one."

"Nah, you can knock on my door tomorrow."

"Yeah, right." She laughed. "Course a woman knockin' on ya door'd wake you up." He laughed as she slung her satchel over her shoulder.

"You ready?"

"Dunno, think so. You ready?"

"Dunno. We gotta have time for coffee." He headed to the door and swung it open, almost knocking himself in the face.

"Watch it!" She laughed again as she followed him out the door. "Yeah, we got time for coffee, but we gotta get it to go. There's a coffee cart on the way." There was edgy, nervous silence as they walked to the elevators and entered after waiting several minutes for the door to open.

"We gotta have time for coffee," he said again.

"Yeah, we got time for coffee, there's a cart on the way," she repeated.

"What's on today?"

"Jeez, you're useless! You'd lose your head if it wasn't screwed on!" More silence until the elevator reached the lobby.

"Shit! I'm panicking," he said as they exited the cabin.

"Me too," she said as they started across the lobby.

"What's on today? What's on tomorrow?"

"Bar Exam today. All day. Professional Responsibility tonight. Performance test tomorrow morning. Essays tomorrow arvo."

"Okay, I got that down."

"You sure?"

"No."

"Fuck you," she laughed as they passed through the front doors of the hotel. "Now *I've* lost it, you bastard!"

They walked in silence to the hall, and into it after speaking barely enough words to identify themselves for roll call, in which they would be sitting for the two day Bar Exams. The seating allocation was random and they had somehow drawn seats next to each other in the same hall. The other two hundred and twenty-six participants noticed them together, the beautiful young woman and the aging man, and found it strange that they appeared to know each other but did not speak to each other. They took their seats in silence; they left the hall together at mealtimes in silence; they returned to their seats after mealtimes in silence; they returned to their separate rooms in their hotel.

*****

It was not until after the essay portion of the District of Columbia Bar Exam was completed on Wednesday afternoon that they spoke to each other again. The participants who heard their conversation found it even stranger than their silence.

"I think I found it, Dick," Jackson said.

"What did you find, Dick?" Giordano asked.

"My mojo."

"Yeah, the mojo. I found my mojo too."

They walked back to the hotel, through the lobby and into the elevator in silence again as both were exhausted, drained, from the experience of Bar Exam. They were the only ones waiting for the elevator. After pushing the button for her floor, he started to raise his hand to press the button for his own floor but he felt her hand grab his and stopped him from pressing it.

"What?" he asked.

"Come back to my room," she said as she pressed herself against him.

"What?" he asked again, he was confused.

"Come back with me, to my room," she repeated. He was startled when she felt her grabbing his buttock with the hand free from holding his.

"You sure?" he questioned. She looked into his eyes, seeing that he wanted her too. She had not been intimate with a man other than her first one, the man to whom she'd lost her virginity; she had not been sure where this would go, but she was sure it would not destroy their friendship as her sexual relationship had destroyed the other friendship. She answered by pressing her mouth to his, parting his lips with her tongue and exploring him.

"What do you think?" she asked as the elevator door opened. He just nodded.

She dragged him out of the elevator barely before the door closed, and to her room, without speaking as she fumbled for her key with the hand she had released from his buttock. She didn't release his hand until after they entered the room and reached the bed. She pushed him back on the bed and undressed herself as quickly as she could, throwing her clothes around the room; it was more difficult for her to undress him as he was lying on the bed, so he sat up and gave her some assistance.

He admired her form and her voluptuous breasts, the meat on her bones; she admired him as, although his form was slight, it was muscular and well defined. He reached for her and grabbed her buttocks, pulling her towards the bed, and slid his right hand to the small of her back as she put her arms around her shoulders. He released his hand from the small of her back, lifted a breast to his mouth and sucked on her nipple. As he released her from his mouth, she moved her hands to his hairy chest and pushed him back down on the bed as she knelt on the bed and positioned herself over him, straddling his groin. She felt him get hard and rub himself between her supple thighs. He skimmed his hand from her breast, down over her belly and parted her and rubbed her groin.

He knew how to please a woman and did so; he pushed her off him and threw her onto her back, pinned her and explored every inch of her for hours with his hands and mouth until she was writhing and screaming in ecstasy. She reached a point where her vocal chords failed her, felt dizzy on adrenaline and she thought she could go no higher. She found she was wrong about that, about not reaching even greater heights of agonizingly painful pleasure, when he guided himself towards her and pushed himself into her. As his thrusting quickened, as he felt her muscles tighten around him and the sensation of her rapture pulsating through him, he lost control of himself and reached his climax quicker than expected.

He did not leave her immediately; but when he did, he did not move completely away from her, rather nestling his head within her breasts. They fell asleep, their bodies intertwined, and did not wake until well into the following afternoon.

*****

The official–looking letter was waiting for her propped up against the kitchen telephone when she got home. Her parents at least had the decency to wait with bated breath at the kitchen table for her to get home from work, without opening it, so she could find out first. Moira jumped from her seat, leaving Gino eating his second bowl of spaghetti, and headed for the front door the minute she heard the keys jangling in the lock.

"Helloooo?" Alyssa called.

"Hello darling!" Moira exuded as she gave her eldest child a hug. Alyssa, arms full, barely in the door, leaned in to kiss her mother on the cheek and dropped her bag.

"How was work?"

"Good. Andrew's come for dinner, if that's okay," she announced, knowing it would be.

"Of course it's okay. You know there's always enough for one more." That caused Alyssa to chuckle. "How are you, Andrew?"

"Good." He kissed her on the cheek. "That's from Grampa Ted."

"How is he?"

"When did you see him?" Alyssa interjected.

"I ran into him at work today, he came in for a checkup," he answered Alyssa first. "He's still kickin', the old codger. Still causing us nurses grief."

Moira, worried about her grandfather's health, heard the respect in Andrew's voice for her grandfather and laughed. If Grampa Ted approved, then Jackson must be okay.

"Just like him. Hungry?"

"Yes," Alyssa and Andrew chimed in unison.

"A letter came for you today." Moira grinned uncontrollably.

"Who from?" Alyssa linked her arm in her mother's as the three of them headed to the kitchen.

"It looks "official". I think it might be your results!" Moira's grin, somehow, Alyssa didn't know how, widened even further.

"Where is it? Hi Dad."

"Hi Lyssie," her father said with a mouthful of pasta. He looked up and saw her companion. "Hi Andy. It's by the phone." Alyssa stopped by Gino and kissed his cheek full of food as her mother retook her seat at the table. "You got your results, Andy?"

Andrew just patted his bag.

"Did you look?" Alyssa enquired of her parents.

"No, but I think you passed!" her mother radiated. "It's too thick for you not to have passed!"

Alyssa walked to the counter where the letter was sitting and, with her back to her parents, stared at it.

"Open it!" Her mother was nervous.

"Yeah, open it," her father, even more nervous, chimed.

"Alright! Alright! Well, here goes nothing." She picked up the envelope as Jackson pulled his envelope out of his satchel and they tore them open together. They read, and exchanged, the letters. She bowed her head and exhaled, as Andrew did.

"Oh, darling!" from her mother and "So sorry, mate," from her father, both thinking that they had failed. It wasn't until she turned to face them that they saw her smirk.

"I passed." Alyssa grinned.

"Me too," Andrew said.

Both her parents jumped up from their chairs, knocking them over, her father upending his plate and sending his pasta across the floor, to hug them both.

*****

She exited one of the numerous elevators stopping on the floor of the offices of Kann Ritchie as if she was walking on air. She smiled and waved at Peter as she sailed towards his desk and saw him raise his eyebrows at her.

He was the first man she had ever met who worked as a receptionist. Well, he really was more than just the average receptionist, his personality more like the warrant officers who ran the Marines, a civilian equivalent of her grandfather, the "go–to" man who really ran the office.

"What's with you," he called. She stopped, sat on his desk, pulled the letter from the D.C. Committee on Admissions from her bag and handed it to him, grinning. "Congratulations. I suppose you'll want another day off?" His laughter distracted her from the sound of the elevator bell ringing and door opening.

"You bet your ass baby!" He covered his mouth as he giggled and pulled the letter to his chest as she said it and looked over her shoulder. She turned to see Eddie Kann and Philippa Watkins standing behind her.

"What is it?" Kann asked, as Watkins just stared quizzically at her. Peter just offered up the letter. After he read it, the senior partner of Kann Ritchie handed the letter he'd received from the unofficial office manager to the official office manager and smiled. After she'd read it, Watkins handed the letter back to its owner. "Congratulations, Alyssa. Of course you can have the day off. Make sure it's in the calendar, Peter." Philippa finally smiled at Alyssa and Alyssa smiled right back at Philippa; both women were headstrong and it had taken some time for Philippa to warm up to Alyssa.

"Of course, Mr. Ritchie," he said to Eddie and Philippa's backs as they headed to his office. Peter pulled a face; Alyssa stifled a laugh.

CHAPTER 19

THE BAR

The Courtroom was packed.

There really wasn't room for the all fresh faced young people let alone even one of each of their family members. She was glad her mother was too busy looking after her father's business, keeping him under her thumb and working on the myriad of work he had to do, to make the trip to the capital; the December weather in Washington, D.C. had snapped cold this year. Alyssa was just too panicky, worrying whether anything would go wrong, to have had to have worried about Mom and Dad being there as well.

Alyssa had flown down from Albany three days before, to file the final certifications with the Clerk; Andrew Jackson arrived at the airport from Richmond the afternoon before the ceremony. He had sent Alyssa his certification to file for him, so she had spent the day and a half before the ceremony first wandering around the Courthouse, seeing a note that Justice Rodriguez was looking for a new Senior Clerk, then around the city, taking in the sights. She had become bored with wandering the monuments to the dead, so she found a public computer, typed a covering letter and printed her résumé. She walked, slowly, just to kill time, back to the Courthouse and asked a junior clerk she'd become friendly with to pass it on to Rodriguez for her. Although her expectations were low, there was always a chance that Rodriguez would consider her for the clerkship; perhaps there was a reason for her to carry the disk, and so much else in her handbag.

Alyssa and Andrew spent the evening of his arrival in his room, catching up and making sure their suits were creaseless and their shoes were spotless. They agreed to meet at the Courthouse coffee shop an hour before the ceremony as Alyssa went to sleep in her own room.

Don't think like that! Andrew made it! she whispered to herself. Andrew had not necessarily always been on time, so Alyssa let the Clerk of the Court know of her attendance and sat down to drink another cup of coffee. When he hadn't arrived twenty minutes beforehand, Alyssa called him at the hotel; he had slept through his alarm. He stumbled up the stairs with barely sufficient time for him to record his presence with the Clerk of the Court and for Alyssa to wipe the toothpaste off his face.

The Court officer ushered the members of the Court of Appeals to their seats. The Chief Judge was out of town, he had always left D.C. early for the Christmas period and his brethren who remained in town always accepted it with some grace; this year the acceptance was a bit more resentful as he had spent more than fair share of time away from the Court this year.

His deputy, Alberto Rodriguez, was presiding, the most senior of the three, over the Bar admissions eight days before Christmas in the year some called the last of the millennium. Well, did it really matter whether 1999 or the next year was the last of the millennium? Alyssa certainly did not care, all she cared about was the fact that she was before the Court to take the attorney's oath. She was in the second group to be sworn in; the room was simply not large enough to fit all the new attorneys in the room to be sworn in one group.

The ceremony went smoothly, blurred, apart from a glass being knocked over and spilling water over the freshly carpeted floor. Alyssa's name was called; she stood, with the rest of them in the room with her, took the Bible and they read the oath of admission from the card as one. As the presiding Judge, it was for Rodriguez to speak to them. Everyone could hear the weariness in his voice; being older than the Chief Judge, he was tired of performing the duties of the more "senior" man without having been properly recognized. He told them to remember their place, to look to their seniors in the profession, good or bad, for guidance. This remark in particular struck a chord with Alyssa, reminding her of Duncan Kennedy; Alyssa knew the remark was not really directed to her specifically, how could he know what had happened, but to instruct all the new attorneys that they still had things to learn and they could also learn by seeing how not to do things.

After Rodriguez concluded his remarks, the judges left the Bench and the new attorneys left the Courtroom; Alyssa and Andrew went back to their jobs in Manhattan and Boston.

*****

The Wednesday before Christmas had been a hectic, strange day.

The Kann Ritchie offices would be closing early for the year–end party, and for Christmas, that day. Alyssa reaffirmed why she carried such a big bag as she pulled her newly framed Certificate of Admission to the Bar from it to show off at the Christmas party. Peter was most impressed and Eddie Kann had offered his best wishes. Even Philippa seemed enthused about it.

As she drove back to Albany, it was as if a great weight had been lifted from Alyssa's shoulders. During her week away from work, her parents had been vociferous in telling her how proud they were; now she could get the job she always wanted. Although she had expected them to say that and for it to weigh on her even more, it was different; she had achieved what she had set out to, albeit five years late, and her mind spun with the possibilities.

*****

A week before her birthday, was even stranger than Christmas.

The ringing cell phone made Alyssa leap from her chair; it was a D.C. number, she only knew the Court clerks in D.C.. *Why would they be calling?*

"Hello, Alyssa speaking," she announced, trying to keep the bewilderment, fear from her voice.

"Hi Alyssa. I'm Judy, from Judge Rodriguez' Chambers."

"Hi Judy."

"Do you have a moment? Can you speak with me now?"

"Yes, I can talk."

"Judge Rodriguez would like to see you about your application to be his clerk. At noon on Monday. He's asked me to confirm that you can make it to D.C. then."

"Hmmm, Monday? Yes, noon on Monday's great."

"Okay, I'll let Judge know to expect you," said the Judge's secretary as she continued with details of how to find his Chambers in the Court of Appeals building.

"Great. Thanks Judy. I'll see you Monday."

"See you then. Bye."

"Bye."

Alberto Rodriguez, second most senior Judge on the D.C. Court of Appeals wanted to meet her! Alyssa was stunned, ecstatic; but she kept her composure, did not tell anyone. There would be no point in jinxing the possibility. She would beg off sick from work; she would not tell even her mother, there would be some plausible excuse she could give.

*****

"Hi Peter, it's Alyssa," she said, hoping the traffic, both aeronautical and pedestrian, would not transmit through the line.

It was not the first scheduled flight out of Albany that, or any, Monday morning and the noises of the passengers in the terminal and the planes taking off was building.

"Hi Alyssa," he chirped, "What's up?"

"Look, I'm not going to make it in today. I have to see... a specialist." That was as close to the truth as she could make it without it really being an outright lie.

"What's wrong?" The concern in his voice was genuine.

"Nothing, I hope, I just have to get something checked out."

"Alright. Look Eddie's just walked in, I'll let him know." She could hear the doubt creeping into his voice, but knew he would accept the explanation on its face. "Eddie, that was Al..." she heard him start as the call disconnected.

*****

Alyssa had meandered slowly to Judiciary Square from the Chinatown Metrorail station. The early flight into Ronald Reagan National Airport had been relatively monotonous, and remarkably on time, for a Monday morning; Alyssa supposed those staffers who had been away from the national capital had been on either the first flight in that morning or on the last flight the night before.

She needed time to compose herself and the walking distance by alighting from the Metrorail a station early accomplished that. Alyssa did not know what she would do with the additional time she expected she would have between the conclusion of the meeting and her return to *Ronald Reagan*; but she did not want to return to Albany too early. At least the arrival time of the early dinner flight would not arouse suspicion that she had not been at work if she was unsuccessful.

The ornate interior of the Court of Appeals of the District of Columbia was even more imposing than its exterior. Alyssa had been sufficiently early to enable her to pass through the security checkpoint just inside the entrance and wander through the building to scrutinize the portraits in the lobby before heading to the Judges' Chambers area; she was unsure of how to get there, but the man who performed the scanning process had given her the instructions she needed after she had told him of the purpose of her visit. Alyssa stood before the painted representation of the man she was about to meet for a few minutes before following the security officer's directions upstairs and pressing the correct button on the intercom to announce herself. A pleasant looking, older woman appeared as the door securing the Chambers area from the public opened and she escorted Alyssa inside the private area to the Rodriguez' outer office.

Associate Judge Alberto Rodriguez was the most senior of the Associate Judges sitting on the Court, only the Chief Judge was more senior, and his reputation was more imposing than the imposing Courthouse, if that was possible. Alyssa was nervous as she sat in the Judge's outer chamber, waiting for him to appear from his inner sanctum. To even be offered an interview was a coup. *How different would my life be,* she reflected, thinking of the offer of the interview with Judge McCoy she had rejected oh so many years ago. The same mistake would not be made twice.

Rodriguez' journey to his current position in life was well known. His family had opposed General Franco's fascism during the Civil War which preceded the second Great War and although many of the anti–fascists sought refuge in France, his had sought refuge in Britain. He had spent only eight years there before relocating to the United States at the age of fifteen. Rodriguez' tough early childhood had given him such drive to succeed, and to give back to his adoptive country. His Navy service while earning his law degree from Harvard Law had served him as well as he had served the Navy. After passing the Bar, he had moved between private and public practice, serving with distinction in both fields, even being elevated to a section chief in the Department of Justice before President Carter elevated him to the District of Columbia Court of Appeals in 1979.

Alyssa looked up as the tall, lean man entered the waiting room a few minutes late. "Good afternoon Ms. Giordano. You've met Judy?" He turned to the woman who had escorted Alyssa into the room, and she nodded and smiled. "Come in, come in."

"Good afternoon, Your Honor. Thank you for seeing me," Alyssa intoned as she followed him back to the inner study and they both sat. The interrogation proceeded with the usual questions to which Alyssa had become accustomed during job interviews: law school, work history, job tenure and the like. The following week would certainly be exciting if she was appointed; meeting one judge was nerve–wracking enough, but to meet so many more at a Judicial Conference would be even more intimidating. His answer to her question about job tenure did not surprise her; after more than twenty years on the Bench, Rodriguez would be retiring on his seventieth birthday at the end of September. Even only eight–and–a–half months as his clerk would serve her in good stead, she thought.

"Thank you for making the trip, Alyssa." Rodriguez said as he escorted her out to the waiting room. "I have some meetings now, but I'll be making a decision today. When are you heading back, will you be about this afternoon?"

"Thanks, Judge." Alyssa uttered, pleasantly surprised at the ease she felt with him now, staggered that he had asked about her afternoon plans. "I'm on the six o'clock flight out of *Ronald Reagan*."

"Ah, good. I'll get Judy to call you by four so you can get to the airport in time."

*****

Alyssa recognized the phone number on her cell phone screen as it buzzed. It was the same number Judy had called her from to set up the meeting.

"Hello?" Alyssa's heart was in her throat as she answered. It was only three-thirty.

"Hi Alyssa. It's Judy, Judge Rodriguez' secretary."

"Hi Judy."

"Judge has asked me to call," she started. "He's still in some meetings, but he would like to offer you the position as his clerk and I've typed up a letter for you. Could you come back to Chambers to sign the letter accepting?"

Alyssa was stunned, relieved. *I've done it, I've really done it!* Alyssa shook her head to end her momentary reverie. "Sure, I can be back in about fifteen minutes. Is that okay?"

"Not a problem. I'll see you soon." Judy replied.

Alyssa felt exhilarated, walking back to the Court, signing her acceptance with Judy in Rodriguez' Chambers, and on the flight back to Albany. In an ironic change in the direction of her destiny, Alyssa's future was turning in her favor. She did not know what she would say, how she would explain her not mentioning the trip, to her parents; but at least she had overnight to work out what to say to Eddie.

CHAPTER 20

CHANGING DIRECTION AGAIN

The day before her birthday, the day after her meeting with Judge Rodriguez, Alyssa had not been able to perform her assigned tasks, or sit still for that matter, at her desk back to Kann Ritchie.

Eddie and Philippa were unusually late, but she really could not bring herself to work and her sleep–deprived state slowed her down. Moira had kept her up talking until some ungodly hour; Alyssa's mother had hindered rather than helped her attempts to finish loading her suitcases, but Alyssa could not bring herself to blame her mother for that. Alyssa had cornered Peter the minute he walked in and told him of her new job, that she needed to finish packing and start driving to D.C. on her birthday. He had shown his usual exuberance for her good fortune and promised to let her know when they arrived.

"Hello?" Alyssa mumbled, picking up the receiver. It was the buzz of an internal call.

"Hi Alyssa, it's Peter. Wake up!" he joked. Alyssa laughed. "Eddie and Philippa have just walked in."

"Thanks Peter." She put the phone back down, missing the cradle and fumbling the receiver. Drawing a lungful of air as she slowly stood, she headed towards Eddie's office. Philippa was gibbering about some nonsense; so they had only been at a meeting at the bank.

"Hi Eddie, Philippa," Alyssa announced as she knocked on the open door.

"Hi, Alyssa. What's up?" Eddie enquired.

135

"Well, um…" Alyssa was unsure how to tell him, so she simply handed over the letter from Judge Rodriguez. He leaned back in his chair and began to grin as he read it, before handing it over to Philippa.

"How exciting!" Philippa exclaimed after she finished reading the document.

"Well, that's an achievement," Eddie added. "So, Friday, hey?"

"Yes. Look, Eddie, I'm sorry to do this to you on such short notice, but I just couldn't pass it up." Although she really was contrite for having to leave them high and dry, Alyssa was relieved that the reason for leaving such a mundane job was such an impressive one.

"I agree. I'm sorry to see you go but I would've been disappointed if you hadn't taken it. When do you leave?"

"I'm driving down, so I think I have to get on the road tomorrow morning. But I can finish out today; I've got to finish the monthly update for you."

"Have you packed yet?" Philippa interposed.

"I started last night, but I haven't finished yet," Alyssa replied as she turned to look at her.

"No, no. Just finish the report, you and Philippa go through it and clear up your pay with you when you're done. Just come by to see me before you go," Eddie said.

"Thanks, Eddie." Alyssa turned and headed back to her desk as Eddie and Philippa went back to the papers from the bank.

*****

The drive from Albany to Washington, D.C. on her birthday had tired Alyssa; she had gotten out of bed in the dark and pulled her car from the driveway, Moira and Gino watching from the garage door, just as the color of the horizon had started to change from grey to pink.

The three–hundred–and–seventy–odd mile drive should only have taken her until lunch time, but Alyssa's journey had been delayed by the commuter traffic entering the city and then by another hour driving around Georgetown, lost. The trip would have been quicker on Amtrak, but to have been without her car would have been unacceptable. At least Moira had had the common sense, as mothers do, to have forced the packed lunch on her: Gino had had the common sense that fathers do to have stuffed some additional bills in her purse and refused to take them back. After Alyssa finally found her hotel and attended to the necessary formalities at the front desk, she followed the bellman to her room, hung a few clothes and wandered the room, unsure of what to do next. As she sat on the bed, Alyssa was glad she had finally given into her father and accepted the extra cash he had left in her purse. Staying in a hotel would suffice for a few days, maybe even a few weeks, but it would be an expensive indulgence if she remained there during her term as Rodriguez' clerk. *What to do, what to do?*

Alyssa looked at her watch; there was still some daylight left in the afternoon. *Right, time to get organized.* So she arose from the bed and moved to the desk to start a list; she spent the rest of the day and the following one attending to basic necessities: pressing work shirts and suits to last a couple of days and starting her search for less temporary accommodations.

*****

The first Friday of Alyssa's twenty–seventh year, her first day as Judge Rodriguez' clerk, certainly had Alyssa in awe.

The ornate interior of the Court of Appeals no longer overwhelmed Alyssa, but the prospect of starting work for a judicial officer intimidated her slightly. She had no difficulty in passing through the security checkpoint as she entered the Courthouse; the officers seemed to expect her, and having her letter of appointment in her hand had expedited the passage through the screening process. Her recollection of the path she had taken the Judges' Chambers for her interview made her trip to her new workspace easy.

"Hello?" Judy's voice answered the noise of the intercom.

"Hi Judy. It's Alyssa Giordano."

"I'll buzz you in."

"Thanks."

Alyssa heard the click of the door; she pulled it open and strode down the hall to her Judge's rooms.

"Hello." Judy's head popped out the doorframe from behind the wall.

"Hi Judy." Alyssa said as she followed Judy into the open space outside her new boss's office.

"This is your desk, mine is in there," Judy indicated to another office space. "Judge is on the phone at the moment."

"So, what are we doing today?" Alyssa asked as she bent down to put her bag in a drawer of the government issue desk.

"We've got to pack up some material for the Judicial Conference next week and take them to the hotel. But Judge wants to show you around here when he's finished his call and get your employment forms filled out." Judy, taller and slimmer than Alyssa, looked up over Alyssa's head as Alyssa turned around at the sound of the door opening behind Alyssa.

"Good morning, ladies," Alberto Rodriguez crooned as he entered the work space that would become Alyssa's.

"Good morning, Judge," Alyssa and Judy chimed simultaneously. Alyssa hoped the tremor in her voice did not convey her nervousness.

"Glad you made it, Giordano," he said Alyssa. "Are you settled in here yet? We have some work to do."

"Yes, thanks," Alyssa replied. "Judy's started to tell me."

"Have you found somewhere to live yet?"

"My great–grandfather lives near the Marriott in Georgetown for part of the year. I'm staying with him."

"That's where the conference is, the Marriott in Georgetown," Judy piped in.

"That's convenient," Rodriguez added. "Let me get you introduced to everyone." He turned and exited to the hallway outside, heading towards the other Judges' rooms, Alyssa on his heels.

The morning had been given to making her accustomed to her surroundings. Alberto Rodriguez had been quite the gentleman, spending her first hour on the job showing her around the private areas of the Courthouse, introducing her to the other members of the District of Columbia Court of Appeals and the payroll officer; but he was of her grandfathers' age group and Alyssa had expected nothing less from him. Alyssa had spent another hour obtaining keys and a magnetic security pass for the building and filling out those tedious and mind–numbing forms required of new employees, let alone new government employees, before returning to her new office; having an office bemused Alyssa. It was Judy's attitude that surprised her. Unlike the secretaries Alyssa had worked with before, she was pleasant, friendly and happy to offer her counsel to a new attorney clerking for a well–respected senior Judge for the first time. Judy had worked for the Judge for many years and seen attorneys, both good and bad, at work in his Courtroom. Both women spent the rest of the morning packing the parcels for those attending the Judicial Conference. One or two of the participants had arrived early from out of the capital, but the remainder would arrive in time for registration on Sunday afternoon.

At least the afternoon had been set aside for setting up the Conference registration desk at the hotel and reviewing the arrangements before the Conference guests arrived on Sunday. Rodriguez had left Alyssa and Judy to pack up the last of the folders and papers and wander down to the hotel's Convention Center, where he would meet them to review their progress. The early part of the day seemed to drag on, nevertheless it was hectic with arranging papers, boxes, and chairs. When Judy told Alyssa that she would not be able to attend the Conference's evening events, she was disappointed about, but accepted, it; the time between her appointment and the start of the Conference had not allowed sufficient time for the security agencies to process the clearance requests. Having to work on a Sunday did not offend Alyssa's Roman Catholic sensibilities, as she had become all too accustomed to it. *At least I'll have Saturday to myself.* Alyssa needed the time to work on her jitters at meeting yet more judges. Rodriguez had invited her to have dinner with him and Judy on Friday night; Alyssa was agreeably surprised that someone so important would be liberal enough to invite someone of such little consequence to dinner on her first night in his employ. Dinner, and the conversation during it, went well; Alyssa had probably indulged in a little too much wine and stayed a little too late, but she had taken her cue from her hosts. Having spent the afternoon at the Marriott, they dined in its restaurant for the simple convenience of not having to relocate.

Alyssa slept late on Saturday morning. Although she had returned to her room in her great–grandfather's townhouse before midnight, after escorting the Judge and Judy to the exit and waiting with them for their cab to appear, the effects of the wine had taken a toll. She made it to the restaurant in time for a late breakfast and spent the rest of the morning reviewing the newspaper. The afternoon was spent readying her clothes, and herself, before Alyssa retired in front of the television.

After spending Sunday morning wandering through the historic quarter of Washington D.C., Alyssa returned to the lobby of her temporary "office" in time to see Judge Rodriguez and Judy walk through the hotel entrance for registration; it was simply an afternoon for the participants to register and the only serious work the participants would need to do would be to renew their acquaintances with their colleagues. But the afternoon seemed to fly past; there were names to check, packages to hand out, directions to be given as the judicial officers, after checking in at the hotel's reception desk, paraded by the table Alyssa and Judy had set up to check them in for the Conference. Alyssa recognized the names, but not many of the faces, from the cases she read at Law School. But she did recognize one face.

"That's Judge McCoy, isn't it?" Alyssa whispered, turning her head to face Judy.

"Yes," Judy whispered back, nodding. "How do you know her?"

"I saw her give a speech a few years ago," Alyssa murmured. "Good afternoon, Judge McCoy." Alyssa raised her voice back to normal conversation level, directing her attention to the woman before her.

"Good afternoon, Judge," Judy also declared. "Welcome to the Conference. Here's your registration package."

"Hello Judy. Hi…" she paused to acknowledge Judy as she moved to attend to another participant and to look at the name tag. "Ms. Giordano, do I know you?" The aging, but still attractive, woman intoned.

"We haven't met, but you spoke at my Commencement at Albany Law School, about seven years ago. And I applied for a clerkship with you about then, when you were on the New York State Supreme Court, but someone else got it." Alyssa did not want to remind Her Honor that she had rejected the interview; nor did she want to relive the memories of that year in Hoboken.

"My word, when was it, 1993? That was a long time ago. You do have a good memory."

"Thank you Judge. Are you enjoying the Second Circuit?"

"Yes. It's certainly a different challenge from the New York State Supreme Court. What are you doing here?"

"I'm Judge Rodriguez' clerk."

"I thought his clerk was a man. When did you start?"

"Friday morning. I interviewed on Monday and got the job, so I drove down from Albany on Wednesday."

"Good for you. Will you be around during the Conference?"

"I'll be at the events during the day. They couldn't process a security clearance in time for me to go to the dinners."

"Oh, well, that's to be expected. I'll see you tomorrow then."

"Yes, Judge. See you then. Have a good evening."

"Thanks." Judge McCoy raised her hand to bid her and Judy farewell as she turned and headed to the hotel's elevators.

CHAPTER 21

MARKING TIME

Engrossed in her research, she jumped; the buzzing startled her.

"Associate Judge Rodriguez' Chambers," Judy announced, beating Alyssa to answer the intercom. "Hello, Judge." She listened, and laughed. "I'll get Alyssa to come and open the door." She exhaled noisily as she replaced the intercom handset. "He forgot his pass again!" Alyssa laughed. "Can you go let him in?" Judy asked as the telephone rang. Alyssa nodded and headed from her desk to the secured door.

"Hi Judge. You forget your key again?" she chastised her boss as she opened the door.

"Yep," he smiled sardonically at his clerk. "Lucky I was only in the Clerk's office. Look who I found there asking for you." Andrew Jackson popped his head out from behind the Judge.

"Hi, Dick," Alyssa exuded as the three walked back to the Judge's Chambers. "What're you doing here?"

"Hi, Dick," Andrew Jackson answered. "Had some motions to file, picked up my certificate of admission and good standing for New York. Happy birthday for last week." Jackson smiled as he hugged Alyssa.

"Thanks," she smiled as he kissed her cheek.

"What were you doing in the Clerk's Office, Judge?" she frowned at him.

"Re–arranging our calendaring."

"What for?" she was surprised that he'd taken on the task himself. "I coulda done that."

"I moved a couple of division panels we were on." He handed her, and Judy, a copy of the revised calendar assignments for February. "Here, have a look."

"Fuck!" she whispered, as she saw that the last Tuesday in February, and only the Tuesday, had been cleared.

"You've cleared the Tuesday of that week," Judy noticed. "What's so special about that day?" She had forgotten what Alyssa had already told her about the importance of the day.

"Alyssa's taking the New York Bar Exam," Rodriguez, his mind still like a steel trap, reminded Judy. "That's the first day."

"Oh, yes," Judy remembered.

"Shit!" Alyssa breathed. "I'll have a hell of a drive to get there and back."

"Don't worry, you won't have to," Rodriguez interrupted as Alyssa looked at the revised calendar again. "You'll take the Exam here; I'll proctor for you."

"What?" Alyssa was confused.

"I told the New York Board of Law Examiners I need you here that week. After I talked to the Chief Judge of the New York State Supreme Court, of course. I got connections, you know." Rodriguez winked at her.

"Thanks Judge!" Alyssa laughed. "Hey, Dick. You got cases here that week." She showed her friend the schedule.

"What?! Crap!" The younger man blushed at having sworn in front of the senior judicial officer. "Sorry, Judge."

"Forget it," he laughed. "I'm a Navy man. You doing the New York Bar Exam as well?" Rodriguez asked him.

"Yes."

"Well, I'll get the Board of Law Examiners to send down another set of papers."

"Whew!" Andrew exhaled, stunned, relieved.. "Thanks Judge!"

"See, isn't it good to know people who know people?" He slapped Andrew on the back as he winked at Alyssa again.

"You busy? Got time for a coffee?" Jackson asked Giordano. She looked at her watch, at her boss; Rodriguez nodded.

"Cafeteria's still open," she answered as she looked at her watch again.

"Don't be stupid. The cafeteria coffee is crap," the old man scoffed. "Take the afternoon off."

"You sure, Judge?" She looked between the Judge and Judy, not wanting either of them to think she was leaving them in the lurch, not fulfilling her duties.

"Judge and I can work on drafting the opinions without you," Judy smiled.

"Yeah, off you go," Alyssa's boss reinforced.

"Thanks, Judge," Giordano and Jackson chimed together before they left the office.

*****

Neither of them was as nervous as they had been the last time they had taken the Exam. Nor were they as nervous as the more than three thousand other participants taking the New York Bar Exam that February as they sat at Giordano's desk. But what did make Jackson nervous was taking the Exam a Judge's Chambers, let alone in the Chambers of the second most senior Judge on the D.C. Court of Appeals. At least neither of them would have to sit the second day of this Exam, having had their second–day test scores transferred from the Exam they had taken the previous July.

"So," the senior attorney intoned as seriously as he could without smirking. "You two ready for this?"

"I think so, Judge," Jackson responded, hoping his nervousness did not show.

"No," Giordano mocked. "Do I *have* to do this?"

"Yes, you do have to do this," Rodriguez' ordered as his eyes flashed over the top of his spectacles. "And you are *not* going to make look bad!"

"Alright, alright," Alyssa laughed.

"Right," the Judge said as he extracted the Exam papers from the envelopes. "You have the whole day. Take your time. Judy and I will be in my office drafting some opinions."

"Thanks, Judge," the examinees chimed together.

The pair put their heads down to start work on the New York local section day of the New York Bar Exam in silence. The silence did not break until Judy brought them lunch. It was dark outside when the silence was again broken, when the outer Chambers door rattled open and the smell of dirty socks permeated the room.

"Good evening, Ms. Giordano," the man intoned as he walked through the door, as if he owned the room. "Is Rodriguez in?"

"Good evening, Chief Judge," Alyssa answered as she and Andrew stood. "Yes, I'll let him know you're here." She walked around her desk and knocked on the door connecting her boss's office to hers before she opened it. Judy was still seated opposite their boss, taking notes, as he looked up. "Judge, the Chief Judge is here," she announced. The old man stood and walked to greet the more senior man.

"Good evening, Your Honor," the "junior" man said to the "senior" man from the connecting door.

"Good evening, Your Honor," the "senior" man answered.

"Of course. Have you met Andrew Jackson?"

"No. Good evening, Mr. Jackson." The Chief Judge extended his hand as he crossed to Alyssa's desk.

"G–G–Good evening, Chief Judge," the older junior attorney stammered as he shook the man's hand, surprised that his friend was not as nervous as he was in the man's presence.

"What are you doing here?" He scowled at Jackson as he wondered why someone not employed by his Court had been allowed into the secured Chambers area.

"I'm proctoring the first day of the New York Bar Exam for them," Rodriguez glared. "I told you that's why I couldn't be on division panels today, remember?"

"Oh. Yes. I remember." The Chief Judge did not remember. "Got a minute, Alberto?"

"You two finished?" he asked the examinees. They both nodded and Rodriguez turned back into his office. "Judy, Alyssa and Andrew are finished. Could you collect their papers and send them to the Board of Law Examiners."

"Of course," Judy responded as she stood exited his office and took the completed Exam papers from Giordano and Jackson. "Will you need anything else tonight, Judge?"

"No. Thanks Judy. You lot can go. Come in, Terrence." He rolled his eyes at his staff as the Chief Judge walked into his office and he closed the door behind them. Alyssa glanced at Judy as she stuffed their Exam papers in the return envelope supplied by the New York Board of Law Examiners, smirked and rolled her eyes.

"What was that about?" the not–so–young attorney asked as they headed for the elevators. Rodriguez' attitude toward his "boss" puzzled Andrew.

"They don't like each other," Alyssa answered as she pressed the call button for the elevator.

"Why?" The simple statement that the two men did not like each other did not satisfy Jackson's curiosity. Judy raised her eyebrows, inquiring whether he could be trusted; Alyssa nodded as they waited for the elevator to arrive.

"Politics. They passed our boy over for the Chief's position, for him," Judy said.

"Our boy offended the Attorney–General's girlfriend at the time the Chief's position became vacant," Alyssa continued. "That pissed the Attorney–General off, apparently."

"And don't forget the Stinking Bishop sandwiches," Judy added, smirking behind the envelope, as the sole elevator working in Moultrie Courthouse that evening arrived.

"Oh, yeah! The Stinking Bishop sandwiches!" Alyssa snickered as Andrew let them into the carriage before him.

"Stinking Bishop sandwiches? What the hell's a Stinking Bishop sandwich? And what's it got to do with anything?" Jackson wondered.

"The Judges have lunch together every Tuesday," Judy explained. "And Stinking Bishop is a cheese the Chief likes. He stacks it on like there's no tomorrow."

"What's so bad about a cheese sandwich?"

"You caught a whiff of his suit, right?" Alyssa inquired.

"Yeah. Smelt like dirty socks." Andrew was still mystified. "Like he hasn't had it cleaned in months."

"Add the dirty socks smell with what wet towels that've been left in the washing machine for days smell like and that's Stinking Bishop cheese." Alyssa feigned fainting.

"Ooooh!" Andrew chortled. "So that's what it was!"

"And now our office is going to reek for days!" Judy complained as the three of them exited the elevator.

*****

It annoyed her that she had to clean up after Anna Sorensen, the Chief Judge's Clerk, before she removed her own Judge's papers from the Bench back to Chambers after the panel's long session. In the five months she'd worked in Rodriguez' Chambers, Alyssa had come to dislike Sorensen, a supercilious woman who was almost as lazy as her boss, almost as much as Rodriguez disliked the only man senior to him on the Court.

After she'd made three trips to carry the Chief Judge's books back to his Chambers, Alyssa was finally able to start clearing her own Judge's papers from the Bench. She jumped, almost dropped the pile of law reports she'd picked up, as the door from Chambers opened into the Court room. Anna had followed her back to the Courtroom. *What the hell does that bitch want?*

"Alyssa." Sorensen barely moved inside the Courtroom.

"Yes, Anna. What can I do for you?"

"The Chief Judge has asked me to pass this on to you for you to deliver it to Associate Judge Rodriguez." She thrust out her hand, with a single sheet of paper in it. She expected Alyssa, arms full of books, to walk to her and take it from her with. Alyssa sighed as she walked to where the woman was standing, put down the books on the end of the Bench, and took the note.

"What is it?" *Fuckin' bitch! Why couldn't you just walk down the corridor and give it to Judy?* Alyssa was barely able to keep her contempt for the woman off her face.

"A memorandum from the Chief Judge to Associate Judge Rodriguez." The woman's tone was, as always, condescending. She always called the Judges by their full title.

"Oh, thank you Anna." *Don't show her how much you disrespect her!* Alyssa chastised herself.

"You'll make sure Associate Judge Rodriguez receives it immediately." Anna turned on her heels without waiting for an answer.

"Of course, Anna. I'll give it straight to him," she said, as sweetly as she could, to the older woman's back. "Okay, so what is it?" Alyssa asked herself out loud as she read the typed note. The memorandum revealed that the Chief Judge could not finish drafting the opinions he'd assigned himself from the February divisions within the 180–day time limit required by the Court's Internal Operating Procedures, procedures he himself had written, and he was reassigning the opinion–writing to Rodriguez. "Aw crap! He's not going to like this!" She scooped up her paperwork and raced back to her own room. The stack of books tumbled out of her arms as Judy came out of the door just as Alyssa went in. The two women laughed as they bent down to reassemble the pile.

"Did Anna catch you in the Courtroom?" Judy asked.

"Yep," Alyssa answered.

"The Chief Judge's secretary brought me a stack of case files. With opinions he hasn't "had time" to write yet." What it really meant was that his clerk was too lazy to do the research he needed.

"Yeah. Anna gave me a note about that!" Alyssa handed Judy the memorandum. The two women rolled their eyes at each other after she'd read it. "Have you told him yet?"

"No, he's on the phone." Judy was as disdainful of the Chief Judge's Clerk as Alyssa was. "He's supposed to be taking his unused vacation time."

"He's just gonna love it!"

"I'm gonna love what?" the man's voice boomed through the internal door to his office. The two women looked at each other. "Come on! Out with it, ladies!" Judy cringed as she passed him the document. "He expects me to finish these before I retire, ten opinions in two months that he can't write in six? *Fuckwit!*" the old man moaned. *He knows I supposed to be on vacation!* his mind raged. "*And* he's got me giving his lecture at that mandatory Professional Conduct and practice course next week!"

"Sorry Judge," the two women groaned in chorus.

"Not your fault, girls. Just means a shitload more work for us."

"Shall I bring them in, Judge?"

"Sure, Judy. You come in too, Giordano. We'd better get started."

*****

The heat blasted the last two attorneys to exit the Ronald Reagan Building. The weather in Washington D.C. was always hot in July; but the second Saturday in July 2000 was hotter than usual. It was a rude awakening after the air conditioning had chilled them in the Atrium Ballroom during the mandatory course on the Rules of Professional Conduct and practice that the District of Columbia Court of Appeals had directed all new admittees take. Although it was only a short walk from the International Trade Center, the heat, the old man's age, and the boxes of leftover course notes that needed to be returned to Moultrie Courthouse made the decision to hail a taxi simple.

"Glad that's over," Judge Rodriguez intoned to his young protégé as they got out of the taxi and entered the Courthouse. "Thank God that'll be the last time I have to do it."

"Me too. At least I got it outta the way now," the younger attorney replied.

"I hated giving those courses."

"You're the one who came up with the Rule, aren't you?"

"Yep."

"Well, it's your own fault then!" Alyssa laughed. "And at least it'll count towards the mandatory continuing education hours I need for New York as well."

"Yeah, it's my own fault," Rodriguez chuckled. "So you passed the New York Bar? You're definitely going back to New York?"

"Yep, passed the Exam. I'm not sure yet, about going back to New York, but I think so." They walked in silence to Rodriguez' Chambers; he beat Alyssa to her keys and opened up. She unloaded the box under her desk as he poured them both a drink.

"So," he motioned to her to sit in the same seat in which she had been interviewed as he lowered himself into the chair behind his desk. "You got a job lined up yet? For after I retire?"

"I got a couple of offers to pick from in New York. And I got an offer here in D.C., to clerk for Judge Kavanaugh on the U.S. Court of Appeals."

"Aren't you related to him?"

"No, no, my great–grandfather's a United States Senator for Massachusetts. But his name's spelt without the u."

"Ooooh!" Rodriguez finally made the connection between his clerk and her ancestor. "So that's how you hear all the gossip about town!"

"Yeah, that's how I hear all the gossip. Grampa Ted's a great source," she laughed again. "He offered me a job too."

"You might want to consider going back to private practice," the soon–to–retire Judge advised. "You don't want to be get pigeonholed, working in the Judicial Branch. You've had enough of an insight into how the Judiciary works. You'll get broader experience in private practice, and be paid better of course."

"Yeah, I've been thinking about that. You're right, about the experience. I just gotta pick which offer I wanna go with."

"So where are the positions you were offered?"

"One was from an insurance company, All Atlantic Insurance, working with their in–house counsel. The other was from a firm called Tait Goldstein."

"Never heard of them."

"They're small. They specialize in family law, do a bit of business law."

"Family law! *Mierda!*" His distaste for that part of the law was clear. "That'd be revolting! You wouldn't want to be pigeonholed in that either. It's up to you, but I'd go with All Atlantic."

"Yeah, that's what I was thinking," she said as they finished their drinks at the same time.

"Want another?" Rodriguez asked.

"No. Better not." Alyssa looked at her watch. "Grampa Ted's expecting me for dinner."

"Good to see you're spending time with the old man." They both laughed.

"Don't you have a dinner on tonight, back at the International Trade Center?"

"Mierda. You're right. Let's go then!"

The pair left together and again hailed a taxi, Alyssa letting the old man out at the International Trade Center on the way back to her great–grandfather's townhouse.

CHAPTER 22

NO—MAN'S LAND

It was an emotional day for him, his last day on the Bench. He was tired, and he hated to be tired. The weariness in his voice was not just because he had not been properly recognized; finishing his last opinions had taken him, his clerk and his secretary had taken quite a few late nights in the last month.

It infuriated him that Anna Sorensen, the Chief Judge's Clerk, had tried to take over the ceremonial sitting of the Court of Appeals for *his* retirement. *Stupid lazy bitch*, his mind grunted. But at least he was able to boot her off the organizing committee, to get his way in managing it, as he had to hand down his last opinions at beginning of ceremony, before his retirement kicked in.

Alberto Rodriguez had spent more than twenty years presiding in the Appeals Court and his only regret was entirely of his own making. *If only I hadn't pissed that dim-witted slut off,* he grumbled to himself. But it pleased him no end, as he and his brother Judges mingled with the members of the Bar in the Moultrie Courthouse courtyard, that the Bar Association had organized a small party for him. He enjoyed chewing the fat with the members of the Bar in more casual settings, when he wasn't presiding over cases they were arguing before him. He spied his last clerk, holding Jackson's hand, across the courtyard. He recognized Giordano's great-grandfather as he turned his head to thank the waitress for the drinks she had just served them and wandered over to them.

"Good afternoon, Senator," Rodriguez interrupted formally. "Thanks for coming today."

"Good afternoon, Your Honor," Ted Kavanagh replied formally. "Wouldn't have missed Alyssa sitting on the Bench with you for the last time for the world."

"Hello, Jackson."

"Hi, Judge."

"So what are you going to do now, Alyssa."

"I took the job with All Atlantic."

"Good, good. So, how about you, Jackson?"

"I'm working in the Governmental Affairs Department for the New York Professional Nurses Union, in Manhattan."

"Oh, so you're in New York now as well? Doing what?"

"Coordinating legislative advocacy for the Association, representing members in labor disputes."

"What made you decide on that?"

"I got into union work at UMass Medical, in Boston, before I took the Bar and I enjoyed it."

"Sounds like good work."

"It is. I enjoy it."

"So what are you going to do with yourself Alberto?" Kavanagh asked. "Now that you're retired."

"Dunno, Ted," Rodriguez sighed. "Gotta do some work on my garden. I might take a cruise."

"So you haven't got any real plans then?" Alyssa could hear, almost see, the cogs turning in her great–grandfather's brain.

"Nup." Rodriguez sighed again, obviously not liking the thought of not working, of his mind becoming inactive. "I think I might become a good–for–nothing lazy bum and let my brain go to mush."

"Hmmm," the Senator muttered, his mind abuzz. He too hated the thought of not workinge.

"What?" Rodriguez' right eyebrow lifted.

"Hmmm," the Senator muttered again. "I think I might have something for you."

"What?" Rodriguez' left eyebrow lifted.

"You two mind if I talk some business with the Judge?" he asked Alyssa and Andrew.

"No, not at all, Ted," Andrew answered.

"Course not, Grampa. Off you go," ordered Alyssa.

"Thanks," he smiled at the two young attorneys as he put his arm around the Judge. "I'm on the Judiciary Committee. I think…" the two young attorneys heard the old Senator start to tell the old attorney as he led him away.

*****

As he showed her through the office, Alyssa Giordano thought his arrangement with his employer was more than a little strange.

The Assumed Name Certificate issued by the Manhattan County Clerk named him as the proprietor of his own law offices. He was registered with the New York Unified Court System and the New York Bar Association as a solo practitioner, he had to have the requisite professional indemnity insurance as if he was a solo practitioner and he would be paying her wages as if she was his employee. But he only ever had one client and did work for no others since he left law school. Although it appeared otherwise, Damien Turner Freeman was really only an employee of, General Counsel and head of the in–house legal department for, All Atlantic Insurance LLC. And although Freeman would be paying her wages as if she was his employee, her pay would really be coming from the coffers of All Atlantic Insurance LLC. *But it's his business,* Alyssa considered. *I 'spose he's got it all worked out.*

"Got a minute, Terry?" Freeman asked as he knocked on the executive suite's door.

"Sure, sure, Damien. Come in," the executive waved him, and the woman with him, in.

"I just wanted to introduce Alyssa Giordano to you. She's starting work in the Legal Department today." He paused as he turned to Alyssa. "Alyssa, this is Terry Macpherson. He's All Atlantic's chief executive officer, and in charge of the claims office here in Manhattan."

"Hello, Mr. Macpherson," Alyssa said formally as she extended her hand.

"Hi, Ms. Giordano," the executive responded slickly as he shook her hand without getting up from his desk. "Please, call me Terry."

"Thanks. Alyssa."

"So, Damien's given you the tour? Run through all the office policies with you. What do you think?"

"Yes, Damien's given you the tour. The offices are very impressive." Alyssa was not impressed by the offices; she had worked in places more impressive than this office. "I've had a quick run through on the Procedural Manual, but I think it'll take me a little time to get on top of that." She was even less impressed by what she had seen in, and been able to glean from, the Policy Manual.

"Hmmm, yes," Macpherson laughed. "It's quite thick. Damien's just updated it for us, rewritten it really. How long did it take you, Damien? Five years, to rewrite the whole thing?"

"Yep, that sounds about right," the senior employee answered. "About five years."

"Has Damien explained the office structure to you? He answers directly to me, and you answer directly to him? That your department is completely separate from the claims department?"

"Yep. He's explained that." Alyssa considered that one of the stranger aspects of Freeman's arrangements with All Atlantic Insurance LLC. "And we only get involved when policy–holders commence litigation."

"Absolutely correct," Macpherson reinforced. "Damien runs a tight ship in the litigation department. How many litigious claims do we have, Damien?"

"We've only got fifteen unresolved actions at the moment. I'm going to be handing five over to Alyssa."

"Good, good." The executive's telephone buzzed.

"Well, we'd better get back to it," Damien indicated as Terry picked up the handset.

"Nice to meet you, Alyssa," Macpherson oozed as he put his hand over the handset's speaker.

"Thanks, Terry. You too," Alyssa called over her shoulder as she and her new supervisor left the executive's suite.

*****

The cigarette hanging from the man's mouth had almost burned down to the butt; the smoker adjusted the box under his arm, pulled the butt from his lips and flicked it across the room as he exited the front door. The smoldering cigarette end dropped into the sofa and lit the accelerant. It took mere minutes for the flames to consume the sofa and spread across the acrylic carpet before it caught the curtains.

The fire swept quickly through the ground floor of the last house in the red brick row. As the interior fire burned, it spewed heat and gases to the ceiling and the temperature hit, and passed, more than a thousand degrees. At that critical moment, everything in the room suddenly ignited and the fire burned downwards from a ceiling as well.

The flames inside the house at number 38 burned so brightly that an orange glow filled the narrow Bank Street in Manhattan's West Village. Neighbors called 911 as one of them a garden hose to try to douse the flames, without much success. The water cooled, and crazed, the windows but they remained intact.

The mid-ship rescue pumper engine from Squad 18 was the first to turn out to the fire box alarms after the phone calls were patched through from the 911 dispatcher. The windows cracked, and exploded, from the frames as water poured from the fire hoses rapidly cooled the superheated glass. As engines from other squads following quickly behind the engine from Squad 18, the flames were extinguished before the complete destruction of the home.

The morning following the fire, an assistant fire marshal examined the burn patterns and concluded that the Bank Street inferno had three points of origin, a classic indication of arson, and he forwarded his report to the New York City Police Department.

*****

Jennifer Tufnell stood in her debris-strewn home next to her attorney. The first floor of her Bank Street row-house had almost been incinerated and although it was uninhabitable, she was glad she'd gone to visit her parents. Now came another blow.

A representative of the insurance company carrying her home insurance police had come to the charred remnants of Tufnell's home to tell her the company would pay just half of the estimated half-a-million dollar cost of rebuilding the house.

"It's devastating," the newly registered nurse cried to her attorney. "I feel absolutely abandoned."

"I know you do, honey," her attorney soothed. "Don't worry. I'll fix it."

"How? Please," Jennifer begged as she waved her arm around the burnt out shell of the first floor of her home. "Tell me how you can fix *this!* Tell me, how I am supposed to fix this if they'll only pay half the repair costs?"

"Don't worry, Jen," Jackson winked. "I'll talk to them. Better if I talk to their in–house counsel. I know one of the attorneys in the legal department at All Atlantic Insurance."

"Oh Andy!" the woman squealed as she threw her arms around the attorney's neck. "Thank you, Andy."

"That's okay, Jen," Andrew Jackson responded as he hugged his nursing colleague. "Just doin' my job."

$$*****$$

The alarm bells had rung in the young attorney's mind after she finished reading the Policy Manual.

Over the last five years, All Atlantic Insurance had paid out less in claims for every dollar spent on premiums by consumers as its profits increased. They had implemented pricing "innovations" that had a disparate, adverse impact on their poorer, and minority, consumers. They had changed policy language to hollow out the coverage offered, particularly for home insurance, and dramatically increased out–of–pocket costs for home owners. They employed ambiguous restrictions that were beyond the ability of consumers to clearly understand.

And their claims settlement practices seemed bizarre to her, to say the least. The insurer had been the first major insurer to adopt claims payment techniques designed to systematically reduce payments to policyholders without adequately examining the validity of each individual claim. And it resulted in what she considered unjustifiably low claims payments.

No wonder they've been cited for anti–consumer practices so often! Giordano screamed silently at the walls. *And they're going to be cited again,* she thought as she reread the opinion she'd just printed for the case file before her. *Andrew will make sure of that!* She stood up, picked up the case file and walked across to her supervisor's office.

"Damien, got a minute?" she asked as she knocked on the open door.

"Sure, Alyssa. Come in," Freeman answered as he waved her in.

"You wanted to see my opinion on the Tufnell claim. I've just finished it." She handed over the case file, her opinion on top, as she took a seat opposite Damien. She waited in silence as he read it, and reread it.

"Hmmm. I don't think you've considered all the claims restrictions in her insurance policy." He knew she had; but his instructions had been clear. He was to deflect all claims, reduce claims payments where he could. "This was robbery and arson, wasn't it?"

"Yes."

"I'll have to run it past Mac, get his approval, before we can confirm paying the full rebuilding costs."

"Right." Alyssa sighed. Damien's aversion to accepting her opinion did not surprise her; he was so entrenched at his employer, he had lost the ability to make decisions on his own.

*****

"Arson is a serious crime, Alyssa," the executive scowled as he lectured the young, no longer naïve, attorney. "It puts fire fighters and innocent people in harm's way. Arsonists are selfish criminals who have no regard for the lives of others. They submit claims to receive insurance money and fraudulently take money out of the insurance system intended for the payments of legitimate claims."

"I know that, Mac," Alyssa sighed, exasperated that Terry Macpherson thought she did not understand the seriousness of the situation. "I agree, *of course* arson is a serious crime."

"As a part of the insurance industry," Damien Turner Freeman interrupted, "we *are* committed to working to ensure that only legitimate claims are paid. And we are working together with the Fire Department and the Police Department to stop arson."

"Look, I know all that, Damien. But Jennifer Tufnell didn't start this fire! She wasn't even in the city when the fire started. She was in Pennsylvania."

"Well, until someone, someone other than her, is convicted for committing the arson, the policy she has is clear." Macpherson retorted. "And our claims settlement practice is even clearer. We are entitled to pay her only half the repair costs."

"Her attorney's going to fight this," Alyssa informed her employers. "He's going to file a claim in the Supreme Court. He's tough and he'll fight."

"How do you know that?" Macpherson asked, the scowl and sarcasm obvious in his voice.

"I know him. We did the Bar Exams together." Alyssa didn't think they needed to know how well she really knew Jennifer Tufnell's attorney.

"Well, then. You know exactly how Damien can fight him back, what tactics he can use, don't you?" Macpherson retorted, the sarcasm in his voice even thicker. "Now, back to work, back to your office. Damien and I need to discuss the SEC filings due next month."

Alyssa left Macpherson's office and returned to own in silence. *Fuck! It's happening again!* She swore at herself. *He's Duncan all over again. I gotta toughen the fuck up!*

*****

Two years had passed before Tom Dickson was arrested, and convicted, for causing the fire at 38 Bank Street in Manhattan's West Village. It was a relief that Abbie Carmichael had been the A.D.A. assigned to the case.

"Hi, Abbie," Alyssa called.

"Hey, Lyssie. I didn't realize you were back in Manhattan. When did you get back?"

"October 2000. What's that, four and a half years now? Yeah, four and a half years."

"Shit. It is four and a half years. I haven't seen you around. You back at Kann Ritchie?"

"No. Wish I was, though. I've been working in the legal department at All Atlantic Insurance since I got back."

"So what are you doing in Criminal Term?"

"That was Tom Dickson, wasn't it? He was convicted of arsoning a house in Bank Street, right?"

"Yeah. And?" The A.D.A. was confused.

"All Atlantic Insurance carried the insurance policy."

"Oh! Right!" Carmichael made the connection and rolled her eyes. "Now they have to pay out if I didn't get a restitution order, right?"

"Not if they can help it." Giordano also rolled her eyes. "So what'd he get?"

"Ten years for aggravated robbery, one for the arson, and five for the theft of property, to run consecutively. I couldn't get the restitution order 'coz of the prison terms."

"Ten years for aggravated robbery? That's tough."

"Yeah." Abbie nodded and winked. "There was more than one count."

"Oh." Alyssa nodded and winked back. "Good work."

"You enjoying All Atlantic?" There was a sly tone in Abbie's voice, a prosecutor's sideways glance in her eye.

"Not particularly. Shit place to work." Alyssa wondered why her A.D.A. friend would ask. "You wanna job there?"

"No." Although she seemed reticent to disclose anything, her tone said volumes.

"Why you asking, then?"

"Can't really say," she confirmed as she winked again. "But I wouldn't want a job there."

"Ah!" Alyssa nodded as she caught Abbie's meaning. "I don't think I'll be around too long after I make the recommendation I have to make on this one."

"Ah!" Abbie nodded as she caught Alyssa' meaning. "I see."

*****

"No, Mac. No, no, no. I will not change my opinion. There is no evidence that the home—owner was involved in lighting the fire. None whatsoever." Her tone was strident. "And the D.A. convicted someone else for the arson."

"You change your mind," Terry Macpherson screamed at her. "We are not paying out on this! We are not changing our disclaimer letter!" Macpherson had signed the letter refusing to pay out Jennifer Tufnell's claim in full, despite Dickson's conviction in Criminal Term, despite the judgment Tufnell's attorney had obtained in Civil Term for the full replacement cost. "You're going to file an appeal against the civil judgment."

"No, Mac. I *will not* change my opinion. I *will not* file an appeal." She moved her defiant gaze from Macpherson to stare at Freeman, expecting some sign of backing from him, particularly as he knew she was right; Damien, who had been silent throughout the heated exchange, unable to bring himself to contradict the man currently holding his career in his hands, he shifted his gaze from Alyssa's insolent glare to look at his shuffling feet. *Hmmm, this is déjà vu,* she

159

chuckled. *But no dread, no fear this time. Maybe I've toughened the fuck up!* She chuckled again.

"Then you quit!" Macpherson's ranting scream escalated. "*You quit!* You give me your keys and get the fuck outta the building! Right the fuck now!"

"No, Mac. I do not quit."

"Then you're fired!" Macpherson shrieked. Alyssa cackled at him. "You heard me! You're fired!"

"You can't fire me," Alyssa laughed and pointed at the weak man sitting next to her. "Only he can fire me."

"She's right, Terry," Damien whispered as Macpherson slumped back into his chair. "She's on my payroll."

CHAPTER 23

LAST DAYS OF SERVITUDE

Although Damien paid her for the following Monday, the first day of the next working week, Friday, February 11, 2005 was her last day working at Turner Freeman. She spent a good part of the day writing up some notes on her case files and cleaning out her desk; although she expected it to take longer, her affinity for organization meant she was finished by three.

"Alyssa?" Freeman started as he reached the doorway to her office, he couldn't see her but he could hear the sound of packing tape being torn from its roll.

"Yes, Damien," Giordano answered as she popped her head up from behind the desk.

"What's happening?" His voice exhibited concern. *What is she doing?!*

"Just finished taping up the box of my personal stuff."

"Oh, okay." His acceptance of the truth of what she had said, that should have been forthcoming, wasn't in his voice, but he wouldn't ask her to open the box. "You ready to go through your case notes with me?"

"Yep, sure." Freeman spent ten minutes reading her notes and it took them the rest of the hour, he peppering questions at her, to discuss the finer details. By the time they had finished it was just past 4 p.m.

"So, that just about does it," he concluded.

"Yep, that does it," she agreed.

"Sorry it had to come to this."

"Well, shit happens."

"That's harsh." He was surprised at her ambivalence towards being sacked. "You're not upset?"

"I got over being upset at being fired a long time ago." She reclined her chair, the look in her eyes cold and unforgiving; he had always believed in the idea that the eyes were the window to a person's soul, inner feelings but he just could not penetrate the wall she had erected around herself.

"Well, as I said, I'm sorry it had to come to this."

"Forget it. I have, I've moved past it already."

"You're not angry?" She just shrugged, pulled a face. "Well, since we're done, I think it it'd be okay if you want to leave now."

"Yeah, it's time."

She stood, silently, and put her hand in her pocket, pulled her bundle of office keys out and her last official act as an employee of Turner Freeman was to toss them on her desk. She slung her handbag over her shoulder and picked up her box; he remained seated and watched her walk out of the room and past the two women in the secretarial pool area. She said nothing to them, not even giving them a "by your leave," as she walked out the door; her stride was determined, rather than angry, as she was determined, relieved, joyous really, to walk away from what she thought was another abysmal job.

The three who remained behind at the offices of Turner Freeman, within the offices of All Atlantic Insurance LLC, were silent, stunned at their former co-worker's ability to walk away without tears, without a fit of anger; what they could not see was that her heart, her emotion, her soul, or whatever one might want to call it, had hardened against all menace that could be thrown at her.

As she walked out of the lobby, box in hand, towards the subway, she was not so much bitter about the way they had treated her and tried to walk all over her, but bitter at herself for not having learnt from her past mistakes, that her judgment was somehow impaired and she was not able to see them for who they really were. She did know that she did not want to again put herself in the position where she would be forced to bow to the will of not quite unscrupulous people again. But how she would achieve that, how she would make her judgment unimpaired, was a question she would need to consider carefully, painstakingly, precisely. She would now treat everyone with suspicion and, if she did decide to work for someone else again, she would investigate them as meticulously as, no more meticulously than, they would investigate her.

That is where I failed! She put her box on the subway platform; it was not heavy but awkward to hold. *I'm too trusting of people! That they consider someone other than themselves! That's not my fault; Mom and Pop shouldn't have taught me to be so considerate!* She laughed at herself, ignoring the stares from the others on the platform, realizing that she should not blame them for that, she could only blame herself for not learning from her mistakes. *Enough of that. Never again. Every man for himself, now.*

*****

The subway ride, and the walk to her trendy condo, was awkward with the box in her arms; she was pleased to see someone exit the front door, and hold it open for her, as she reached it. She was surprised to see her parents sitting in the lobby as she entered. It had been a while since they'd come to Manhattan just to see her.

"Hello! What are you guys doing here?" she enquired. Alyssa moved the box to one side to accept kisses from them.

"Hello darling," her mother said.

"Hello, babe," from her father.

"We're going to dinner and a show and we thought we'd pop in to see if you wanted to come with."

"Okay. Come up so I can dump my stuff and change. I've got time, haven't I?" she asked as they headed for the elevator.

"Sure darling," her mother replied. "The reservation's not till seven–thirty."

"What's with the box?" her father asked as the elevator door closed behind them.

"I quit my job today." She knew what their reaction would be if she told them that she'd been fired again; she did not want to deal with that.

"What for?" they chimed together. "I thought you liked it," from her father as they left the elevator on her floor.

"They wouldn't give me a pay raise." She put the box down and fumbled with her keys in her door deadbolt keys. She finally got the sticky lock unbolted and pushed the door in.

"Why not?" from her mother as her father picked up her box and they followed her in.

"They said they didn't have the money." They sat on the couch and her father turned on the television as she walked into her sleeping quarters. This would mollify them; she had asked for a pay raise and they didn't need to know what she had refused to do for them. "Which is bullshit," she called from the bedroom, where she was changing.

"Wash your mouth out!" Her mother didn't like it when her daughter, any of her children for that matter, used what she considered foul language.

"Oh, come on, Moira!"

"Come on what, Gino? You know I don't like that language!"

"Alright, Moira," her father laughed. "Whaddaya mean bullshit?" he asked as she returned to the living room.

"I saw their fiscal reports for last tax year before they went in the corporate reports for the SEC. I might not know everything there is to know about money, but I know how to read a balance sheet. The money was there."

"Bastards!"

"Gino, language!"

"Well, they are, Moira! Let me talk to them."

"No, Dad! Can you please just leave it? I was bored there anyway."

"Okay, darling. Whatever makes you happy. You need money?" He thought money could fix everything.

"I'm right for now; they gave me a severance check for three months' pay and the holidays I'm owed." Her parents jumped off the couch simultaneously, startled by the rattling of keys in the door.

"You expecting anyone, darling?"

"It's Andrew, Mom."

"Andrew? Andrew who?" from her father, who had put it out of his mind that she'd told them that she and her friend had exchanged apartment keys. Even though he had accepted Jackson as his daughter's boyfriend, as a son really, he would be forever the overprotective father, who would always have difficulty in accepting that his eldest daughter, any of his four daughters for that matter, was dating a man fifteen years her senior.

"Me, Andrew Jackson," the male voice answered as he shut the door behind him. "Hey, Dick," he called through the bedroom door.

"Hey, Dick," Alyssa called back.

"Hello, Andrew," Gino and Moira chimed together. "We're going to dinner and a show," Moira continued as she hugged and kissed her daughter's friend and sat back down. "Would you like to join us?"

"Only if I'm not imposing."

"Course not, Andrew," Gino confirmed as he too hugged her daughter's friend and retook his seat.

"Come on, Dick," Andrew hollered. "I'm hungry!"

"Yeah, you are too thin, Andrew," Gino growled. "We need to fatten you up like a good Italian man! Like me!" Jackson laughed.

"You, hungry? That's a first!" Alyssa mocked him as she returned to the lounge room. "Okay, I think I'm ready. Do I look okay?"

"You look perfect, darling," her mother cooed.

"Oh, come on, Mom!" she laughed.

"Right." Gino sprang off the couch and offered his hand to his wife. "Let's go!"

*****

February 28, 2005, two weeks after she became unemployed and almost a week after it had been suggested to her, she had spoken to the Bar Association about what was necessary to establish her own office.

Alyssa Giordano had spent the weekend after her parents had taken her to dinner and a Broadway show mulling over what she wanted to do and the following week searching the classifieds for a job, updating her resume, contacting head hunting agencies. Poppy Ian asked why she didn't start her own office over lunch in Albany the next Sunday, and Nonno Paul pulled his check book out and asked how much she wanted, needed, to get started, and Mom and Pop just oozed support. Her three sisters and lone brother jibed that she couldn't do it; they were just jealous, or maybe not – maybe they knew she needed to be told not to do it before she would decide to oppose them.

I don't know, Poppy.

165

Mama Mia! Course ya can! Nonna exclaimed.

Come on, Lyssie, Nanna had added as Nonno handed her a check, signed but the amount blank, for her to fill it in. She had been stunned, mostly at herself. She had always thought that she would rather work for someone else than struggle to start as the two generations of her ancestors sitting with her had struggled.

Why should I bother? It's too hard! A light bulb went off in her head. *Fuck! Why not? I can do it the right way. My way. Nobody pushing me around ever again.* Except for her parents of course, but they only wanted her to succeed more than they had.

From that point, the decision to establish her own law office was made easy. She had discovered that she had fulfilled all the requirements needed to work for herself and establish her own law office, with the exception of arranging the required insurance. There would be other tasks that she would need to complete, but obtaining insurance would be the first.

Alyssa walked into the New York State Unified Court System Office of Court Administration to pay the biennial fee to renew her registration as an attorney. Although was not due for another couple of months, it was only three hundred and fifty dollars and Alyssa had preferred to pay the fee while she had the funds to cover it. It was the first time she had to pay the fee to the Office of Court Administration herself, as the last time it had been paid by her former employer. At least she had been able to use the courses she had done there to fulfill the Continuing Legal Education requirements needed for her to continue her registration. Arranging the insurance had cost Alyssa nine hundred dollars.

The office space at 305 Broadway had proved satisfactory. The first time Alyssa visited it was to inspect the suite on the ninth floor and the second visit was to sign a six month lease and pay the security deposit and first month's rent. The lease would be necessary to renew her registration as an attorney, this time as a solo practitioner, with the New York Unified Court System.

The office was really a virtual office; it was serviced office space and the other tenants were comprised of a number of other professionals, some attorneys, some accountants. The area which was hers was a medium–sized office on the floor, big enough to comfortably accommodate two people, and the lease she had signed gave her use of the reception area, administrative and secretarial support, which included access to the floor process server, the copier, internet and computer network, the conference and lunch rooms. The main attraction was that she had access to a telephone system with her own number and custom voicemail, which the receptionist would answer when she was out, and access to the building twenty–four hours a day, seven days a week, all for the measly sum of three hundred dollars a month. Because there were other businesses already operating in the same space, the company running the office space had already obtained the required Certificate of Occupancy for the whole floor.

The lease was necessary to allow her to obtain her Assumed Name Certificate and federal tax identification number. It had taken a week of hard searching to find the location, but it was perfect; it was only a short walk to the Courthouse and to City Hall.

In the two weeks since she had signed her lease, Alyssa Giordano had been busy with administrative tasks. The first week had been consumed with registering the business and sorting out the state and federal tax requirements. The telephone call to the Internal Revenue Service about obtaining an Employer Identification Number was simple; she was issued with a number immediately, with the certificate to follow by mail within a week. Filing the Assumed Name Certificate with the Manhattan County Clerk, and obtaining four certified copies, had been time consuming and cost a couple of hundred dollars. The second week was consumed with banks. After all her searching she found that the Bank of America had the best deal; she would not have to pay the monthly maintenance fees on her business checking accounts gave her for as long as she maintained her personal account with them. And there were several branches close to her new office.

And then it was done, she thought.

CHAPTER 24

JUSTICE SHARED, ENHANCED

March 9, 2005 was a prominent, and prodigious, day for Alyssa Giordano and her career. The day would be marked as the day she declared to the world she had established herself as her own boss.

That Wednesday, she had caught the subway to the center of midtown and walked from the station to the office building at 305 Broadway. Although she had been there before, the building entrance daunted her. She stood outside the lobby for half an hour, staring at the entryway while she sipped a coffee, letting the other workers who occupied the building pass by her. It was just the third time she had approached the entrance to the building. She finished her coffee and decided it was time to enter her office.

As she neared the revolving door that granted access to the lobby, she stopped short. She shook her head, she was hearing things; nobody, apart from her family, yet knew that this would her first day as a solo practitioner so why would she be hearing someone call her name as she walked to her office.

"Alyssa!" She heard the voice again. "Alyssa, I thought it was you!" She turned to see a woman hurrying towards the building, and her.

"Hello Peggy! I thought I was hearing things!" The women squeezed each other in a fashion to avoid emptying the remnants of coffee over each other.

"Hello, Alyssa. I wasn't sure it was you."

"What are you doing here?"

"Second job interview," Peggy Cooper puffed, breathless from the swift pace with which she had taken the steps leading up to the building. She bent over to catch her breath.

"Are you okay?" Alyssa touched her friend's shoulder.

"Yes," she breathed more easily. "I'm outta shape!"

"Me too!" Alyssa laughed. "When did you start looking for a new job?"

"A month ago. Fuck, it's hard!"

"Looking for a job? Tell me about it!"

"You wouldn't believe how many jobs I've been for in the last month! And how many I've missed out on!"

"Yes I would! I've been going through the same thing!"

"What are you doing here?"

"I'm starting work in the building today."

"Great! Thank God at least one of us has a job. At least I'll know someone in the building if I get this one."

"Why did you leave?" The inquiry was not just concern for her friend.

"They were dodgy and they were screwing me on my pay." Alyssa just groaned at that statement. "I thought it would have been easier."

"What, getting a job? It's a pain in the ass! It's tough to compete with the grads they can pay zilch."

"I thought my clients wanting to follow me woulda made it easier."

"Have you ever thought about going out on your own?"

"I wish I could! I don't have the money! I barely had enough for the subway here today, let alone a coffee! And I don't want to do it all by myself just yet. I'm not ready yet. I don't think I could do it all alone anyway, with all the work they want me to do. And I hate all that administration shit!"

"I do. And neither do I."

"What?" Peggy was confused.

"I do, have the money I mean."

"Well, why haven't you done it then?!"

"I have. My new office is in this building. Wanna join me?" Alyssa smiled slyly, wryly.

"Whadda ya mean?" Peggy's jaw dropped.

"I mean fuck the interview. I don't want to do it all alone either. I don't mind all the administration shit; I love it. And I haven't really thought it all through: I haven't told my clients that I've to go solo yet, so I really don't have any work just yet. You got more work than you can handle alone and I got time and an office. Between the two of us, I bet we can do it."

"But how would we work it?"

"Let's get more coffee and talk about it."

"Okay." And they turned away from the building together, arms linked, and headed towards the closest coffee house.

Alyssa Giordano never made it into her new office that day. When she returned the following day, Peggy Cooper accompanied her as her new partner. It would work for them; as friends they would make it work for them: the partnership load would be divided in what they considered to be equitable. Peggy would bring her clients and work with her to keep herself busy doing billable hours all day and Alyssa busy only part–time, so she could dedicate the rest of her time to sending out the bills, and the rest of the administrative paperwork that Cooper so loathed, and bringing in new clients when she could.

*****

Johannsen's inner stylist did not like the look of the man sitting in front of his desk: he was scruffy and smelly and he definitely did not match the decor, or the class, of the office which he deemed to be his own personal protectorate. And he had become quite adept at identifying, and weaning out those who would be good for nothing.

In the two and a half, no almost three, years he had been with them, Eric Johannsen had not come to understand why Ms. Giordano and Ms. Cooper let people like him into their office. His social conscience understood that these people had rights too, but didn't his taxes pay for Legal Aid? Well, whatever their reasons, his bosses, two wonderful women, had decided that they occasionally needed to use their legal acumen, and the money they had made from it, to give back to the community by working on the occasional case for free. *Pro bono publico,* they told him: for the public good. He was startled out of his trance as the door defending one of the office spaces behind him flung open.

"Your messages, Ms. Cooper." He had written the man's name on a message slip and handed it to her with the other slips.

"Thank you, Mr. Johannsen. Mr. Xiang Lian, is it?" The scruffy man stood and nodded. She looked him up and down, taking in his appearance.

"Yes."

"I'm Peggy Cooper. Please come in."

"Thank you." He followed her into her office and she closed the door behind her. He remained standing until she reached her desk.

"Please, sit, sit. Did I pronounce that right? Your name?"

"Yes, thank you," he answered as they both seated themselves on opposite sides of the desk. "But, please. Call me Liam. I call myself Liam Xiang here."

"Thanks. I'm Peggy. Your English is excellent. How long have you been here?"

"My wife and I've been here five years. I'm a financial advisor and Kylie was a pediatric surgical nurse before we moved here." He paused and sighed, tears started to flow down his cheeks. She waited for him to continue, handed him a tissue. "Please forgive my appearance. We haven't been home in days. After Jimmy was born and we went home, we gathered some things and just fled the house," he said softly.

"We?"

"My wife and I and our two sons."

"How old are your boys?"

"Michael's three and Jimmy's just a week old."

"Why haven't you been home?"

"My wife gave birth to Jimmy a week ago, at St. Luke's–Roosevelt Hospital, and the doctors wanted to vaccinate him."

"What for?"

"Hep B. My wife contracted it when she worked as a nurse, she got cut during a surgery. That's why she doesn't work now."

"Why don't you want him vaccinated?" Peggy was shocked. If it was her choice, and she had put either of her children at risk for such a disease, or even if she could have made such a decision for her grandson, she would have had doctors given them whatever shots they wanted immediately.

"Look, I know it doesn't sound reasonable to most people. But we're his parents and it's our choice. We know it can cause liver cancer and cirrhosis, but hepatitis B can be managed more effectively without the vaccine." Peggy did not immediately reply; the thought of her grandson, and her single daughter's decision to circumcise him, changed her mind and she understood. "You don't believe me? Kylie's done it; she knows more about it than I do. We're more worried that the aluminum in the vaccine has more potential to do neurological damage."

"No, no. That's not it. I just remembered something." She paused again. "I'm not sure how I can help you."

"They offered to give Jimmy immunoglobulin straight away and said that he should get vaccinations over the next six months. We told them thanks but no thanks."

"Well, vaccinations are not compulsory in New York."

"That's what we thought. Then doctors and midwives on the ward told us that we'd be arrested and OCFS or ACS would take custody of both our kids if we left the hospital without having the vaccination." Peggy immediately recognized the acronyms for the State Office of Children and Family Services and the City's Administration for Children's Services. She wished she had never heard of them, given the number of times she had dealt with them before.

"Why did they say that?"

"They told us it was abuse not to give him the vaccination. Look, Michael was born after Kylie was diagnosed and he doesn't have it."

"They allowed you to leave the hospital?" Peggy was confused.

"We agreed to visit a Department doctor with someone from OCFS and someone from ACS to get more information about the risks involved. As if we don't already know the risks! But we didn't go. And now they've gone to Court and got an order forcing us to hand over our kids and forcing Jimmy to have the shots!" The exasperation in his voice ascended. "Look, my wife is tired. She's just given birth and we are on the run with a newborn and a three–year–old. The tactics that have been pulled so far are unbelievable."

"Yes, they are unbelievable." She lost herself in thought, dredging up vaguely remembered case law from college.

"What is it?"

She held her hand up, continuing to search her memory. Finally, it came.

"I think we can get an injunction to stop them." The man smiled and sighed in relief. "But my partner's away until Friday, so I'll need a day to get the papers drawn up. Can you come back tomorrow?" He just nodded.

After she had closed the office's main door behind him, Peggy Cooper's head did a double take as she saw the reporter's face filling the television screen, the building behind her barely distinguishable as a hospital.

"Could you please turn it up, Eric?" He obeyed and they were both entranced by the news. "Where's Alyssa?"

"She's still in L.A. She hasn't left for the airport yet." Peggy picked up the handset of the telephone on the reception desk and dialed her partner's cell phone.

"Hello? Alyssa?" A pause. "I got a good pro bono case in today." Another, longer, pause. "Yes, yes, I'll tell you about it when you get back. But that's not what I'm calling about. You near a television?" Another pause. "No, you have to see it to believe it. Angela Ryan's on CNN right now." Another pause. "You there, Alyssa? You there?"

She pulled the hand piece away from her ear as she heard Alyssa Giordano's cell phone clatter to the floor and handed it back to Eric. She had paperwork to do if she wanted to get that injunction she had promised.

CHAPTER 25

MISTAKING IDENTITY

The violence Ben Walker experienced on what would be his last overnight shift happened suddenly.

Officer Walker and his partner, Dillon Anderson, had no obvious reason to believe they were encountering a man now suspected in the shooting of another officer when they set out to follow him for a routine traffic violation on a New York Street. That chance meeting unfolded about ten minutes to three that morning. With Officer Walker driving, the two officers were assigned to a "conditions car," deployed to check certain areas, like nightclubs, because of the potential for trouble. Though riding in an unmarked dark green Chevrolet Impala, the officers were both in uniform. The wet weather had made the pavement slushy. They had stopped, but Walker had not yet turned off the engine, outside The Pussycat Lounge, a club on Greenwich Street, just south of the Stock Exchange.

A man in a maroon 1990 Infiniti Q-45 sedan sped past them and drove through a red light in the swanky Lower Manhattan financial district.

"Shit, Dillon."

"Yeah Ben, shit."

"Wish I was back on Long Island in this weather."

"So do I." Walker just laughed as he made a U-turn, crossing traffic and causing more than a few irate New York horns to sound, and gave chase as Officer Anderson picked up the radio microphone.

"Command: this is Anderson, in CC27. I need a 10-27 on a Jersey plate, D-8471, a maroon Infiniti sedan: it just ran a red and we're in pursuit."

"CC27, this is Command," the dispatch officer answered. "Hold while I check." Only seconds passed before the radio operator's voice garbled back. "CC27, this is Command: it's a New Jersey dealer plate, the New Jersey Department of Motor Vehicles records show that it should have been turned in to the Department a week ago. Approach with caution."

With the officers in pursuit, the Infiniti followed a roundabout route around the neighborhood, and headed towards Brooklyn. Anderson, constantly updating Command over the radio, requested that more cars, both marked and unmarked, join them in the pursuit as the Infiniti approached the Brooklyn Bridge at speed. The Infiniti driver did not see the casino–bound bus on the Bridge as it sped along the on–ramp, or was more concerned with evading Walker and Anderson, and pulled in front of it. The bus driver and Walker slammed on the brakes of their respective vehicles, the bus barely missed hitting the rear of the Infiniti, and Walker was just able to shoot around the back of the bus. Skidding on wet and slushy pavement, the bus spun its wheels, ran off the left side of the roadway, swerved back to the right, and shot fifty feet down the Bridge. The police cars following Walker and Anderson reduced speed and began weaving around to avoid the bus and the other traffic on the Bridge.

"Shit!" Walker cried. "The bus has gone off the Bridge!"

"Command: this is CC27 again," Anderson hollered over the radio.

"CC27, this is Command."

"Command, we are still in pursuit of the Infiniti across the Brooklyn Bridge and it forced a bus off the Bridge. I repeat it forced a bus off the Bridge."

"CC27, are there any other cars on the scene?"

"Command, CC48 and CC91 were behind us. They'll need backup and paramedics!"

"Copy that, CC27: more cars and paramedics on the way to the Bridge. Remain in pursuit of the Infiniti, remain in pursuit of the Infiniti."

"Copy that Command, will remain in pursuit. Out."

"I hope he stops soon!" Walker piped up.

"You're doin' good, Ben," Anderson responded. "I'll spot him and you just drive where I tell ya!"

"Yeah right, Dillon," Walker spluttered as he tried to laugh, "like you can give directions!"

"Just shut the fuck up and drive," Anderson laughed as he punched Walker's right arm.

"Fuck! Don't do that!" Walker screamed. "My arms hurt!"

As Walker and Anderson kept close to the Infiniti, police, firemen and paramedics worked tirelessly to treat wounded bodies at, and to clean up the mess that had surrounded, the chaotic accident scene Two men were killed instantly and the remaining twenty–eight injured passengers suffered varying degrees of injury; the bus driver was the only person unhurt when the bus skidded and rolled after speeding Infiniti cut it off. The surrounding emergency rooms were also chaotic: doctors and the emergency room staff throughout Manhattan and Brooklyn treated those who were injured by, but survived, as they arrived in multiples. The two men who died were identified and their families notified. Of the twenty–eight injured passengers, nine remained hospitalized in critical condition at Jersey Shore Medical Center, Toms River Community Medical Center or Kings County Hospital Center. There was confusion as the families arrived: two had been sent to Kings County instead of Jersey Shore and another three had to reroute to Toms River after being sent to Brooklyn City Medical Center.

*****

After a circuitous chase, the cars ended up next to each other at Flatbush and Church Avenues, Brooklyn.

The police car came to a stop nearly parallel and to the right of the Infiniti, which had also stopped. With both cars in the intersection, the man in the Infiniti pulled a gun and aimed through the open passenger side window, firing five shots and hitting the police car in the front and rear doors. The man fired again and one of the bullets hit Officer Walker under his left armpit just above the panels of his bullet–resistant vest and pierced his left ventricle. The gunman floored the accelerator and turned left on Church Avenue.

"Oh fuck," Anderson squealed into the radio microphone as Walker pulled off after the Infiniti. "Command, shots fired, shots fired! We need back–up now!"

In spite of his wound, the adrenaline pumping through the officer's body seemed to dull the pain, allowing him to drive for blocks in pursuit of the gunman. The gunman went another block, sped up and swung wide and turned north onto the wrong side of East 21st Street into the path of another car. The man in his newly purchased Toyota Camry slammed on the brakes and swerved to miss the Infiniti as it fishtailed. The Camry driver's reaction time was inadequate: he was unable to correct his swerve in time to avoid bouncing into a LeSabre parked in front of the corner drug store. The gunman's reaction time was better: he was able to pull out of the fishtail. The driver of a Honda Civic, although not following closely behind the Camry but with his eyes focused on the backup police cars in his rear–view mirror, did not see and was unable to avoid the rear of the Camry. Both men were thrown from their cars. As the Camry was shunted further into the rear of the LeSabre, it caused a chain reaction of the three parked cars in front of it striking each other. The final parked car in the chain, a Pontiac Firebird, immediately caught on fire as it hit a man exiting the drug store. Three squad cars, this time marked and responding to the call of shots fired, pulled up behind the accident scene. Officers jumped out of the cars which had pulled up at the scene to check the injured men. This second accident scene was not quite as chaotic as the first, but still frenzied, with the bodies of the three injured men, and the groceries of one, strewn on the ground amongst car parts. Just as the Fire Department truck pulled up next to the burning car to start working on the fire, two ambulances arrived and paramedics took over from the policemen working on injured men lying on the roadway. Emergency workers found the wallets of all three men, whom looked remarkably alike, with graying hair and similar pot–bellied builds. It was no wonder that their wallets were confused.

*****

With Anderson gripping the dashboard to stop himself from thumping into the door beside him, Walker swerved in the opposite direction to miss the Camry and accelerated in pursuit of the Infiniti. A fourth marked car did not bother to stop at the accident scene but joined Walker and Anderson's pursuit of the gunman.

The gunman turned left on Church Avenue, went a block, turned north onto East 21st Street and pulled into the basement garage through an open metal door. As the gunman's car went into the garage, the metal door closed and the sound of the tires of the two squad cars squealing as they pulled up to the garage door echoed through the street. All four officers jumped out and Anderson and an officer from the second car fired a maelstrom of bullets at the door behind which the gunman had hidden before Walker could pull his weapon.

"I'm shot, I'm shot," whispered Walker as he staggered and fainted. Anderson turned to see Walker put his hand to his chest and fall to the roadway.

"Call a bus! Call a bus! We gotta get him to a hospital!" Anderson screamed at the other officers as raced towards his fallen partner and knelt beside the collapsed man.

"They're on their way," one of the other officers shouted as he tended to one of the other men.

"How many coming?" the third officer screamed over the sound of the wailing sirens.

"Don't know, but they're coming. More backup's coming too," the officer who had also drawn his weapon and fired called back.

"Ben can't wait. I'll take him in our car!" Anderson hollered back.

He grabbed Walker under his arms and dragged him towards the bullet–ridden Impala. He laid him back on the street next to the passenger door, and opened the door. As the firemen and paramedics started working on the fire and the two other injured men lying on the roadway, Anderson again grabbed Walker under his arms and struggled to drag him backwards into the unmarked patrol car. At the same time as Anderson was struggling to get his wounded partner into the car, paramedics attending the scene outside the drug store dragged one of the other men onto a gurney and shoved it into the back of the ambulance.

As the ambulance's back doors slammed shut and it reversed direction and started screaming towards the closest medical facility, Walker was able to drag the door of the patrol car shut behind him and Anderson climbed into the driver's seat and started the engine. The wheels of the Impala squealed as they started off towards Kings County Hospital Center as Emergency Services Unit officers cordoned off the garage and nearby rooftops. The Infiniti was found in the building's garage, and its vehicle identification number led them to a man in the neighborhood who said he had recently sold the car to the gunman and knew where he lived. With that information, detectives located the address of the gunman's sixth–floor apartment, about two blocks from the scene of the shooting. Police officers, including hostage negotiators, went to the building later in the morning and determined that the gunman was not inside.

*****

The entrance, surrounded by armed men, to Building C of the Kings County Hospital Center in Brooklyn is designed for ambulance traffic, but the bullet–riddled unmarked green Impala that stopped at its painted curb, behind an ambulance that had just pulled in, around quarter after three, counted as an emergency vehicle.

The emergency room staffers saw bullet holes in the doors, and the front–seat passenger, Officer Ben Walker, was bleeding from a massive heart injury. His wound was critical and dangerous, but there was cause for optimism. Just a few hours earlier, surgeons at the hospital had opened the chest of a seventeen–year–old gunshot victim, saving his life, and now Officer Walker, thirty–five, was delivering a robust, thick–walled heart into their care.

The professional lawman was cognizant when he arrived in his unmarked cruiser, but the slug had crossed through both his left ventricle, the heart's main pumping chamber, and his left anterior descending coronary artery, which delivers blood to that ventricle. The projectile had not exited the heart muscle. Deep inside Officer Walker's chest, contradictory and incompatible forces were at work. His pericardium, the rigid sack that surrounds the heart, was filling with blood from the hole in his ventricle. The sack was probably helping keep the man from bleeding to death. But the blood had to go someplace. As it filled the sack, it pressed on the heart, choking the muscle's capacity to pump. Within minutes, the burden inside the officer's chest besieged his cardiac system, and his heart stopped.

Inside the emergency room, the team of doctors and nurses grew to more than a dozen. Their patient was now in full cardiac arrest. Pumping drugs, blood and clotting agents into his veins, they cut open his chest. One of the surgeons took Officer Walker's heart in his hands, rubbing it in a gentle clapping motion until it resumed pumping. To relieve the pressure on the muscle, surgeons cut open the outer sack. With a long, narrow pair of metal pliers, the surgeon gripped a curved needle and drew an inch–and–a–half–long blue, nylon–like suture across Officer Walker's heart.

Officer Walker was then taken to a second–floor operating room, where his chest was sealed. The surgical team performed transfusions to keep up his blood pressure. They wrapped his body in a "bear–hugger," a blanket with circulating heat. They implanted tubes to suck air from his chest. And their efforts seemed to be working. Their patient's blood pressure was responding to the treatments. The hole in his artery had clotted. His bleeding was staunched.

The doctors transferred their patient from his stretcher to a bed in the intensive care unit. There, Officer Walker was a room away from his bosses, the Mayor and the Police Commissioner, who had arrived and were waiting with the officer's wife, his children and other family members. But behind the door, Officer Walker went into cardiac arrest a second time. Surgeons reopened his chest and tried one method after another to restart his heart. In a last desperate maneuver, the surgeons opened his chest cavity in the Intensive Care Unit bed. As Officer Walker lay there, his heart massaged in a doctor's hands, a scrub nurse left the room and found Mrs. Walker outside her husband's room.

"Mrs. Walker, could you please come into your husband's room."

"What? Why?"

"If you could come in please. The doctors would like to talk to you." Stunned, Mrs. Walker simply followed the nurse into the room. But the officer's wife was unable to move beyond the cusp of the door.

"Who's that?" one of the doctors screamed at the nurse.

"His wife," the nurse snapped back. *Doctors who think they're gods,* she thought as she rolled her eyes and immediately went back to her station. The screaming doctor handed over to another and approached Mrs. Walker and described her husband's condition to her as gently as he could. Her screams could be heard by those outside the room as she fell to the floor. Tears welled in her eyes as the doctor helped her up and guided her to the table; the medical staff parted a path to a position close to her husband's head and she kissed him on the forehead. Walker was pronounced dead, with his wife by his side, at twenty minutes to nine.

CHAPTER 26

FIGHT FOR SURVIVAL

As the fight to keep Officer Walker alive played out over roughly five hours, other battles raged within the hospital. Two other surgical teams at Kings County Hospital Center doctors fought to save two men, as yet unidentified, involved in the crash in Brooklyn.

The first ambulance had arrived shortly before the bullet–riddled unmarked green Impala carrying Officer Walker. The second ambulance that had arrived at East 21st Street had also taken the second man from the street to the same Hospital as Officer Walker and the first man from the street. A team of another dozen doctors spent substantial hours in another operating room repairing a lung punctured by broken ribs and pinning severed leg bones and in the intensive care unit trying to control the bleeding around the man's ruptured spleen. The facial fractures and bruising took second place as an emergency splenectomy did nothing to control the bleeding; but it could not control the bleeding as the bleeding in the man's liver went undetected for too long. He too was pronounced dead, shortly after Officer Walker

The third team treated the other man for right subarachnoid hemorrhage and a left subdural hematoma with a shearing injury, which now threatened his life. An emergency aspiration tube was fed down his throat, in case he needed to be resuscitated. Doctors induced a coma. This man's other broken bones, facial swelling and cuts and bruises could wait; he would remain in the induced coma for weeks.

The men looked remarkably alike, with similar colored hair and similar builds. But with so many policemen at the hospital, it was apparently not hard to sort out the identification of one of the men. The man with the punctured organs, who was pronounced dead at almost the same time as Officer Walker, was officially identified as Duncan Kennedy, originally of Millbrook and now of Hoboken and New York; the man with the brain injuries was identified and then unidentified: his driver's license proved to be counterfeit.

*****

It was during a news conference at the hospital that the deaths of the two men at Kings County Hospital Center, and the bare survival of the third, were announced by the co–directors of trauma surgery, with the third man's condition described as critical.

"The heart has a mind of its own," said one of the policeman's surgeons, "and his was the heart of a fighter. It's called a double–hit phenomenon: a glancing blow that leaves two injuries from the same hole. I only know of one patient I've treated who survived it, and that was a knife wound," the doctor said. "Bullets do a lot more damage. And the bullet wound had to be closed quickly or he's going to bleed to death right in front of our eyes.

"Officer Walker went into cardiac arrest a second time. Surgeons reopened his chest and tried one method after another to restart his heart. That's a desperation maneuver, to open his heart in bed in the I.C.U.," the doctor said.

"We asked his wife to come into his room so she could be with him when he died. She was muted, traumatized," the doctor said. "At 8:40 a.m., her husband was pronounced dead in his bed in intensive care. She had tears in her eyes," the surgeon said, "and she kissed him."

"Officer Walker showed remarkable tenacity and courage in pursuing his assailant," said the Police Commissioner. "Despite his horrific wounds he continued to drive his police car, keeping the shooter in sight."

The Police Commissioner then took over to describe the chaotic accident scenes caused by the Infiniti and the pursuit of it, in which bodies, wallets and personal items were strewn on the ground.

"Based on information from emergency workers, hospital staff and friends of the victims, rescuers have identified two of the three men who died at the accident scene in Brooklyn as Michael Halliday and Duncan Kennedy. Halliday was pronounced dead at the scene and Kennedy died here, at the Hospital, after the wonderful medical staff did all they could for him. We haven't been able to identify the third victim as his driver's license proved to be a forgery. The unidentified man suffered brain and other injuries and he remains in a coma in the Intensive Care Unit. We'll be circulating a picture in the hope that someone will know who he is."

"What about the condition of the man who survived?" piped up a reporter. "What is his condition?"

"I'll take this one," one of the doctors indicated. "He's alive, but we've had to induce a coma. He's suffered broken bones throughout his body, severe bruising to his face, and gravel rash on his back but these are the least of his injuries. His spinal cord was undamaged, but he's suffered a right subarachnoid hemorrhage and a left subdural hematoma with a shearing injury"

"What?" several reporters screamed at once.

"Basically, bleeding and bruising in his brain," the doctor explained. "Now those injuries threaten his life. We've induced a coma and fed an emergency aspiration tube down his throat, in case he needs to be resuscitated. He could remain in this condition for weeks."

"Do you know who he is?" The question was from only one, the most senior reporter. A woman this time.

"At this point, we haven't been able to identify him properly yet," the Mayor indicated. "The identification he had seemed to be forged and we'll need to wait till the doctors deem it appropriate to take him out of the coma before we'll be able to ask him."

"Is it the man who shot Officer Walker?" the same reporter asked.

"No," the Police Commissioner indicated, "but our investigations are continuing there."

"When will Officer Walker's funeral be?" the reporter asked.

"Now that will be up to Mrs. Walker," the Mayor said. "Now, Officer Walker was a five-year veteran of the force and a decorated professional. He's already been recognized four times for distinguished police duty. He was also a devoted family man with two young daughters. The Police Commissioner and I agree that the City will be giving him a funeral with full Police Department honors if Mrs. Walker wants. But the arrangements will be up to her."

*****

She could not believe what she was seeing before her eyes. She dropped her cell phone as she collapsed onto the bed, her eyes glued to the television.

The man she loathed was dead. He would not suffer the pains of facing the wrath of the justice system, but he was gone. She felt let down, but relieved at the same time. It was as if the burden had lifted and she would not shed tears over it. Her fight to get on with life, just barely surviving, was over.

CHAPTER 27

CHANCE ENCOUNTERS

It was one of those coincidences that are believable only in real life. A million–to–one chance.

The airport in July, myriad strangers crossing each other's paths as they make their way from one side of the globe to the other.

The eyes of the two met for a mere split second as they rode the moving walkways in opposite directions. Over ten years had passed, but each face retained enough of its youthful appearance to produce in the other a flash of startled recognition, a sudden racing of the heart beneath the designer jacket in one case and the crumpled T–shirt in the other, as the shock of memory and emotion hit home.

And then they were past each other. Swallowed up into the safety of the anonymous crowds. One a woman, now slim and smart but the minor crow–lines on her face showed that she matured elegantly and with poise, the other a man who had aged just as gracefully as grip on youth had tightened after his marriage to a college girl and the birth of his biological child, whom he had strapped to his back.

Still shaken from that split–second confrontation with her past, Alyssa Giordano approached the airport exit gates. The blood pounded in her ears and her legs in their high heels felt leaden as she stumbled off the walkway with her trolley of matching luggage. For a moment she tried to convince herself she had merely dreamed it. Surely that man who had slipped by her so swiftly couldn't be Bill. It just wasn't possible.

But she had caught the swift double take of recognition, had seen her own trepidation reflected in that other startled face and knew she hadn't been mistaken.

It was an omen, Alyssa shivered, a sign telling her that she should never have come. But she'd had to; she had to make sure the funeral was really happening. There'd been no choice about that. And she'd been sure that the risk after all this time would be minimal.

Only now did she realize how wrong she might have been.

*****

The woman emerged from the clinic and stood for a moment on the sidewalk as if unsure where to head next.

Her narrow face was pale and drawn and she shivered in the chill drizzle that was already frizzing her short brown hair. She'd been gone so long, she thought, she'd almost forgotten the bite of the New York cold, but it was not much from Sofija she realized.

Despite the rain, Rebecca decided to walk. Her hotel wasn't that far away – and she was still fit enough for that. But more than anything else, she needed time to think. To comprehend the news that had just been so delicately but unequivocally relayed to her. She hoped her husband would have picked up his room key and settled their child, now a rambunctious toddler, by the time she got there. They had named him David; Rebecca had sentimentally insisted that he have her husband's, and his father's and grandfather's, middle name as his first. Lost in thought, she wasn't noticing, couldn't help but not notice, those around her; she mumbled an apology as she helped the woman, the one entering the clinic she had just departed and she'd bumped into as her mind galvanized, pick up the few small items which had fallen from her handbag before she recommenced her stride.

In truth, it hadn't really come as a shock. For almost a year now the pains had come and gone. Sharp and severe, they would hit without warning but had always subsided eventually. Until these last few weeks. That was when she knew she would have to do something more than rely on the aloof assurance of the doctor she'd visited in Sofija, the cool, patrician Bulgarian who, after barely bothering to examine her, had diagnosed her problem as 'mere gastric upset' of the type common among tourists faced with unfamiliar diets.

But, back in New York, Rebecca Morisette wasn't a tourist, and neither was her husband.

She'd met him not long after they'd both left New Jersey, each with a backpack in March of 1999. She was on the tour that her parents had given her on her triumphant graduation from the Conservatorium and having had minor success in the theater. He was escaping his ex–wife and the vocation which he thought would destroy him. Their first meeting at a foreign airport information desk, despite being on the same flight to the same destination, was a quirk of fate: they had both hoped that someone at the kiosk spoke enough English to direct them through the quagmire of locating a place to bed down for the first night of separate expeditions, and he'd wanted to help the young American girl who'd seemed nervous. Since then, they had run into each other so often that it made sense to combine their travels; they subsequently holidayed together in some odd places: Romania, Turkey, Macedonia, Iran, Lebanon, and even Albania.

Bill Morisette had taken to teaching English during their travels, and found that he liked it more than the law, and even got himself a Masters in Applied Linguistics. His language skills had drawn them to Oman for two years, which were okay years, and the money was great. But it wasn't good enough to keep them there. He found the Saudi heat, and the subjugation of his wife in a culture so completely different from their own, vile.

For someone who hated the heat, living in the Middle East seemed strange to Bill, which was partly why Bulgaria became home despite the fact that neither of them spoke the language. But Bill came to understand quite a bit and could read the menu in pretty much any restaurant around. They, especially Bill, learnt to appreciate the change of seasons, the cold desolation of winter and the baking hot summers and loved it in late spring when the poppies came out in full bloom and the first cherries started to appear in the markets. He especially loved his new vocation of being a slacker.

She and Bill had lived in Sofija for almost four years now, and she was scratching out an additional living for the love of her life, as his salary teaching English in the Eastern Bloc was substantially less than it had been in Saudi, and insufficient to maintain them, now that their child was growing. She would endure the indifference of an audience who talked and laughed or, worse still, heckled drunkenly as she took the stage every evening, for the man she worshipped from the depths of her soul. Occasionally her name would strike a chord and someone in the mainly tourist audience would come up after the show and say how much they'd loved her "in the old days". Meaning, of course, when they were all young, when they'd all had hopes and dreams, when anything was possible. Rebecca could see the pity in the eyes of some. The sympathy for someone who might have made it big but who was now reduced to earning her living in third–rate foreign bars.

They had not previously felt a burning need to return to their homeland and, since their first meeting, had spent only eight days in the United States, simply to revisit friends and relations. But now the need was different, her physical pain had made sure of that. Wherever they had run – backpacking through the Eastern Bloc countries, Bill teaching in the Middle East despite his loathing for the heat, and landing finally in Bulgaria – he'd, and therefore they'd, never been able to escape. The guilt he felt had followed her husband everywhere; he had only wanted to help and he had, but he did not know it. Sensing his remorse, his self–reproach, at the thought that he had had a hand in destroying her had eaten at his new wife inside, and in the end, she felt sure, contributed to the disease that she'd just learned would soon take her life at twenty eight. Even though the death of the cruel menace had assuaged his guilt somewhat, it had come too late.

Rebecca walked the wet pavements of New York, the city where she had arrived so young and so full of wild dreams, bitter tears welled in her eyes. She *could* have made it too, she thought defiantly, but the dream had been snatched away by his guilt over what had happened. And from that time on, her husband, and therefore she, had paid the price.

At once, hot panic fluttered in her throat. Four weeks, the specialist had told her. So little time to try to put things right. To try to right that terrible wrong, if only to ease his guilt.

But that didn't mean she wasn't going to try.

*****

After he'd put the now not so small child down, Bill had fallen on the bed and immediately dozed off without turning down the covers; he was dog–tired after the flight from Sofija, particularly as it was the first time he had really had to manage the child alone. That was hard and now he understood, he thought, Rebecca's dog–tiredness at the end of each day, particularly after she'd had a singing gig the night before.

He jumped, knocking the glass of water from the bedside table, startled as he heard the lock click and the hotel room door push open.

"Shit. Hello?" As he threw his legs over the edge of the bed and bent down to pick up the glass, he hoped he hadn't missed the knocking of room servicing staff in his sleep.

"Hello, darling! You made it!" He looked up to see his second wife enter the room and approach the traveling crib first. "Hello, my young man!" Rebecca Morisette tickled her young son's stomach as he smiled and flailed his arms at his mother, wanting to be picked up. But she wanted to kiss her husband first. "How long has David been awake?" she asked as she wandered over to Bill, kissed him on the top of his head, tousled his already mussed hair and sat next to him on the bed.

"I don't know. I must've zonked out." He took her hand, kissed her on the cheek.

*****

She had waited until the service was under way before slipping in at the side door of the church.

The rear pews were empty and she slid onto the polished wood, a now petite, fine–featured woman wearing an elegantly simple black dress, her hair drawn back in a gold clasp. As she took her seat, a couple of curious heads turned, then looked away.

Alyssa Giordano didn't really expect to be, hoped not to be, recognized.

At thirty–one, she was a long way from the jeans–clad nineteen–year–old whose hair had hung in a thick curtain to her waist.

The number of mourners in the inner–city Anglican Church surprised her. But then, Alyssa reminded herself, Duncan Kennedy had always been well–known, at least with those who had known of the as–yet–unsolved tragedy which had befallen his first wife and daughter, and well–respected by most but not by all given the financial concerns which surrounded the death of Janet and Kristie Kennedy.

From behind her dark glasses she scrutinized the rows of heads. An impossible task to pick out anyone she might know. It was so long ago.

Everyone and everything had changed. On the way in from the airport the day before, she'd been amazed by the differences that twelve years had wrought. The choking traffic and crowded streets, the forests of mid–rise apartments, the sense of bustle and energy. It was almost like being back in New York, she'd thought. Except for the sun; the Hoboken mid–rise apartments could never approach the dizzying heights of the Manhattan skyline.

Now, shifting her head a little to the left, Alyssa could just see the woman in the front row. Lydia "the second". It had to be. The curls were the same, although a different, lighter color. She was flanked by Lydia "the first" on one side and two young girls on the other, and had a comforting arm curled around one of the young girls. Duncan Kennedy's business partner, second wife now a widow and his living daughters. The screaming toddler in the arms of the couple sitting next to "the two Lydias" seemed to represent the mourning of all those, apart from her, at the service. The woman turned to take the child from the man sitting next to her and Alyssa saw her profile; she looked familiar, she looked like the woman who had knocked her bag out of her hands on the street outside the clinic.

Alyssa wondered how it felt to be a widow in such turmoil, with such responsibility to try and protect her children from the dishonor of her dead husband's fall from grace. Then a glimmer of bitterness lit her hazel eyes. At least he was dead now; she felt the same. Maybe not that much different from the bitterness she felt when she left Hoboken, the bitterness she felt at the disintegration of the relationship with the only man she thought she would ever love. Pain and loss. A life needing to be reshaped. Pointed in a new direction. Exactly what she had faced twelve years ago. Only there hadn't been any children, thank God. The prospect of motherhood, without him, had seemed unbearable. After what had happened.

Abruptly, she brought her attention back to the ritual. The minister was calling on one of the mourners to step forward and deliver the eulogy.

A man, blond, very tall, the male half of the couple with the howling child sitting next to "the two Lydias," rose to his feet with quick, easy grace made his way to the pulpit.

Alyssa frowned. There was something strangely familiar about that walk. Then, as he turned to face the congregation, she saw the aquiline nose, the confident set of the mouth and chin, the serious green eyes.

And her face paled with shock, again, the same shock she had felt at the airport.

CHAPTER 28

AWKWARD REUNIONS

The trip to the cemetery had given her churning stomach time to settle, her mind time to form so many questions. Was it really him at the airport? Was it really him at the church? The woman sitting next to him didn't look like Theona, or maybe her mind had failed her; it had been years since she had seen them both.

The mausoleum in which he, her former boss, her nemesis as she had come to think of him, was being interred was crowded, full when she arrived. Alyssa Giordano didn't want to be inside anyway: she just wanted to observe from a distance as she had done for the funeral mass, to give a chance to look about her and reminisce while the ritual of burying the man she detested unfolded. She had wanted to make sure that Duncan Kennedy was really in the ground, so to speak; he had fled and now he had been found. She was not unhappy that he was dead; she was disappointed that he was dead before he had faced what he had done, the fitting end would have been for him to have lived and been wounded by Lady Justice.

And she had wanted to make sure that her eyes had not deceived her and that she had really seen who she thought she had seen at the airport.

Again she had waited until the ritual was under way before edging her way to the side door of the mausoleum; the people congregating several feet outside the door huffed, their looks indicated their annoyance that they were being pushed aside by this young upstart. As she reached the door, she saw that those inside were also standing, packed tightly around the coffin. Such a crowd! Surely they couldn't all like him? Surely some of them had come, as she had, to make sure that the asshole had really gone, got what was coming to him in some twisted way?

Her eyes caught a glimpse of Bill Morisette, and the woman with whom he had been seated at the church, on the opposite side of the expanse. His head turned as he noticed the movement which made way for her and, as he noticed her, he smiled ever so slightly and blinked a nod to her, then looked away towards the coffin. She did the same and saw the two Lydias, and Mrs. Kennedy's children, standing next to the minister at the coffin's side. She heard the minister droning, hearing the words but not taking them in, as the coffin slid into its niche. *Strange,* she thought as she noticed the engraving on the niches next to and immediately below his. *Why is she burying him next to his first wife?* She shrugged. *Maybe to be near his daughter?*

Alyssa snapped from her reverie as the sea of people in the catacomb chamber parted for the minister to lead Mrs. Kennedy, with her children by her side, to the front entrance; as the mourners parted, they pushed those in her door outwards. Caught in the pack, she drifted with it to the front of the building; she drifted slowly, allowing others to pass so she would fall to the back of the pack. Her nerves fluttered in her stomach again; she felt some duty to offer condolences, if that was what it should be, but probably something else, to the widow if she remained at the cemetery long enough. But she did not really want to see or speak to his former business partner. The motion of the crowd in front of her slowed; Lydia Kennedy had stopped in front of the tomb to accept greetings from those who had come to witness the burial.

"Hello, Lydia." Alyssa saw the redness of the tears in her eyes as she tousled the hair of the widow's children. Morisette and the woman were standing behind the two Lydias; she nodded to him. "You have my, um, sympathies. I think that's the right word."

"Thank you, dear. Thanks for coming." Lydia Kennedy laughed as her accent slipped back into the Manchester dialect of her youth. "Yes, sympathies will do. How are you?"

"I'm well. How are you? Do you need anything, help with anything?"

"I'm alright, we'll be alright. No, Lydia's helping me." Her voice was low as she turned to Lydia Price.

"Hello, Alyssa." Price's voice seemed stilted, she seemed unsure how to react to seeing her former employee.

"Hello, Lydia."

"We've got to go, Lydia." Price seemed anxious to leave. "Bye, Bill, Rebecca. Call me later."

"Bye, darling." Mrs. Kennedy shook Giordano's outstretched hand. "Thanks again for coming."

"That's alright, darling," Alyssa replied, smiling. "Let me know if you need anything."

"I will," the widow called over her shoulder as she headed across the lawn with her children and her husband's business partner.

*****

"Hi," the woman intoned to Alyssa, causing both her and Bill, holding the small wriggling child, to break the stare they had held for a quarter hour. They shook their heads and turned towards her. "Did I hear Lydia call you Alyssa?"

"Yes. I'm sorry; I don't know you, do I?"

"I'm Rebecca, Bill's wife." She tickled the boy's side. "This is our son, David." She grabbed Alyssa and hugged her with all her might. "I really must thank you."

"What for?" As she returned the woman's hug, Alyssa was stunned: at the idea that he was married for a second time, at the idea that he had a child. She didn't understand why the second Mrs. Morisette wanted to thank her. Rebecca pulled back from the embrace, but didn't let go of Alyssa.

"He's told me all about you. He said you made him see the light, gave him the impetus to get out of marriage to that frightening sociopath!"

"What?!" Mr. and Mrs. Morisette could see the horror on her face as she turned her head between them. He smiled wryly before laughing nervously.

"On, come on, Becky!" he exclaimed. "I never said that!"

"Well, alright," she jibed at him as she finally let go of the hug. "But I think you helped! You wouldn't have realized how unhappy you were with that bitch without her."

"Yes I would." Alyssa could see that he wasn't trying too hard to deny it.

"Oh, don't give me that!" She laughed at her husband. "You see, Alyssa, I know him too well." She turned back to her husband. "You told me all about Theona and Alyssa. You never would have gotten out. Here, give me Davey and give her a hug!" She had to pull the boy from his father's arms. "Come, on, darling. Give him to me." He finally released his son and put his arms around Alyssa as his wife hugged their child. She was nervous when she did the same, not knowing how she would react; the feeling of her first lover in her arms sent shivers down her spine.

"How are you?" he asked as he pulled back.

"I'm well. Surprised." The surprise was evident on her face. "How are you?"

"Well. Surprised at what?"

"You're married, you have a kid."

"You really shouldn't be surprised that I divorced Theona." They both laughed.

"No, not really surprised about that. But, marrying again! And a child! You being a pa surprises me."

"Yeah, that surprises me too. I did see you at the airport the other day, didn't I?"

"Yeah, I was visiting my sister in L.A. and I heard about the funeral. I wanted to make sure it was true." She paused. "You wanted to see it too?"

"Yes and no. Lydia asked me to come and Becky had to come back to the States for an appointment."

"You don't live here anymore?"

"No, we live in Bulgaria."

"Bulgaria! What the hell!" The shock on her face heightened again. He laughed.

"Yeah, Bulgaria."

"What are you doing there?"

"I'm an English teacher."

"Jeez! You are full of surprises today. How did that happen?"

"Well, after my marriage to Theona broke down, that frightening sociopath opened the door for me to escape from the legal profession and to take up my real vocation of being a slacker." It was her turn to laugh at him.

196

"Yeah, that sounds like you! How did you do it?"

"Yep, that's me. And I enjoy being a slacker! I never liked the law, not from day one and I haven't practiced since 1996. I never liked it, till the day I woke up and decided I was not going to work; I just phoned up Terry Garrick and told him I wouldn't be in."

"That's a shame, you not liking your chosen profession. What did you do? How did you two meet?"

"Yeah, I found being a teacher was something I loved. We met at the airport."

"Now, there's a story!" his wife chimed in. "We were both lost, and I didn't have a translation book and my beloved did when we ran into each other. After that, we stuck to each other like glue."

"Huh?" Alyssa was confused.

"I spent 1997 traveling Europe, came back and did a few short stints as a locum in 1998 and early 1999 for traveling money," Bill continued his wife's story, "and when I went back in March of 1999, Becky and I ran into each other at an information desk at some airport looking for a hotel. And we traveled through Europe, Romania, Macedonia, Iran, Lebanon, even Albania and spent a couple of years in the Middle East."

"The heat in Oman and Saudi was vile!" his wife spat. "That's why we ended up in Bulgaria."

"Oh, come on Beck, it wasn't that bad," he giggled at her. "The money was great, but we both hate the heat. But we loved Bulgaria, and we can appreciate the change of seasons, the cold desolation of winter and the baking hot summers."

"Bulgaria is so beautiful," Becky oozed. "It's late spring now, and the poppies are out in full bloom and the first cherries are appearing in the markets."

"Sounds wonderful." Alyssa smiled at the child and tickled him. She was pleased that Bill seemed to have found happiness. "What's this young man's name? David? How old is he, two?"

"Yep, David's two." Bill said. The three of them laughed as Alyssa caught a couple of slaps in the face from the toddler and stepped back to move her head out of his reach.

"He seems to like you! He never takes to anyone!" If her son could like her, Mrs. Morisette's opinion of her could only increase. "Wanna hold him?"

"Sure." Alyssa took the child from his mother and blew raspberries on his cheek.

"So, what have you been doing since you went back to Albany?" Bill asked as watched his former lover play with his child. "You still there? You married, got a boyfriend?" Bill asked.

"No, I'm in Manhattan now. I am seeing someone, but I'm not sure how serious it is."

"Oooh, tell us about him!" Mrs. Morisette exclaimed.

She told them of the dead end clerking jobs she had taken, how she met the man with a President's name, how she finally retook the Bar and moved to Manhattan.

"Andrew Jackson!" the Morisettes chimed together as they laughed.

"Yeah." She rolled her eyes and laughed. "Andrew Jackson."

"I'm happy you found your niche," Bill smiled at her.

"Yeah. Me too," Alyssa smiled back. "I'm hungry. Wanna get some dinner?"

The pair looked at each other.

"No, sorry, we can't." The disappointment on her face as Mrs. Morisette looked at her watch was obvious. "We've got to pack tonight."

"Oh, you're leaving tomorrow?" Disappointment crossed Ms. Giordano's face. Even in their brief encounter, she had taken to the second Mrs. Morisette as the second Mrs. Morisette had taken to her.

"We have time, don't we?" Mr. Morisette asked his wife. "What time to we have to be at the airport?"

"I don't think so, darling. We have to be at the check–in counter by five–thirty."

"We got plenty of time."

"Oh, don't be silly, Bill." Alyssa understood the demands of getting just herself to the airport, let alone a family with a rambunctious toddler. "That's too early for me, even without a baby. We can have dinner another time, next time you come back."

"Sure. That'd be great." Rebecca sounded a little disappointed as David started fidgeting and grabbing at her in Alyssa's arms. Bill just nodded, sadness passing across his face. "Oh come here baby doll," Rebecca whispered to her child as Alyssa handed him back to his mother.

"You'll let me know when you're coming back?"

"Sure," they both said, their sadness deepening.

Alyssa didn't understand the sorrow she sensed in them as they parted company; but it dawned on her as she entered her own car where she had seen the woman before and wondered why she had been there.

*****

The voice announcing dinner service and the lights being turned up in the main cabin startled the dying woman and she jerked upright, jostling her son, asleep on her lap, awake and he began to whine; the early start had drained both her and her son and neither were able to sleep easily in the uncomfortable position. The din had not woken her husband; she didn't want to wake him, his face was so serene and peaceful, the guilt seemingly dissipated. But she needed to get her son off her lap and she shook him.

"You alright, baby?" Mr. Morisette asked his wife as he ran his hands over his face.

"Just perfect, darling. Just perfect." She arched her back, the pain starting to echo from her awkward sleep in the seat of the plane. "Take David, will you?"

"Yes, you are perfect." He kissed her lips as he took his son onto his lap.

"I'm so glad I met her."

"I'm glad you met her too."

"She seems quite happy."

"Yes." He sighed. "Yes, she does. Things seem to have worked out for her."

"You feel better, don't you." A statement. No response. "You do feel better, don't you darling, knowing that?" A question, her voice softer.

"I don't understand."

"Yes, you do. You know what I mean." She let him consider his answer.

"Yes," he whispered, tears rolling down his face, the burden of his guilt lifting and pressing back down on him at the same time.

"I want you to see her after you take me home."

"But–"

"But nothing. I want you to promise me you'll see her after you take me home."

"I'll think about it."

She kissed his cheek, and left it at that, hoping he would honor her wish in death, as the plane taking them to their foreign home crossed into French airspace.

CHAPTER 29

FAIRNESS LEFT WITHOUT

"How was the funeral?" Peggy Cooper and Erik Johanssen articulated together as the outer office door opened; they did not care to say good morning yet, as whether or not it was depended on Alyssa Giordano's mood.

"Good." Giordano smiled and nodded. "As good as a funeral can be."

"Who was there?" Peggy asked, meaning specifically was *he* there.

"Hell of a lot of people I didn't know, but I said hello to his wife and kids. And all the old work people were there."

"Was he there?" Erik seemed like an eager little beaver wanting all the gossip.

"Yes, he was there. We spoke. Okay, what have we got on today?"

"Liam Xiang's here." Peggy looked at her watch "We're in Court at noon."

"Who?" Alyssa asked.

"Liam Xiang." Eric handed Alyssa a copy of the petition the City's Administration for Children's Services had filed with the Family Court. "The pro bono case, about the vaccinations."

"Oh, that case? Where are we at with it, Peggy?"

"It's the dispositional hearing today. Judge Kaye left the kids with the Xiangs, but she wants to hear testimony from the doctors again today."

"Noon? Want me to come with?"

"Sure, we were just about to head down to the Courthouse. Come meet Liam first," Peggy said as she led Alyssa into their joint office. "Liam, this is Alyssa Giordano, my partner."

"Hello Ms. Giordano," he uttered as he stuck his hand out.

"Mr. Xiang." She shook his hand. "Please, call me Alyssa. Do you mind if I come with you and Peggy today?"

"Liam," he sighed, relieved. "Please do! I could use all the support I can get right now!"

"Alright, let's go then!" Alyssa was excited to have something useful to do, to take her mind off the last few days.

"You're right, Alyssa. We better head out if we want to make it on time," Peggy said as she looked at her watch again.

*****

"Silence, all rise," the court security officer announced as the door between the courtroom and the Judicial Chambers opened. "The New York County Family Court is now in session, the Honorable Judge Judith Kaye presiding."

"Calling the matter of Xiang," the Court Clerk announced as the presiding Judge took her seat. They had been waiting in Judge Kaye's Courtroom for almost twenty minutes before she took her place.

"Thank you for waiting, ladies and gentlemen. The Chief Judge insisted I finish my caramel slice over lunch," Judge Kaye intoned. The attorneys sitting at the Bar table laughed, knowing her penchant for sweets. "Right, who do we have here today?" she laughed as she requested the attorneys to announce their appearances.

"Anastasia Specht for ACS, Your Honor."

"Peggy Cooper for the Xiang family, Your Honor."

"I also see Ms. Giordano here today," Kaye indicated.

"Your Honor, Ms. Cooper will be conducting the case today," Alyssa said. "I'm just observing."

"Ah, yes. Thank you Ms. Giordano. And you, sir?"

"Kenneth Campbell for St. Luke's–Roosevelt Hospital, Your Honor."

"Kenneth Campbell?" the Judge enquired.

"My middle name is John, Your Honor. I'm neither delinquent nor deceased," said the man with the name similar to two others who had been admitted to the New York Bar. The room erupted with laughter.

"Yes, alright," Judge Kaye said after she had stopped giggling. "Where are we up to with this case? Ms. Specht?"

"Your Honor, this is a continuance of a case ACS brought against Mr. and Mrs. Xiang. Your Honor made an order last Thursday requiring Mr. and Mrs. Xiang to immunize their son Jimmy against hepatitis B. I had also applied on behalf of ACS for ACS to take over responsibility, wardship, for the both the Xiang children, which Your Honor granted. And Your Honor wanted to hear more medical evidence today."

"Just a moment, Ms. Specht. I see Angela Ryan in the back of the Court. Ms. Ryan, what are you here for?" Giordano turned to see the veteran reporter and they smiled at each other.

"Yes, Your Honor, I'm here to report on this case."

"Does anyone have any objections?" Specht and Campbell shook their heads whilst Cooper and Giordano conferred briefly with their client, then with each other and with Mr. Xiang again.

"My client has no objections," Cooper said.

"Okay, Ms. Specht, go on."

"Yes, thank you, Your Honor. As I was about to say, Mrs. Xiang has hepatitis B and gave birth to the couple's son, Jimmy, not long ago at St. Luke's–Roosevelt Hospital. The Xiangs were offered the hepatitis B vaccine but refused it and have not reported back to ACS after Mrs. Xiang was discharged from the hospital."

"Yes," the supervising Judge of the Manhattan Family Court interrupted. "I remember now. They have a second child, don't they? Is Mrs. Xiang here today?"

"Mr. and Mrs. Xiang have two sons, Your Honor," Cooper was on her feet quickly. "Mrs. Xiang isn't here today, but Mr. Xiang is. You were going to hear from the doctors from the Hospital today and didn't require Mrs. Xiang to be here with the children."

"Thank you, Ms. Cooper. Are the children in the custody of ACS?"

"No, Your Honor," the ACS attorney answered.

"Thank you, Ms. Specht. Now Mr. Xiang, do you understand what's happening here today?" The Judge liked to be informal with parents appearing in her Courtroom and often liked to address them personally.

"Yes, I think so. Peggy, I mean Ms. Cooper, explained it to me."

"Okay, Mr. Xiang. I just want to make sure you understand," the Judge started to launch into her usual sermon on the workings of her Courtroom. "I'll just explain it for the record. When it appears that a child under eighteen has been abused or neglected, the Administration for Children's Services may file a petition asking the Family Court to assist in protecting the child. The court then holds hearings to decide if what ACS says is true and what action the court should take to protect the child. Now this is just a dispositional hearing to find out some more facts from the doctors. Okay? Do you understand?"

"Yes, ma'am, I understand." Liam Xiang felt like rolling his eyes, he was not stupid, but was able to keep himself from doing so.

"Right, Mr. Xiang, good. Okay, Mr. Campbell. I think it might be time to call your witnesses."

"Thank you, Your Honor. I call David Shapirov." An aging man stood in the gallery.

"David Shapirov?" the Court clerk called.

"Yes, that's me," the standing man answered and he approached the witness box and the court clerk duly sworn.

"Yes, thank you Bruce," Judge Kaye said to her clerk. "Mr. Campbell?"

"Yes, thank Your Honor. You are David Shapirov?"

"Yes."

"You hold a Bachelor of Science and a Doctor of Medicine?"

"Yes."

"You hold a number of other post–graduate degrees in infectious diseases?"

"Yes."

"What is your current position?"

"I'm a professor in pediatric infectious diseases at St. Luke's–Roosevelt Hospital."

"Do you know Mr. and Mrs. Xiang and baby Jimmy?"

"Yes. Mrs. Xiang gave birth to Jimmy at St. Luke's. Mrs. Xiang's obstetrician called me after she'd given birth and asked me to speak with her."

"Why?"

"Well, Mrs. Xiang has hepatitis B and her obstetrician wanted me to discuss his parents the risks of not having Jimmy vaccinated.

The initial vaccine has to be given within twelve hours of birth for effectiveness."

"Did they agree to have Jimmy vaccinated?"

"No, and that's why I contacted ACS. It angered me and the other staff at the hospital."

"What did?"

"Well, the baby's rights were being ignored."

"So what are the risks?"

"A baby born to a mother with hepatitis B has a five to forty percent chance of contracting hepatitis B from its mother and about thirty per cent of people with hepatitis B will develop cancer or cirrhosis and die young."

"So being vaccinated will prevent Jimmy contracting the disease?"

"No, not completely, but it will reduce the chances of him contracting it to a very small percentage. Look, I'm a strong believer in vaccinations being voluntary but not getting this baby vaccinated is a form of child abuse," he said. "We are talking a potentially major and awful outcome for this child and it is our job to protect children when they can't make decisions for themselves. I don't understand why these people are willing to sacrifice their child for a warped idea when the benefits far outweigh the risks."

"So the benefits outweigh the risks?"

"Yes."

"Thank you, Professor. I have nothing further for this witness, Your Honor." And he sat.

"Yes," Judge Kaye said. "Thank you Mr. Campbell. Ms. Specht?"

"I have nothing for this witness, thank you Your Honor."

"Thank you Ms. Specht. Ms. Cooper?"

"Yes, thank Your Honor. Professor, so you've met baby Jimmy."

"Yes."

"You know he has an older brother?"

"Yes, Michael should be vaccinated too."

"Why?"

"Again, for the same reasons Jimmy should be vaccinated."

"So, if Mrs. Xiang gave birth to Michael after she contracted hepatitis B, he should have been vaccinated within twelve hours and then had a course of vaccinations over a number of months?"

"Yes. The first dose should be administered within twelve hours of birth and then it's administered in four doses of the vaccine over six months."

"Does the weight of the baby affect the amount of the vaccine you give him or her?"

"I'm not sure what you mean."

"Do you give the same amount of the vaccine to a baby weighing, say five and a half pounds as you'd give to a baby who weighed, say ten pounds?"

"Oh, I see. Yes."

"So you give the same amount of vaccine to all babies?"

"Yes."

"So it's a one-size-fits-all policy?"

"I don't agree with that."

"Does the vaccine contain aluminum?"

"Yes."

"How easily can an adult break down aluminum?"

"If a baby gets hepatitis B at birth he or she will become a chronic carrier of the virus," the doctor said. "And about a third of those chronic carriers will die young from cancer of the liver or cirrhosis of the liver. This is a horrible disease, and the child's rights were being ignored," he said. "It's policy, state health policy mandates that parents of all babies born to hepatitis B-positive mothers must that be offered immunoglobulin for the child."

"Could the aluminum in the vaccine cause the baby more damage than contracting hepatitis B?"

"Look, if you do not immunize a baby in this situation, you're putting that baby's life at risk."

"Don't even bother, Ms. Cooper," the Judge interjected as Peggy looked at her. "Look, Doctor, just answer Ms. Cooper's question. Could the aluminum in the vaccine cause the baby more damage than contracting hepatitis B?"

"Well, in some cases," Shapirov started.

"Don't give me in some cases." Judge Kaye's frustration at the non–answers was becoming evident in her tone. "Yes or no, could the aluminum cause more damage than contracting hepatitis B?"

The pediatric specialist sighed, knowing that the answer would hurt. "Yes, but that only happens in a small percentage of cases, say five to ten per–cent."

"Thank you Doctor. Any more questions, Ms. Cooper?"

"Yes, thank Your Honor," Peggy sighed. "So what's the risk of the baby contracting hepatitis B again?"

"Five to forty percent. And the first stages of vaccine needed to be administered by tomorrow for it to be ninety–two percent effective."

"So, there's a sixty to ninety–five percent chance that a baby won't contract hepatitis B without the vaccine? And the vaccine is not one hundred percent effective?"

"I suppose you could put it that way."

"Do you know if Michael's been tested for hepatitis B?"

"No."

"If I were to tell you that he has been tested," Cooper stopped mid–sentence to hear the other attorneys objecting.

"What are your objections, Ms. Specht?" the Judge asked.

"Foundation."

"Mr. Campbell?"

"The same," he answered the Judge.

"Ms. Cooper?"

"I have medical records, Your Honor."

"Subject to connection, Ms. Cooper."

"I tender a copy of Mrs. Xiang's medical records, Michael's birth certificate and a copy of his test results. I have copies for my colleagues," she said as she handed copies to the court clerk and the other attorneys.

"Overruled," the judge ruled on the objections.

"Thank Your Honor. Professor," Cooper started her question again, "if I were to tell you that Michael was born after Mrs. Xiang contracted hepatitis B, that he has been tested and that he has tested negative, what would you say to that?"

"I'd say he was very lucky."

"Okay, thank you Professor. I have nothing further for this witness, Your Honor."

"Thank you, Professor. You may step down. Thank you Ms. Cooper." She paused for a moment. "Do any of you have any submissions?" The three attorneys each stood spoke over each other at the time, the racket causing Judge Kaye to raise her hand to quiet them.

"Alright, alright. I think I got all that!" The attorneys laughed, Mr. Xiang was confused. "So you, Ms. Specht want the children to be placed in the care of ACS. You, Mr. Campbell, want the child Jimmy vaccinated immediately. And you, Ms. Cooper and Ms. Giordano, want the children to be left in the care of their parents and for them to be able to go home and sleep in their own beds." The attorneys all nodded in unison. "Well, none of you will be satisfied, but I will do what is in the best interests of the children for the moment. I'll discharge the orders I made previously for the children to be remanded to ACS and that they be vaccinated. I order that the children be remanded to the care of their parents, but I'll order that they be tested for hepatitis B. Can that be done by next week, Mr. Campbell?"

"Yes, Your Honor. But–" the hospital attorney said.

"But, Your Honor," the ACS attorney started.

"But I don't understand," Mr. Xiang almost screamed as his attorneys pulled him back into his seat.

"No, no, no, Ms. Specht and Mr. Campbell, no vaccination yet. Now, Mr. Xiang, I did say that none of you will be satisfied. What this means is that your children will remain in your care and you and your wife can return to your home without the fear of ACS taking your children into foster care."

"Okay," Liam said, still confused. "So my wife and kids can come home?"

"Where are they now?"

"Um, they're in Albany."

"Yes, they can come home," the Judge smiled. "They can sleep in their own beds tonight. But I want you to just get your children tested to see if they have hepatitis B. Just tested, mind you, not vaccinated yet." Kaye continued. "It will help me make my decision. Do you understand?" Alyssa whispered in his ear for a few moments and he nodded at every statement.

"Yes, Your Honor," the naturalized American said, a look of comprehension dawning on his face. "Yes, I understand." He smiled and collapsed back into his seat.

"Alright then. Off you all go. I will go off the Bench to consider my decision. My clerk will let you know when I'm ready to deliver my judgment."

The wait until his wife and babies came home would be agonizing for Mr. Xiang.

CHAPTER 30

BODIES REPAIRED;
MINDS REPAIRING

The unidentified man was still unidentified, not remembering yet who he was, as he began recuperating in the rehabilitation center attached to the Kings County Hospital Center some three months later. Seated at a table in the recreation room, he was surrounded by young nurses, girls really. Despite his injuries, he was in a flirtatious mood. Off in the corner some classical music played tenuously on the stereo.

The man watched as a young woman massaged his right hand. His still swollen eyes grew wide. He looked at her, looked at the veteran reporter. The reporter was following up on the unidentified man after the slaying of Officer Ben Walker some months earlier. He looked at the eight and a half by eleven sheet of paper in front of him – the one with all the alphabet letters laid out like a keyboard; the one in the black loose–leaf binder that had become his constant companion –– and shook his hand loose. He began to move his index finger fast and furious across the page, pointing at letters.

"N–O E–N–G–A–G–E–M–E–N–T R–I–N–G?"

"No, no engagement ring," Angela Ryan smiled nervously at him as Ray Jensen snickered from behind the camera. Despite his facial injuries, there was something about him which she recognized. Jensen saw it too.

With the man's permission, Angela Ryan had reviewed his medical records before arriving at the Rehabilitation Center to interview him. He had spent twenty days in the Hospital, ten of them in the Intensive Care Unit before being transferred to the Rehabilitation Center. But his basic itinerary could not truly indicate what he had lived through. The brain injuries caused a severe high tone condition; his muscles were shortened and locked as if in a state of constant, severe cramp. They twisted his aging body into absurd, even grotesque, angles. A weakened diaphragm, stressed vocal chords and tightened facial muscles make it almost impossible for him to talk. He had been receiving Botox injections to deaden nerves in his extremities. There was also Valium to control muscle spasms, Lidocaine patches to ease pain in his wrists, Pepcid for stomach uneasiness and Allegra for allergies.

He had undergone numerous cranial surgeries to stop further hemorrhaging in the brain, numerous facial surgeries to repair the damage to his face. He had also undergone physical therapy to strengthen muscles and balance so he might one day walk again, speech therapy to strengthen his diaphragm so he might one day talk again and occupational therapy so some day he might be able to function on his own: bathe, dress and feed himself without supervision. He had made significant progress since the accident and could now lift a glass by hooking the rim with his crooked index finger. But even the most basic chores were an ordeal and the future remained uncertain. For now, he was traveling in a wheelchair.

"What made him up before the accident, whomever he is, was his personality and independence and when you take that away you take away a lot of who he was," one of his physical therapists had said during a discussion with Ryan. "That is why we are working so hard on trying to get that back."

Already, the hospitalizations, medicines and tests had cost more than half a million dollars. As he was still yet unidentified, insurance from the accident covered only a small portion of the bills and, although some further expenses would be covered by Medicaid, that would not cover all his in–patient care. The Rehabilitation Center had instead resorted to fund–raising to help pay the monstrous bills. Angela Ryan had reviewed some of the pictures taken not long after his accident, which police had tried to use to identify him.

"Why do they upset you?" Ryan enquired.

"I G–E–T F–R–U–S–T–R–A–T–E–D   W–I–T–H M–Y–S–E–L–F," he indicated. "G–E–T A–N–G–R–Y A–B–O–U–T W–H–A–T H–A–P–P–E–N–E–D."

He went on to say he just wanted others to learn from the mistakes. That he hoped they will drive safer, that they would not speed. Because for him every day, every moment, was now a struggle.

"Do you miss the things you used to take for granted?"

"Y–E–S," he messaged.

"Like what?"

"R–E–C–O–G–N–I–Z–I–N–G M–Y–S–E–L–F. K–N–O–W–I–N–G W–H–O I A–M." There was drool dripping from his mouth, onto his shirt. On his cheek, there was a tear. A therapist saw it and silently motioned to Ryan that her time was up, she should really leave.

"Do your doctors think you'll recover your memory?"

"T–H–E–Y D–O–N–T K–N–O–W Y–E–T. B–U–T P–O–S–S–I–B–L–E." It was a struggle, but he went on to say that the specialists had told him that they did not know enough about brain injuries, about the brain itself, to be able to tell him whether he would recover his memory. As the unknown man began to cough on the tube in his throat, the therapist repeated her silent plea for Ryan to wrap up the meeting and leave.

"Well, I think that's enough for today," Ryan said to the man in the wheelchair, acknowledging the therapist's second plea to leave with a nod. "Thanks so much for the interview."

"N–O. T–H–A–N–K Y–O–U."

"Would you mind if I came back again? When you're up to it?"

"N–O–T A–T A–L–L. P–L–E–A–S–E C–O–M–E B–A–C–K S–O–O–N. L–I–K–E P–R–E–T–T–Y W–O–M–E–N." Ryan and Jensen laughed at that.

"Okay, I'll come back soon! Thanks again."

Angela Ryan and Ray Jensen packed. He waved them off and they left the rehabilitation center and loaded the equipment in their vehicle. They sat quietly for a few minutes silently after climbing in.

"You saw it, Ray?"

"Yeah, saw something Ange, but I don't know what."

"Thank the gods I'm not going crazy."

"But what did we see?"

"We know him. He looks different but we know him."

"Whadaya mean, he looks different but we know him?"

"The metal cage around his head, his face is thinner, all wrong, smashed out of place. But I think I've seen him before."

"Where? When?"

"I don't know yet. That's what we have to find out."

"You got a better eye for faces than me, Ange." Angela Ryan just laughed as her cinematographer, shaking his head, started the car and headed back to the studio.

"Fuck, Ray! I wish I could work out where I know him from!"

"You'll remember, babe."

"Yeah, I hope it's soon. It's going to bug me until I do." Angela Ryan did not yet know how long it would take for her to remember the face, to discover the time difference between the recovery time for the man's brain and the recovery time for his body.

CHAPTER 31

ECCENTRICITIES OF DESTINY

Johannsen tightened his lips in frustration as the girl dropped the envelope on the desk in front of him. What the hell... demanding overbearing vixen... still, it might be the only way to get rid of her short of calling security. With a curt nod, he rose from his desk and, aware of the woman's silent scrutiny, crossed the room and tapped at the door to the inner office.

Alyssa Giordano was on the telephone, chatting in her familiar quick fire fashion. She glanced up with a probing frown as her aide passed the envelope across the cluttered desk and signaled towards the reception area. Still speaking, Alyssa cradled the receiver between her shoulder and ear. Her thick brown hair fell before her green eyes as she carefully tore open the envelope. A split second later, her eyes grew wide in astonishment and she stopped mid–sentence. The blood froze in her veins as she looked at the hand–written pages. *It was impossible... totally impossible...*

Alyssa couldn't believe the name she saw at the bottom of the last hand–written page. Lydia Kennedy – it was totally impossible; but maybe it wasn't.

"Sorry, what? I was interrupted; my aide brought me a note. Look, I'll have to deal with this and get back to you," Alyssa mumbled. As she listened to the sycophant prattle on the other end, she regained her equanimity as her blood warmed back up.

"No," Alyssa retorted back harshly, "the hearing is months away and the discovery doesn't have to be completed for months. My clients will not be forced to concede anything yet. I'll get back to you."

As she terminated the call and flipped back to the first page, Alyssa punched the intercom. "Eric, tell Mrs. Kennedy I'll be out in a minute."

"Yes, of course, Ms. Giordano," he replied. A minute turned into ten, then into fifteen, then into thirty.

*****

Alyssa carefully read and re–read the carefully crafted epistle; it was a plea for help from a woman who thought her conniving husband was dead, and whose funeral she herself had attended.

Duncan Kennedy was alive, but that revelation did not surprise her. What troubled Alyssa the most was his contact with his second wife and the "deal" he proposed for her to keep her children. It was just another of the scammer's "wonderful" schemes to extort every last penny and destroy one's self–esteem: either she let him move back in with her or he would drag her through the New York justice system to take her children, and the money which was now hers, from her.

I can't let that happen! She could do nothing less than return the favor and help the woman who had been so kind to her all those years earlier. She took another lungful of air and stood from her chair and turned to the bay of windows facing New York Harbor and stared at the Statue of Liberty for an instant. As she turned towards the door, she contemplated upon the first time she'd met the second Mrs. Kennedy and smiled imperceptibly.

Alyssa Giordano would give her friend nothing but her full attention. "Lydia," Alyssa called. "I'm so sorry to keep you waiting."

"Oh, Lyssie," Lydia sobbed in her Manchester accent, as her eyes welled with tears. "That's okay. I'm sure it's just as much of a shock for you as it was for me!"

"Shock?" Alyssa sighed. "That's an understatement!" As she looked her up and down, Alyssa could see that Lydia Kennedy's face confirmed the suffering she had been through in the last couple of days. The two women embraced and as they did, Erik wondered what could have been so important to have interrupted Ms. Giordano from putting that creepy lawyer she'd been on the phone with in his place. "Come into my office and you can tell me all about it. Would you like a drink?"

214

"I think I need coffee; I really haven't been sleeping all that well."

"I think I need a coffee too." Alyssa, turning to Erik on the way back to the internal door, and he nodding in understanding, led Lydia to the couches at the far end of the office. "Take a seat." They sat next to each other. "Could you tell me what happened?"

"You read my note?" Lydia thought she had been clear enough.

"Yes, but I'm not quite sure I understand what happened." Alyssa had understood what the note contained, but what she really wanted to see for herself was the effect that recounting the tale would have on Lydia. "I know he disappeared before he was declared dead in that accident. Could you tell me what happened from then, from the day he disappeared?"

"He was controlling," Lydia dropped her head as she sighed, "a very controlling man just before he left."

"Hmmm, yes. I sensed that. He tried to control me as well." Alyssa paused, seeing the tears welling in Lydia's eyes. "He beat you, didn't he?"

"Yes," Lydia sobbed. "But he wasn't always like that. He was very debonair when we first met. He really knew how to turn on the charm."

"Did he ever hurt your kids?"

"No, no, he never touched the children. I would've killed him if he'd tried!" She pulled a handkerchief from her purse and patted her eyes. "How did you know?"

"Most women I know aren't as accident prone as you were then." She shook her head. "I wish I'd known what to do. When did it start? How?"

"It was just verbal at first, after it became just Lydia and him in the practice. He lost a lot of money from that." Alyssa just nodded. "You remember Bill Morisette? He left the same time you did."

"Yes, I remember him." Alyssa smiled wanly as she saw Lydia relax a little.

"Things started going downhill for them again about a year before he left, well when both of you left really." Lydia seemed to relax a little more, relieved to be able to get the weight off her mind. "He was just so lazy, just wanting to sponge off everyone who worked for him. He started taking money out of the business and he ran up big debts all over town. That's when the authorities came after him. The IRS came after him as well."

215

"Ah," Alyssa nodded, things falling into place in her mind. "When did that happen? About a year after we left?"

"Yes," Lydia's eyes squinted as her mind churned to remember the date, "that sounds about right. No, wait. A couple of IRS agents turned up on our doorstep before that and it took them a couple of months to tear through our house. They ripped through everything."

"So what happened? When he left?"

"He left for Court one day, well I thought he left for Court, and just never came back."

"That was in 1998, the middle of 1998, right?" Alyssa vividly remembered the day when the trial, when the jury voir dire, was supposed to start

"Yes, that sounds right. He was gone, out of my life, out of our children's lives; I thought I was free. He was quite pleasant that morning. That surprised me." She paused momentarily, reflecting on the strangeness of her husband's attitude that morning. "He got ready for work kissed me and the children and walked out the door. Lydia called me ranting that he didn't turn up to Court."

"Bet that was pleasant!" Alyssa chortled.

"Yes," Lydia rolled her eyes. "Real pleasant! That bitch is a real piece of work!"

"Yeah, I know. So what did you do?"

"Nothing at first. I was just so glad he was gone! The houses were in my name, so I just sold up the Montauk beach house and got a job when the money I'd put away started to dry up."

"You didn't go to the police straight away?"

"No. I didn't care about that. I was just so happy to have gotten away from him." She smiled at the thought. "Lydia told me I should and she begged me for a while to do it. I didn't care so she went herself. Then one day, she dragged me to the police to report him missing, get them to try to find him."

"Why?" Alyssa had seen followed Angela Ryan's broadcasts about the case at the time, but the news reports did not, could not, have the detail behind the other Lydia's attitude. "They would have already been looking for him."

"She said that they wouldn't do it on her say so, she was only his business partner. They needed the "next of kin" to do it and it was the only way to get what was left of our assets put in my name, to get a payout on his life insurance. She said it was the only her to clean up what was left of the business!"

"The police obviously didn't find him."

"Nope. He just went "poof". I would have been happy to have just left it; I didn't care about the insurance, or the business for that matter. Then that fucking bitch dragged me through Court to get him declared dead." The woman's anger grew, as she thought of Price's dictatorial stubbornness and the ignominy she suffered as a result. "She said needed more money than I did to clean up the mess he'd left her. Then the insurance company appealed!"

"I don't remember the Court of Appeal ever ruling on that. It must have been easy when everyone thought he'd been killed." Alyssa saw Lydia's anger dissipate and her spirits lift at the thought of his death.

"Oh, it was so easy! He was dead, that was all there was too it. But it took another six months to go through Probate."

"You weren't asked to identify him?"

"Well, they didn't ask me to look at him at the morgue. They wouldn't let me. They told me his body was in pieces and his face was badly damaged and the police said that it was him from his wallet. I had no idea that wasn't him!" Lydia sighed. "And the funeral home wouldn't let me have an open casket. You were at the funeral, Alyssa. If it'd been open, someone else might have seen it wasn't him."

"Yes, I remember the casket was closed." It was Alyssa's turn to sigh: she remembered the news reports, that the multiple accident scenes were strewn with multiple bodies and multiple automobile parts, and there were cars burning. *The hospital, that's where they must have they mixed up the wallets!*

"Why couldn't these people do a proper identification? None of this would have happened if they had just done an autopsy!"

"I know, Lydia. Mistakes happen," Alyssa sympathized. "Do you know why he waited so long to contact you?"

"Well, he says it took him that long to remember who he really was! Because of brain damage, because of the head injury he suffered. But I don't believe him." Lydia's breathing started to heave as she barely held her emotions in check. Alyssa handed Lydia another tissue as the tears welled in the non–widow's eyes again.

"Well, it could be true, it could be a lie. Head injuries are funny things." Alyssa paused as Lydia calmed herself ever so slightly. "When did he turn up?"

"A couple of days ago."

"So let me get this straight: he wants money, or he drags you to Court to take your kids away from you."

Lydia nodded as she burst into tears. The now hardened lawyer was more than appalled at the man's impropriety: it offended her and wounded her sense of justice that he would even consider such an obscenity. At least she could now return the favor Lydia had done for her. *Fuck!* Alyssa cursed as she put her arms around the bawling woman in what she hoped was some small measure of comfort. *How do I fix this?*

As her tears subsided, the former Ms. Tobin jumped, startled by the office door opening behind her.

*****

It had taken the sobbing woman almost an hour to vent her tears, when the office door opened.

"I'm so sorry Alyssa," Cooper started. "I didn't know you had someone with you." She began to leave the room.

"No, no, Peggy," Alyssa motioned for her not to leave. "Lydia, this is my partner, Peggy Cooper and she's way better at this sort of litigation than me. We share this office." Giordano's partner shook the older woman's hand. "Peggy, this is Lydia Kennedy."

"Oooohh!" Peggy started to make the connection of this woman to her partner's past. "So you were married to Duncan Kennedy?" Alyssa just smiled at Peggy's confirmation of her own thoughts.

"Yes," Lydia answered.

"Read this," Alyssa said as she handed over the letter.

"So how did this happen?" Peggy asked.

"How did what happen?" Lydia was confused.

"How did it end up that Duncan wasn't really dead?" Peggy clarified.

"Oh, okay. You remember that car chase in Brooklyn a couple of years ago? The one where the policeman was shot and the bus overturned on the Brooklyn Bridge. He got hit by a car that caught on fire." The attorney nodded. "Well, they mixed up the driver's licenses at the Hospital and the Medical Examiner just declared Duncan dead based on who the Hospital said he was."

"But let's not worry about that now. He's back and he wants the money." Alyssa recounted the details Lydia had just given her for her partner.

"I didn't know what else to do, who else to turn to," Lydia uttered after Alyssa had finished passing on the details for her. "I didn't want to go to Lydia, spiteful bitch."

"Of course you wouldn't want her sticky fingers on it!" Alyssa agreed.

"Fucking bastard!" Peggy extolled. "Alyssa told me he was an asshole, but I didn't realize he was *this* much of an asshole! Don't worry, we'll fix it." Peggy intoned, drawing her coffee to her lips in one hand while she lifted the note in the other.

"So, let's get things set up. Let's get Erik to get the paperwork started," Alyssa agreed. The attorneys started towards the door to get her very modern model of a modern secretary working.

"What?! I don't understand!" As Lydia twisted on the couch to look back at Alyssa clutching the door handle, coffee spilt all over her, the suede cushions and she jumped up. Alyssa couldn't conceal the laugh; which set Lydia off laughing as well, so much so that more coffee spilt on her shoes and the rug under them.

"Don't worry, Erik knows who to call to get those stains out." Alyssa said, still chuckling. "Look, here's how I see it. He died, well we thought he died, you got his money and you got on with your life thinking he was dead. You don't need that entire red tape nightmare he'd put you trying to pick up your relationship where it left off or trying to get all your money out of you by claiming you're still married now that he's not dead."

"But we are still married, aren't we? And it's not my money, really, it's his."

"Do you want to be married to him? Do you want to give him any money?" Peggy asked.

"No way in hell! On either count!"

"Okay, then. What we need to do is get to Court as soon as possible and get a declaration that the marriage is over because he was declared dead." Peggy turned to Alyssa. "Aren't we back before Family Court tomorrow? Our pro bono case?" Alyssa looked at her diary.

"Shit, yes! Tomorrow, two in the afternoon. You reckon we can get an urgent motion on this before Judge Kaye for the same time?"

"You bet your ass, baby!"

Lydia shook her head at the two attorneys laughing at each other as Peggy walked out to the reception desk to put Erik Johannsen to work.

"Now look," Alyssa turned back to Lydia, "the Court will probably say you'll have to give him some money, and we'll need to get some research done on that, but we'll argue that you shouldn't have to give him one red cent because of what he did."

"Thank you! I can live with that! Thank you really isn't enough, but thank you!" Lydia's eyes welled with tears again as the two friends embraced again.

"Isn't it amazing how things just turn out?" Alyssa smiled as she pulled back from the hug to look at Lydia. Lydia just smiled back.

Chapter 32

Onward and Upward

It was the first time since law school, more than fifteen years ago, since the two women had "pulled an all–nighter". They had had late nights since their partnership began, but never like this; they had specifically agreed when they started their law office that it was to be avoided at all costs except for the most dire of emergencies.

But now they had the emergency, to prepare yet another motion to go before the supervising Judge of the Family Court building down the road at the same time as their child–protective proceeding. To avoid duplication of trips to the Courthouse would be worth the effort. The internal buzzing of the telephone startled them both from sleep; Alyssa Giordano's hand reached the receiver first.

"Yes, Erik?" A pause. "All of them?" More listening. "Okay, let them know we'll be out in a moment."

"They're here?" Peggy Cooper yawned.

"Yep." Alyssa also yawned.

"All of them?"

"Yep."

"We done?"

"Yep."

"How long we got?"

Alyssa checked her watch. "Oh, 'bout an hour."

"Which one do you want?"

"Liam's up first, right?"

"Yep. I'm ready on that."

"And I'm ready with Lydia. You wanna take it that way?"

"Yep. How you wanna 'splain it to 'em?"

"Like it is."

"Right. Let's go."

"Right. Let's go."

They exited their office. Peggy took the Xiang family in her charge, and Alyssa took Lydia in hers, as they obtained separate taxi–cabs to go from their offices on Broadway to Lafayette Street in lower Manhattan, between Franklin and Leonard Streets, to the New York County Family Court.

*****

Judge Kaye was on time to deliver her decision; she did not want to keep the cameras waiting. Angela Ryan, in particular, had an early deadline today.

"Quiet please," she said as she banged her gavel. "Quiet please." She waited for the din in the courtroom to calm down. "As I was saying, ACS originally applied to take over responsibility for the baby boy and his brother after Mr. and Mrs. Xiang refused to have him vaccinated. I originally granted ACS wardship and that Jimmy be vaccinated. They also applied for a lesser order that Mr. and Mrs. Xiang present their children for medical assessment to encourage them to come forward.

"Mr. and Mrs. Xiang were represented by Giordano Cooper, who advised them, quite correctly, to get their children tested, which they did. Michael was tested for hepatitis B and he does not have it. Jimmy has now also been tested and he does not have it.

"Professor Shapirov said he is a strong believer in vaccinations being voluntary but not getting this baby vaccinated in this case was a form of child abuse. He also said that there was the potential for a major and awful outcome for this child and he saw it as a part of his job to protect children when they can't make decisions for themselves. While I accept Professor Shapirov's evidence that there is scientific evidence to prove that vaccination can be beneficial in preventing a baby born to a mother with hepatitis B from contracting it, the scientific evidence in this case is that it would *not* be beneficial.

"I too am a believer in vaccinations being voluntary but I disagree with Professor Shapirov that this case is a form of child abuse. In this case, the potential awful outcome did not occur. From the legal point of view, given that the first dosage of the hepatitis B vaccine must be administered within a week of birth, it is not justified to pursue it in an active legal sense after that week has passed. And ACS has decided not to pursue further action against Mr. and Mrs. Xiang for refusing to vaccinate their baby.

"In this case, it is *not* a form of child abuse not to get the child vaccinated. But I am not saying that this will be the case, that not getting a baby vaccinated against any number of other childhood diseases is not a form of child abuse, in every case. I am sure that there would be cases, certain diseases, where it *would* be a form of child abuse not to get a child vaccinated. There are so many diseases that have been wiped out by vaccination. Every case must be decided on the facts of the case if and when it comes before the Courts. I am not going to order Mr. and Mrs. Xiang to vaccinate either of their children against hepatitis B and it is not appropriate to take punitive action against the Xiangs.

"I therefore discharge the wardship order and ACS will no longer have parental responsibility for the Xiang children. I also discharge the order that Jimmy be vaccinated. I also dismiss the summons to have the Xiang children medically treated. I also release the children into their parents' care. I will ask the attorneys whether they want any further orders."

"No Your Honor, ACS does not seek any further orders."

"Thank you, Ms. Specht. Mr. Campbell?"

"Not for the Hospital, Your Honor."

"Thank you, sir. Ms. Cooper?"

"On the question of costs, Your Honor."

"Yes, yes of course, Ms. Cooper. The Xiangs' will have their costs paid."

"But—" Anastasia Specht started.

"No buts, Ms. Specht."

"Yes, Your Honor."

"Thank you. The parties in the matter of Xiang are excused. Bruce, call the next case as soon as the courtroom clears, please," she directed her clerk as Peggy escorted her ecstatic clients out of the courtroom. The ACS and Hospital attorneys followed them, as did the majority of the journalists who packed the gallery. But two journalists remained, seemingly not interested in taking shots of the Liam and Kylie Xiang hugging each other, then their children, or the statement made by ACS and St. Luke's–Roosevelt Hospital that while this case was highly individualized all parents should still vaccinate their children; they were more interested in the news that would arise from the case that they had heard would be determined next.

"Next case, Bruce," her Honor intoned as the commotion in the courtroom quieted.

"Next case," Bruce started. "Kennedy. All parties in the matter of Kennedy."

"Yes," Alyssa Giordano started. "I am conducting that case."

"Ah yes," the Judge replied, with a wink. "I remember this originally went all the way to the nine wise men in Washington D.C., Ms. Giordano."

"Yes it did, Your Honor."

"Is your client here? Is Mrs. Kennedy here?"

"Yes my client's here, but she would prefer to be called by her maiden name, Tobin, Your Honor."

"Of course, Ms. Giordano. Mr. Kennedy?"

"No, Your Honor. This is an ex parte motion. I, well my client and I are looking for an annulment of the marriage, but my client's primary concern is for some urgent interim orders regarding custody."

"Yes, well, we can deal with temporary custody and the other injunction on an ex parte basis. But there'll need to be a full hearing on the annulment issue and on final custody orders. You'll need to serve the papers. Your client understands all that?"

"Yes, Your Honor. I've explained it to her and she's cognizant of what needs to occur to enable her to obtain final orders."

"Yes, well I've read the papers. Let's proceed."

*****

Alyssa Giordano saw that the veteran reporter and her director/cameraman had already left the Courtroom by the time she had finished packing her briefcase. Damn!

"Alright Lydia," she started with the woman standing next to her. "Let's get back to my office and get these papers served."

"Whew!" Lydia Tobin sighed. "That was quick. I just don't know how to thank you," she said as they headed to the courtroom doors. Alyssa pulled the door open and let her out first.

"Well, no need to thank me just yet," she replied as they started down the hall towards the building's main entrance. "This is just the beginning. We've only got you an interim custody order for the kids and the injunction to stop him from moving into your house. We've still got a ways to go."

"But it's a start. It's a relief. At least I'm not married to him again now he's not dead! I just wish he didn't have to see my babies. Bastard!"

"Well, I know. He's a real big bastard! He's been away and they don't know him. But they have the right to know their father. But we can convince the Judge to keep the visitation limited, and supervised, while they figure out who he is again. And the U.S. Supreme Court has already ruled on that, and the State Courts can't change that. But we may have to give him something, just to get him to shut up."

Lydia knew that when Alyssa said "we" she meant "you". This time she pulled the main door open for Alyssa. "So what do we do now?"

"That was some fancy footwork in there, Ms. Giordano," Alyssa heard and jumped, startled, as she and her client reached the top of the courthouse steps.

"Thank you, Ms. Ryan," she replied to the journalist. Lydia stood back, surprised that the two women knew each other. "I thought you'd gone."

"Ray," she indicated to the man standing a few feet away, "thought it would be a better shot out here." The two women laughed. "You spoken to Martinez lately?"

"Not in a while. You?"

"He called me this morning."

"Ah! Okay. Lydia, this is Ms. Angela Ryan. Ms. Ryan, this is Ms. Lydia Tobin."

"Nice to meet you, Ms. Tobin. Call me Angela." She stuck out her hand and noticed that the woman's handshake was very genteel, very English. "Sorry you have to go through this. That asshole is a real piece of work!"

"Please, call me Lydia. You know my husband, well ex–husband now? How do you two know each other?" Ryan and Giordano looked at each other and understood that the poor woman did not need to know all the details or the extent of the help they had given each other.

"I met him when I was reporting on the house fire and the death of his first wife – it was my first big assignment for my network when I switched to them, what was it, eighteen years ago now? And I interviewed his mother while he was recovering back then. I can't remember how I met Alyssa."

"Neither can I!" Alyssa interjected and both women laughed again. "I think it was at some courthouse somewhere."

"Yeah," Angela appeared to remember. "Probably at some courthouse somewhere."

"Oh," Lydia sighed. "And you interviewed him when he was in rehab this time didn't you? I didn't recognize him then, when I saw the program."

"Neither did I." Ryan had been kicking herself for that. "Look, do you mind if I get some comments from you?"

"Hmmm," Alyssa looked at her watch. "We got some work to do. We're back next week."

"Just one question, for you Lydia?" Lydia looked at Alyssa, who nodded, and looked back at the reporter, and nodded. "Were you told how they misidentified him?"

"Well, they told me the driver's licenses were mixed up at the scene, and they wouldn't let me look at him because he was all mashed up. But they didn't do any tests to confirm who the dead man really was! They were sorry for the mistake, but that doesn't help me now!"

"Okay, thanks Lydia," the reporter said. "We'd better let you go."

"Thanks, Angela," Lydia said.

"Yeah, thanks Angela," Alyssa repeated. "Call me?" Angela just nodded as she watched the two women who had suffered at the hands of the nasty troublemaker walk off.

*****

The frantic sound in her receptionist's voice caused her, and her companion, to race madly back to her office. The telephone reception was good enough for them to hear in the background a madman screaming, the sounds of glass smashing, furniture being overturned and her partner shrieking back. As the door was pulled back, they saw the destruction, the havoc that the man had wreaked on the reception area.

"You had enough, Duncan?" Before he brought the cane down on the glass table, he looked up to see the aging policeman looking through, and then step through, the broken door.

"Wh–wh–what?" He lowered the cane.

"You had enough, Duncan?" the aging policeman asked again. Kennedy saw his former employee standing behind the policeman who had led the investigation into the death of his first wife. While Hugo Martinez had become more distinguished than he had with age, Alyssa Giordano had grown more stunning in the years that had passed since she left Hoboken. The expensive, well tailored suit was unnecessary to make her any prettier, but it certainly spoke of her success.

"No, I haven't! Alyssa, please! Why are you doing this to me?"

"I'm not doing this to you, Mr. Kennedy," Alyssa retorted.

"You want me to arrest him, Alyssa, Peggy?"

"Yes, of course we want him arrested Hugo!" Peggy Cooper was furious. While she expected the parties opposing their clients to be mad, angry, she had never experienced such a maniac.

"Me!" Kennedy was shocked at the thought that it could be suggested that he should be arrested after what this stupid bitch had done to him. "Arrest me? You should arrest them! Who the fuck are you anyway to want to arrest me!"

"You don't remember me, do you Duncan?" Duncan stared blankly at the man, shaking his head. "I'm Hugo Martinez," the policeman identified himself.

"Who?"

"I'm Hugo Martinez," he repeated. "I was the Chief of Police in Millbrook twenty years ago." He, and the two attorneys, caught the dawning of recognition on the man's face.

"No," Alyssa uttered, deep in thought. "No, Hugo. I don't think we want him arrested. I think we can resolve this privately. Don't you, Peggy?"

"Yes," Peggy started as the thought in her partner's mind dawned on her. "Yes, I think you're right, Alyssa. No we don't want him arrested, Hugo. But I think we need to call Lydia to see if we can get this resolved." Erik, in his infinite wisdom, had already dialed Tobin's cell phone and asked her to attend the office immediately.

"You got an attorney, Duncan?" Alyssa asked.

"No. Not yet. I want you to stop this, right now."

"No, Duncan, I can't. We can't," Peggy intervened. "Our client has told us in no uncertain terms that she wants to proceed. And you need an attorney." Kennedy's nostrils flared.

"You wanna call Lydia Price?" Alyssa asked, already knowing the answer.

"No."

"I know a few attorneys. You want me to call someone for you," Martinez interfered. "Someone really good."

Kennedy saw the writing on the wall. "Yeah," he acceded. "Whoever."

"Here's the number," Martinez said as he handed a business card to Erik.

"He'll be here in twenty minutes," Erik intoned after a short and stilted conversation with the owner of the business card he'd been handed. "And Ms. Tobin will be here any minute." They all looked toward the empty space of the reception door, from which the glass had been smashed, as they heard the lift doors open and a gasp emanate from the lift well.

"Do you mind waiting until your friend arrives?" Peggy asked the policeman as Alyssa stepped through the broken door to escort Lydia into a conference room.

"Not at all, Peggy. Not at all."

CHAPTER 33

ROLES REVERSED

Duncan Kennedy evaluated his life as he watched her, as she stood at the top of the Courthouse steps in Foley Square. It had been only a couple of months since he had last seen her and she had humiliated him: he hoped against hope that she had forgotten.

His eyesight, as well as his memory, had diminished but he could still recognize Judith Kaye, the supervising Judge in Manhattan for the Family Court of New York, and John Walker, the Chief Judge of the United States Court of Appeals' Second Circuit. The head injury was tough to recover from, but he still had enough of his wits about him to feign an increase in its significance. The others he did not know or could not see clearly enough to recognize. But two of the most senior judicial officers of the State of New York seemed to know them well enough. There were a few obvious security workers standing close, but not too close.

This time, he had sat the Bar Examinations in Manhattan rather than near the Board of Law Examiners office in Albany, hoping the difference in locale would help. The Examinations seemed so much different, harder, from when he sat them in Trenton so long ago, forty years ago. But the difference in location made no difference to his results; Duncan had failed for the third time.

He understood but disliked the Board's reasons for why he had to be re–examined. He'd been in "retirement" from his partnership with Lydia Price for a few years now, especially after his accident and subsequent rehabilitation, and not kept up with the fast changing pace of the law. Duncan had heard of her passing the Bar eight years before, but disbelieved it at the time. Had she told them of what happened, what he had concealed, in Hoboken? He certainly hoped not, but did he really want to try again?

Duncan looked again at Alyssa, at the high–ranking members of the Judiciary she was standing with, talking to. How did she know so many of them? Maybe she could help; would she though?

It was his turn to be at a juncture, albeit so late, in life. Without knowing, what he did next would make the decision for him.

"Alyssa? Alyssa Giordano?" he called to her from about halfway up the steps, hoping she would think he was questioning his sight, or memory. Alyssa turned towards him at hearing her name; she turned back to those she was engaged in discussion with and appeared to sign off. She started gracefully down the stairs towards him. The other woman, one of the group who seemed vaguely familiar but he did not yet recognize her, walked with Alyssa. He did not know how she could be so friendly with the senior judiciary.

"Good morning, Duncan," Alyssa uttered, her disdain evident. "You remember my partner, Peggy Cooper."

"Yes," he said. The face clicked. "Hello, Ms. Cooper."

"Mr. Kennedy."

"How are you, Alyssa?" he asked.

"I'm well, we're very busy. How are you?" He could see she was trying to be pleasant; he also understood that she really was uninterested in his responses.

"I'm well, much better thank you. So what have you been up to?" Out of the corner of his eye, Duncan could see Chief Judge Kaye and Chief Judge Walker still chatting, seemingly now uninterested in Alyssa; their security officers had drawn in closer to them.

"You know what I'm up to, what I've been up to for the last couple of years." Her glare said, *you can't be that stupid, that forgetful?* She knew about head injuries and she knew Kennedy and his propensity for deceit and falsehood. "We're still running our own practice, here in Manhattan. Peggy's my partner. The Family Court just handed down a decision in one of her cases. What are you in the city for?"

"Studying for the New York Bar, the Board of Law Examiners wants me to re–take the Examinations here." Duncan started to stammer. That was something that had not come up in the Court case. "Maybe, if you're willing, you could help," he uttered, looking at his feet. Duncan was not taken aback to see the scorn and ridicule on Alyssa's face as he looked up.

"Look, Duncan, do you really think that's appropriate? No, I don't think so. Not after what's happened. And *especially* not after I represented Lydia. I've got a lot of work to do so I must go." Peggy was already at the bottom of the stairs as Alyssa turned and started down towards her.

"Wait, please," Duncan begged as he grabbed Alyssa's arm, the papers flying from her grip all over the steps. "Please don't hold that against me. Don't hold the past against me!"

"Duncan, let go." She had said it firmly and sufficiently stridently for a security officer to turn, step towards them. "Duncan, please let go," she reiterated, pulling away. His fingers lost their grip on her jacket; she miss-stepped. The sounds of Alyssa's ankle splintering, her head cracking as it met the concrete banister, horrified Duncan and his jaw started flapping.

*****

This time, it really was déjà vu all over again.

Except this time, the players did not need to pick up the calls they were receiving. This time, they were already there, watching it as it unfolded. They had all attended the retirement of the outgoing Chief Justice and the swearing in ceremony of the new Chief Justice: Martinez and Olsen had felt compelled to attend as public administrators, police officials; Ryan and Jensen were there for news value, for another one of their specialty current affairs bulletins. Their attention, and Ray's camera, was drawn to the sounds of the human form crashing against the concrete and bones breaking.

This time Jensen was not the sole cameraman. As the action unfolded, his cinematographic instincts caused his camera to retain focus on Giordano while his directorial instincts caused his spare hand to wave the other cameras to cover the rest of the encounter. Angela almost broke a Manolo as she jumped back, out of her director's way as he fell back into his role as her main cameraman: she watched what her mind could only think of as her drill sergeant hand silently directed, with the barest movement of his fingers only noticeable to her, the most exquisite parade drill.

Jensen caught Hugo Martinez race towards the young beautiful lawyer and he hoped one of the other cameras would catch Olsen racing towards, and then dive on, Duncan Kennedy, hurtling with him down the stairs. Other officers followed swiftly behind him. As Olsen pulled Kennedy up from the recently positioned pavement, he glanced at Martinez and saw that Martinez was taking a quick look back at him. *Do we have him his time?* They both thought as a single psyche. Ryan and Jensen saw the two men look at each other and it was as if they could read their minds.

*****

Kennedy was watching it all happen from above the statue of the Goddess of Justice, yet his body was in the thick of it.

He saw the more junior of the senior police administrators flying towards his body, crash tackling him down the stairs, the more senior of police administrators cradling Alyssa with a bloodied cloth to her head as Peggy held her hand. The cuffs clacked shut, tight on his wrists; the two Chief Judges talking to men in police uniforms, probably giving statements; the protection detail cordoning off the front steps of the Courthouse; the sirens wailed in, ambulance, police cars.

It was karmic, coincidence in a way. *Black fly in your chardonnay...* *Isn't it ironic...* The tune of that Alanis Morisette song Alyssa liked so much swirled around in Duncan's head over the sounds of the sirens.

I wonder if she's related to Bill.

It was almost déjà vu for him too. The wail of the sirens, the click of the handcuffs, and the disdain on the faces of the growing crowd. Except he was in the back of a patrol car instead of an ambulance this time. Suddenly Duncan could taste the bile from his nervous stomach reaching his taste buds. He made a gagging sound and emptied the contents of his mouth on the newly laid cobblestones.

How could I have been so presumptuous? Duncan muttered to himself, angrily. *So desperate? So arrested?* He felt his body being jerked upright and had one final glance at Alyssa, pale and still sitting supported on a step, her leg outstretched and being tenderly cared for by the highly placed police official.

"You're coming with us, now move those feet!" growled one of the cops. Flashes went off in Duncan's eyes. News reporters and photographers, maybe. He thought he saw Angela Ryan. Maybe tourists, taking shots to sell later. "Aw, shit." He muttered. "Well, there goes the Bar."

And, here come the bars.

Really, now he only had one hope to keep him out of confinement for aggravated assault on an officer of the court. Only one hope. Shoved roughly into the back of the patrol car, Duncan Kennedy finally began to take stock. One thing he didn't know and couldn't consider was that twenty minutes before, his unwitting intervention had prevented a reprehensible exploit.

*****

The sniper had lowered his sight from where Alyssa had been standing, realigned it on her again as she lay on the steps, and just before he could breathe in, then out, and slowly depress the trigger, the first security guard's body moved between him and his target flying towards the man who had seemingly pushed her. More people crowded around.

Idiot! Damned fool! A tirade of expletives entered his mind: he recognized the man from Millbrook.

Sighing, the figure unscrewed the barrel, silencer and stock, and gently placed the pieces of his weapon into his padded guitar case. He would have need for them later. He left the room in the vacant building across the way.

*****

There they were in the midst of the gathering spectators; each lost in their own thoughts. Despite her lapses in consciousness, Alyssa, worrying about her disheveled appearance, tried to think back to a time when Duncan was not messing up her orderly life.

The only time he hasn't been messing up my life was when I didn't know him! Alyssa thought to herself. She had been young when they met, when she first went to work for him, and mistaken his lustful interest in her for him wanting to be a mentor for someone new entering the legal profession. Towards the end of her time at his office, his licentious intent had grown to such a degree that he had trouble hiding it from Alyssa and his second wife. Both had rebuffed him in the end.

Well, at least all I will have to do is testify against him, she meditated as the trolley was pushed into the back of the awaiting ambulance. *I never understood till now the cliché of revenge being best served cold...*

*****

Kennedy had finally washed the taste of bile out of his mouth with the small sip of water an officer had allowed him with the aspirin. But the aspirin did not have much effect on the pounding in his head that hitting the door of the patrol car had given him. The car had had to wait till the crowd, which was heckling him, dispersed before it could move him to the cell which would be his new home.

Duncan refocused from his dream state as he turned to look out the car window at the crowd just as the man from the roof with the guitar case walked past the car, peering in. The man with the guitar case squinted through the window, recalling a time well past, and a smile entered his eyes. "Hello, Duncan," he mouthed through the window as his lips curled upwards.

Duncan's eyelids grew wide with shock, terror, as his eyeballs expanded out of their sockets. The bile grew in his throat again. He leaned forward and what little was left in his gut exploded over the floor of the patrol car as the executioner merged into the foot traffic and flowed with the increasing crowd. Six blocks away, he hailed a cab, and after a mile ride and a three–block walk, another cab. After alighting from the second ride, he walked four more blocks to his Lexus. Driving to his hidey–hole, he used the unregistered, disposable telephone.

"Okay. I didn't get the shot. Somebody knocked her down and people showed up." He listened. "It was an accident, but now you get one more at no cost. You only pay for the girl." He smirked. "The doofus? Now he knows, but he ain't talkin'. Nobody would ever believe him." He listened again. "Yeah, I'm sure. I just wanted him to get an idea what his future will be like. You run and you run and you run and then you die." More listening. "Oh, yeah. The doll. You can say she's already dead. She just don't know it yet."

The maniac stroked his guitar case lovingly. He then rolled down the window and tossed the phone into a canal. He had more.

CHAPTER 34

IRONY BEGINS AT HOME

The roving hired gun for hire finally received the call three days later. His masters did not want to leave her alive; they could not afford to do so if they wanted to wreak the havoc on the United States Marine Corps Warrant Officer who had thwarted them so many years ago. The revenge was cold enough after sixty years, but revenge was even better if it was served cold and if the person on whose behalf it was served was alive to see it.

The security at the hospital had been downgraded now that Kennedy was in lockdown. He had spent hours waiting outside until the graveyard shift was well and truly weary. He did not need to ensure that he was the only survivor this time; it would appear that her death had commenced with, and had been concluded by, Kennedy's actions.

He prowled, he planned, and he did everything under the sun to ensure she would not survive. He knew it was irrelevant that the security cameras were rolling as he stalked through the infirmary. This time he was armed with a syringe instead of a .22 caliber rifle, but he still carried his instrument case. He had courted the staff for so many years, playing for the children, keeping them entertained, distracted from bothering the harried nurses, that they were happy to see him. The case had always covered his real reasons for being there on many an occasion.

It took him an hour to find the room in which she lay.

Damn! Alyssa Giordano had visitors. *Those two cops!* The menace in committing the act was too great with them there: he was not suicidal. They would still have to pay; but he would give them the same discount he had given them for the first attempt. *Why are they here so late?* The answer to that question bothered him less than it bothered him that they were actually there, at the hospital, visiting her at all.

Then, in front of the security cameras, he gesticulated in defiance and disappeared off–camera through the exit.

Why won't she die?! Why the fucking hell won't she die?! He did not know why they wanted who he presumed to be such an inconsequential woman dead. The reason for the contract did not concern him; the money did. *They're not going to be happy!* He pulled an unidentifiable, disposable telephone, one of his many, from his pocket and dialed. He would leave his masters to ponder the question why the two powerful police administrators were visiting her.

"Couldn't get the doll."

Why? he heard.

"Cops and a couple of others outside her door." He paused, sighed. "Woulda been identified if I'd tried. The hospital staff know me."

Don't tell me you couldn't have executed the policemen. The pompous, oddly accented, voice sounded as if it had learnt pompous English from a proper Englishman, but in a place far from where proper Englishmen lived.

"Look," the anger was growing in the assassin's voice. "I got my cover with them for a reason. I been in before, and I'll get in again. But only if my cover's not blown." What he heard next was unintelligible, but its meaning apparent.

What do you mean you have your cover with them?! the voice screamed.

"Look, they think I'm a musician and I go play for the kids' ward when I got a job there. It's the way I get in and out of the hospital. Nobody notices me; nobody cares who I am. With the cops there, I woulda been noticed."

Ah, yes. Alright then. I see. A slightly different English pomposity, followed by more gibberish unintelligible to his ears. *When can you go back?* The original voice again.

"Gonna take a while for me to set up. Gotta go outta town for... a few days."

What? Why? The first, unreasonable, haughty voice.

"Look, I had to ditch the drugs and I gotta get some more. She ain't goin' anywhere for a while. It'll give me a chance to set it up right."

What do you mean "set it up right"?! The first, unreasonable, voice. *It was set up correctly!*

"No." There was a patience in his voice, as if he was explaining the simple workings of a toy to a simple child. "It wasn't. The cops were there. If I set it up right, I can get in, get out, nobody sees me, no cops around. So I won't get caught."

Ah yes. I see. The simple child now understood how to play with the simple toy.

Where will you get your... supplies? The second, more reasonable, snobbish voice interjected.

"Colombia." He smiled, to himself, pleased that he never went anywhere without more than one means for a fast exit out of any nation into any other nation.

You can exit and return safely from there? The second voice now carried astonishment.

"Of course."

Ah! Yes! Perhaps we can consider some other business. The first voice said, not so astonished. *After this matter is concluded? Let us know when it has been finalized.*

"Yeah, sure," the killer with the guitar case answered as he heard the call abruptly terminate. *Fuckin' assholes. Arrogant shits.* He laughed to himself. *You're really gonna pay me well for this one!* he thought as the phone washed down the open drain.

*****

As her eyes opened, she coughed on the intubation tube.

Alyssa raised her hand to pull at it, but another hand, not her own, stopped her. Her eyes finally focused on the lab coated woman in front of her; there were four others, all men, standing outside the glass wall, her eyes were able to identify them but her brain would not let her attach names to them yet.

As the tube came out of her throat, she smiled at the irony of it all; *Black fly in your chardonnay... Isn't it ironic...* The verses and words of the chorus muddled up a bit, but she knew what she meant. Alanis Morisette had said it all. Her doctor was talking to her, but Alyssa couldn't quite make out her words over the tune of the song yet; all she could do was nod and smile. *Ironic* finished, then came the words to her other favorite, the other one about finding the man of her dreams but the one where he was without the wife. *What was its name?*

What was his name? Alyssa couldn't quite make the logical leap yet, make the connection to one of them standing outside the glass.

Why that one?

*****

Olsen jumped out of his chair as he heard pounding on his wall. Martinez's method of communication still startled him even after all the time that it had been happening.

"Hey, Tim! Timmy boy, we got him!" he heard Martinez holler through their connecting wall after he'd stopped pounding the wall.

"What! Got who?" Olsen hollered back.

"Kennedy!" Olsen saw Martinez walk through the connecting door between their offices, holding his right hand out with a wad of paper in it. There was a digital tape in his left hand. Olsen took the sheaf, collapsed back into his chair and started reading. Martinez watched him read for what seemed an eternity.

"Whoa! That the tape?" Olsen raised his eyebrows.

"Yeah. Whoa is right." Martinez grinned slyly.

"You seen it?"

"Yeah."

"Wanna put it in and see it again?"

"Righto." Martinez, knowing the revelation had stunned Olsen just as it had stunned him, left Olsen to his chair and walked to the cabinet where Olsen kept his television.

It was a digital rendering of the CCTV footage that the two had recovered together in Millbrook oh so many years ago. It would solve the "mystery" of the burned–out mansion that has riveted them, and the rest of New York, for close to a month nearly thirty years ago – the millionaire businessman owner apparently being dragged on an hour–long violence spree that killed his wife, daughter and their horses and pets before their house was set alight and he was almost himself killed. The footage showed Duncan Kennedy being dragged through his house by a man with a guitar case, apparently aware that the security cameras were rolling, holding his gun as he stalked through the house and the barns and sheds around Millbrook House. As the horror spree could see Kennedy being dragged to the barn, and then from it as it started to burn, forced into a horse float to the mansion's gates. They then saw the man with the guitar case shooting out the tires and forcing Kennedy back to the main house. At one stage, they saw the man with the guitar case even gesticulating at the cameras in defiance, apparently knowing that they were still running. How the cameras, placed around the grounds, escaped the flames would flummox them, but it would just be one of the unsolved and unsolvable pieces of the crime.

Both men sat silently back for a quarter hour after the tape concluded. Neither wanted to break the other's concentration while they pondered the ramifications of the tape and the forensic report.

"Jeez Louise, Hugo."

"That says it, Tim"

"Whydaya think he did it?"

"Money. If it's not cheating, it's always the money."

"Yeah, money. So where did the forensic guys get the reports from? I thought the property clerk woulda sent it all back when we closed the case."

"Kennedy didn't want 'em so I kept it. I s'posed it was all too hard for him at the time. Something bugged me about that, him not wanting it back, so I kept it."

"Oh, okay." Tim thought for a moment. "So why did you give it to forensics now?"

"The Giordano case. I thought since we were putting together the assault case against him on that, they might as well have another look." Tim Olsen raised his eyebrows at the man who'd been his chief since he was twenty–three.

"Technology, eh?"

"Yeah, technology. I don't understand it, but I love it!"

"I don't get it either. My grandkid tells me he just got some Apple cell phone that's also a record player that can hold my vinyls ten times over. Jeez, I'm too old for that!" Martinez laughed.

"That's an iPhone you idiot! See," Hugo pulled one from his pocket and tossed it to Tim, "you just plug it into your computer and you can download all your songs onto it. Well I had to get my grandkid to do it for me, but I love it."

"Put that away!" The younger man tossed it back, not being able to work out how to activate what he thought was an infernal, useless gadget. "I just told you I'm too old for that shit! I still can't even work out how to turn on my Department cell phone!" Martinez laughed again. "Gimme a two–way any day!" The younger man paused for a beat. "You let the DA know yet?"

"Nup, not yet. Wanna head over with me?"

"What the hell. I wanna see the look on his face too!"

*****

The Manhattan District Attorney was stunned, staggered, horrified by what he saw and read. It had taken him longer to come to grips with it than it had taken the two policemen: more than half a day. Martinez and Olsen watched him in silence after they'd handed over the tape and the report.

The reports from the forensic accountants showed that Kennedy faced bankruptcy with business debts in the millions. The FBI psychiatrist concluded Duncan Kennedy had suffered a breakdown as he chose to murder his family and destroy his wife's family home rather than handing his wife's money over to his creditors as well as his own. Apparently Kennedy did not want to lose his ostentatious lifestyle: he would rather lose his family and the house. The crime that had particularly shocked the local community would shock them again.

At first, the suggestion that Kennedy may have been responsible for the nightmare seemed implausible to the District Attorney: family, friends and neighbors described a man content with his lot and flamboyant in his displays of success. But as the years had passed, Kennedy's business associates began to tell a different story, one which showed that the smiles in that last, grotesque family tableau his mother had displayed on national television hid much more than it revealed.

In fact, behind Kennedy's showy lifestyle, the self–made billionaire was on the cusp of financial ruin, a bankruptcy that would have seen him lose his beloved house and cars to his creditors. Kennedy's financial success story began early in his career when as a junior lawyer in a backyard firm he won a large anti–trust against a major financial institution. Entrepreneurial from the very beginning, Kennedy established his own law offices and began to tout for business for petty grievances against large corporations. Soon he had a staff of twelve. While he had some degree of skill and clients began clamoring for his services in earnest, it appeared that Kennedy's legal skills did not match his flair for sales or entrepreneurship. His company was turning over millions, adding to his first wife's family money, and Kennedy embarked on a billionaire's lifestyle in earnest. He bought and sold property, trading up each time, finally settling back in Janet Kennedy's gamily mansion in leafy Millbrook. He renovated, bought luxury cars, sent his daughter to a private school nearby.

Kennedy then nabbed a really big overseas land deal, but despite the deals and turnover, debts were also mounting and had reached almost the total of just his, rather than his and his wife's combined, fortune. The accounts also showed some discrepancies, including a six–figure loan to an unidentified company director. Kennedy was told he needed to cut costs and it is here he made his first, disastrous decision: he chose to bypass a major client and secretly act against them for another company that had offered a larger retainer. He was found out and sued for breach of contract and ordered to pay millions to the slighted client. The case opened Kennedy's books to scrutiny and revealed the extent of his mounting debt – billions to the taxman and millions to other creditors. Terrified, Kennedy moved to strip client funds from his escrow account into another company. How he wasn't caught, particularly after the mandatory audits, the District Attorney couldn't explain. But Kennedy was no stranger to the courtroom. Before the sitting District Attorney's time, he had apparently alleged blackmail during an offshore land deal – and there had been counterclaims that Kennedy threatened violence in return. Kennedy had identified the man with the guitar case, the one on the film the District Attorney had just seen, as one of the men involved in the land scam but those he and his partner accused were never identified, never caught.

"Damn shame we couldn't ID Guitar Man. How sure are you, Hugo? You got it all lined up for the grand jury?" The District Attorney had known the two policemen, had played poker in Millbrook with Martinez the day Olsen brought the news of the Millbrook fire and had fought many a case with them over the years. They knew as much of the criminal law and procedure of his District as he did and he trusted their judgment. They took on the procedure and he took on the law.

"Yeah, I'm pissed about that. Guitar Man I mean. As sure as I can be. It's circumstantial, no better no worse than some of the other cases we had. It'll be a tough sell, but ya just gotta take the financial stuff slow for 'em."

"Tim?"

"I say we got him. Nail the sucker. Maybe he'll give us Guitar Man."

"Witnesses?"

"All ready," the policemen chimed together. A short pause.

"'Cept the butler." Tim said.

"Yeah. 'Cept the butler," intoned the District Attorney, "the dead butler."

"Pity we don't have that technology yet. Wish he could pull a Lazarus," droned Martinez, showing his colors.

Another, slightly longer, pause as they contemplated the case without him.

"I think I'll take this one personally." The two policemen looked at each other, smiled and nodded at Manhattan's chief prosecutor. The District Attorney walked them out to the reception and checked his diary and the grand jury calendar his executive secretary kept for him.

"Okay to start Monday?" The detectives looked at each other again.

"Yep," Martinez said solely as he and Olsen left.

*****

The guard grabbed at the prison garb as the attorney left the meeting room.

The hand shaking his shoulder Duncan awoke him out of his daze. His attorney was not confident about the trial; but it was not his fault, it was all an accident, not his fault.

As he walked the halls of Rikers Island, feeling as if he was walking the gauntlet, Duncan's mind turned back to the day before Veterans Day 1994 and considered the irony that he was now in the position in which he had put Alyssa; he wondered if he could make them understand he had done nothing wrong, as she had tried, but failed, to do with him.

He knew the New York State Chief Judge would not be presiding at his trial. He only hoped it would not be someone Alyssa had become as friendly with as she had with the Chief Judge.

So began his downward spiral into depression.

THE END